The Sister Jane series

Outfoxed

Hotspur

Full Cry

The Hunt Ball

The Hounds and the Fury

The Tell-Tale Horse

Hounded to Death

Fox Tracks

Let Sleeping Dogs Lie

Crazy Like a Fox

Homeward Hound

Scarlet Fever

Thrill of the Hunt

Out of Hounds

Lost & Hound

Books by Rita Mae Brown with Sneaky Pie Brown

Wish You Were Here

Rest in Pieces

Murder at Monticello

Pay Dirt

Murder, She Meowed

Murder on the Prowl

Cat on the Scent

Sneaky Pie's Cookbook for Mystery Lovers

Pawing Through the Past

Claws and Effect

Catch as Cat Can

The Tail of the Tip-Off

Whisker of Evil

Cat's Eyewitness

Sour Puss

Puss 'n Cahoots

The Purrfect Murder

Santa Clawed

Cat of the Century

Hiss of Death

The Big Cat Nap

Sneaky Pie for President

The Litter of the Law

Nine Lives to Die

Tail Gate

Tall Tail

A Hiss Before Dying

Probable Claws

Whiskers in the Dark

Furmidable Foes

Hiss & Tell

The Nevada series

A Nose for Justice

Murder Unleashed

Books by Rita Mae Brown

Animal Magnetism: My Life with
Creatures Great and Small

The Hand That Cradles the Rock

Songs to a Handsome Woman

The Plain Brown Rapper

Rubyfruit Jungle

In Her Day

Six of One

Southern Discomfort

Sudden Death

High Hearts

Started from Scratch: A Different Kind
of Writer's Manual

Bingo

Venus Envy

Dolley: A Novel of Dolley Madison
in Love and War

Riding Shotgun

Rita Will: Memoir of a
Literary Rabble-Rouser

Loose Lips

Alma Mater

The Sand Castle

Cakewalk

FOX AND FURIOUS

FOX AND FURIOUS

A NOVEL

RITA MAE BROWN

ILLUSTRATED BY LEE GILDEA

BANTAM

NEW YORK

Bantam Books
An imprint of Random House
A division of Penguin Random House LLC
1745 Broadway, New York, NY 10019
randomhousebooks.com
penguinrandomhouse.com

Hardcover ISBN 978-0-593-87411-0
Ebook ISBN 978-0-593-87412-7

Printed in the United States of America on acid-free paper

1st Printing

First Edition

BOOK TEAM: Production editor: Andy Lefkowitz • Managing editor: Saige Francis • Production manager: Jennifer Backe • Copy editor: Pam Feinstein • Proofreaders: Kate Hertzog, Megha Jain, Allison Lindon, and Barbara Stussy

Series design by Victoria Wong

The authorized representative in the EU for product safety and compliance is Penguin Random House Ireland, Morrison Chambers, 32 Nassau Street, Dublin D02 YH68, Ireland. https://eu-contact.penguin.ie

Dedicated with gratitude
to
Mrs. Lynda Bird Johnson Robb.
Her warmth, wisdom, and sparkling good humor
have been a gift to the state of Virginia.

CAST OF CHARACTERS

THE HUMANS

Jane Arnold, MFH, "Sister," has been a Master of Foxhounds for Jefferson Hunt since her late thirties. Now in her middle seventies, she is still going strong. Hunting three days a week during the season keeps her fit mentally and physically. She is married to Gray Lorillard, choosing not to take his last name, which is fine with him.

Gray Lorillard isn't cautious on the hunt field but he is prudent off of it. Now retired, he was a partner in one of Washington, D.C.'s most prestigious accounting firms. Often called back for consulting, he knows how "creative" accounting really works. Handsome, kind, and smart, he has dealt with decades of racism. Doesn't stop him.

Betty Franklin has whipped-in for Jefferson Hunt for decades. Her task is to assist the huntsman, which she ably does. In her mid-fifties and Sister's best friend, she can be bold on the field and sometimes off. Everyone loves Betty.

Bobby Franklin especially loves Betty; he's her husband. They own a small printing press, work they enjoy. Bobby is a good businessman. He leads Second Flight, those people who don't jump but might clear a log or two.

Sam Lorillard is Gray's younger brother. A natural horseman, he works for Crawford Howard, who has a farmer pack of hounds. After hitting the skids, he finally overcame his alcoholism with Gray's help. He is a bright man and a good one.

Daniella Laprade is Gray and Sam's aunt. Somewhere in her late nineties, she can be outrageous. Stunningly beautiful, she even now looks good considering her years. No one in Jefferson Hunt has known life without her. Having three rich husbands helped her live comfortably. As to her numerous affairs, she was discreet.

Wesley Blackford, "Weevil," hunts hounds for Sister. He loves his work and, being young, is learning, soaking up everything. Aunt Daniella had an affair with his grandfather, whom he greatly resembles. He is in love with Anne Harris.

Anne Harris, "Tootie," is another natural horseman. She whips-in to Weevil. Betty is her idol, as Betty exhibits incredible instincts in the hunt field. Tootie left Princeton to hunt with Jefferson Hunt. She is almost finished at the University of Virginia. She looks very much like her famous mother.

Yvonne Harris was one of the first Black models. She and her detested ex-husband built a Black media empire. Divorcing him, she moved to Albemarle County to be near Tootie in hopes of repairing that relationship. She wasn't a bad mother, but unwittingly neglectful. She can't understand that Tootie has little interest in racial politics. Tootie is the product of her parents' success. She has no idea about earlier struggles.

Winston Bradford, Master of Beagles, hunts the Bradford Beagles. In his mid-fifties, he is a stalwart in his community, ready to help.

Beryl Bradford, Winston's wife, follows the beagles on foot. It's a good marriage.

Andrew Bradford, MB, occasionally hunts the pack but is more useful on foot. Having inherited a great deal of money, he wants to prove he can make money himself. He can't.

Solange Bradford is Andrew's new, young, gorgeous wife. She is learning about country life as well as about Andrew.

Olivia Bradford, the mother of Winston and Andrew, keeps the peace. When her husband died, she ran the huge timber company, further securing the great Bradford fortune.

Georgia Bradford is Andrew's first wife. She is much loved by the community; people stuck by her when she was thrown over for the bombshell.

Ann Howlett has been a dear friend of Solange's since college. She works on the farm as a gardener and as a companion to Solange—a companion who, while well treated, is not really part of the community.

Scott Howlett, married to Ann, has known Solange since college. He is the gardener of the estate, loyal to Solange, and keeps clear of Andrew.

Crawford Howard was best described by Aunt Daniella, who commented, "There's a lot to be said about being nouveau riche, and Crawford means to say it all." Given his ego, large as a blimp, he learned about Virginia and hunting the hard way. He made his first fortune in Indiana. They may have been irritated by him, but the Hoosiers were used to him. He is restoring Old Paradise, a great estate built with funds stolen from the British during the War of 1812.

Marty Howard, married to Crawford, patiently guided him to less bombast. She has a passion for environmental projects and the funds to pursue them.

Walter Lungren, MD, jt-MFH, practices cardiology. He has hunted with Sister since his childhood. He is the late Raymond Arnold's outside son. His father accepted his wife's indiscretion, raising Walter as his own. It wasn't discussed and still isn't. He and Sister have a warm relationship.

Ronnie Haslip is the hunt's treasurer, indefatigable in raising funds. He was the best friend of RayRay, Sister's late son. He is a good rider, loved by his Chihuahua, Atlas.

Raymond Arnold, Jr., "RayRay," died in a farm accident in 1974. Loved and remembered by Sister, Ronnie, and others who knew him, sometimes they feel his spirit. He was a good athlete and a good kid.

Kasmir Barbhaiya, born and raised in India, was educated in England, like so many upper-class Indians. He foxhunts with gusto and rides well. When his wife died, he left India to come to Virginia to be near an Oxford classmate and his wife. He fit right in. He is a man with broad vision, knowing the world in different ways than an American.

Alida Dalzell brought Kasmir back to life and happiness. They met on the hunt field. She adored him but never made a move out of respect for his late wife. Ultimately, Kasmir realized his beloved wife would have wanted him to be happy. These two are made for each other.

Edward and Tedi Bancroft are stalwarts of the hunt. After All, their property, abuts Roughneck Farm, Sister and Gray's farm. Now in their eighties, they are slowing down a bit but fighting it every step of the way.

Ben Sidell is the county sheriff. He got the job coming from Columbus, Ohio—good training, as that is a university town. In Virginia, towns and rural areas have separate political structures, so Ben is not responsible for policing the university. There's enough to do in the county. He rides Nonni, a saint. Sister found the mare for him and told him to learn to hunt. It's the easiest way to understand Virginia, which is not like Ohio.

Adrianna Waddy, MFH of Bull Run, is friends with Sister Jane. She owns a successful realty company and has a sense of the land. Her work helps her as a Master of Foxhounds. She and Sister Jane greatly enjoy each other's company. Magnum is her retired foxhound.

Birdie Goodall, recently retired from running the office of Walter Lungren, MD, suffered a devastating loss when her son, Trevor, was murdered. It's fair to say Trevor did not live up to his potential, but did he deserve to die for it?

Cynthia Skiff Cane hunts Crawford's pack. She gets along with him. He went through three huntsmen before her. She also gets along with Jefferson Hunt.

Shaker Crown hunted Jefferson hounds for decades. A bad accident ended his hard riding. He fell for Skiff, and helping her helped him, as he was lost without the horn. Hunting hounds was his life and he loved it.

Freddie Thomas hunts First Flight. She rarely talks about her profession, which is accounting. She, Gray, and Ronnie are all accountants, which sometimes amuses them. She is Alida Dalzell's best friend.

Kathleen Sixt Dunbar owns the 1780 House, a high-end antiques store. Her husband left it to her even though they rarely saw each other, living hundreds of miles apart. They never bothered to get divorced. She drives Aunt Daniella around to follow the hunt. She absorbs so much about the hunt, plus everything else. Aunt Daniella is a fount of information.

Rev. Sally Taliaferro is an Episcopal priest who hunts. She is always there if a parishioner or anyone else needs her.

Father Mancusco is the priest at St. Mary's. He's fairly new, having been there only three years. He and Sally get along, both more than happy to give people's prayers in the hunt field.

THE ANIMALS

J. Edgar Hoover, a young box turtle with a beautiful shell, has landed at Roughneck Farm. Golliwog, the cat, is appalled.

Miss Priss is a retired Bradford Beagle living with Winston and Beryl.

Tidbit is a Yorkshire terrier owned by Winston and Beryl.

USEFUL TERMS

Away. A fox has gone away when he has left the covert. Hounds are away when they have left the covert on the line of the fox.

Brush. The fox's tail.

Burning scent. Scent so strong or hot that hounds pursue the line without hesitation.

Bye day. A day not regularly on the fixture card.

Cap. The fee nonmembers pay to hunt for that day's sport.

Carry a good head. When hounds run well together to a good scent, a scent spread wide enough for the whole pack to feel it.

Carry a line. When hounds follow the scent. This is also called working a line.

Cast. Hounds spread out in search of scent. They may cast themselves or be cast by the huntsman.

Charlie. A term for a fox. A fox may also be called **Reynard.**

Check. When hounds lose the scent and stop. The field must wait quietly while the hounds search for the scent.

Colors. A distinguishing color, usually worn on the collar but sometimes on the facings of a coat, that identifies a hunt. Colors can be awarded only by the Master and can be worn only in the field.

Coop. A jump resembling a chicken coop.

Couple straps. Two-strap hound collars connected by a swivel link. Some members of staff will carry these on the right rear of the saddle. Since the days of the pharaohs in ancient Egypt, hounds have been brought to the meets coupled. Hounds are always spoken of and counted in couples. Today, hounds walk or are driven to the meets. Rarely, if ever, are they coupled, but a whipper-in still carries couple straps should a hound need assistance.

Covert. A patch of woods or bushes where a fox might hide. Pronounced "cover."

Cry. How one hound tells another what is happening. The sound will differ according to the various stages of the chase. It's also called giving tongue and should occur when a hound is working a line.

Cub hunting. The informal hunting of young foxes in the late summer and early fall, before formal hunting. The main purpose is to enter young hounds into the pack. Until recently only the most knowledgeable members were invited to cub hunt, since they would not interfere with young hounds.

Dog fox. The male fox.

Dog hound. The male hound.

Double. A series of short, sharp notes blown on the horn to alert all that a fox is afoot. The gone away series of notes is a form of doubling the horn.

Draft. To acquire hounds from another hunt is to accept a draft.

Draw. The plan by which a fox is hunted or searched for in a certain area, such as a covert.

Draw over the fox. Hounds go through a covert where the fox is but cannot pick up its scent. The only creature that understands how this is possible is the fox.

Drive. The desire to push the fox, to get up with the line. It's a very desirable trait in hounds, so long as they remain obedient.

Dually. A one-ton pickup truck with double wheels in back.

Dwell. To hunt without getting forward. A hound that dwells is a bit of a putterer.

Enter. Hounds are entered into the pack when they first hunt, usually during cubbing season.

Field. The group of people riding to hounds, exclusive of the Master and hunt staff.

Field Master. The person appointed by the Master to control the field. Often it is the Master him- or herself.

Fixture. A card sent to all dues-paying members, stating when and where the hounds will meet. A fixture card properly received is an invitation to hunt. This means the card would be mailed or handed to a member by the Master.

Flea-bitten. A gray horse with spots or ticking that can be black or chestnut.

Gone away. The call on the horn when the fox leaves the covert.

Gone to ground. A fox that has ducked into its den, or some other refuge, has gone to ground.

Good night. The traditional farewell to the Master after the hunt, regardless of the time of day.

Gyp. The female hound.

Hilltopper. A rider who follows the hunt but does not jump. Hilltoppers are also called the Second Flight. The jumpers are called the First Flight.

Hoick. The huntsman's cheer to the hounds. It is derived from the Latin *hic haec hoc,* which means "here."

Hold hard. To stop immediately.

Huntsman. The person in charge of the hounds, in the field and in the kennel.

Kennelman. A hunt staff member who feeds the hounds and cleans the kennels. In wealthy hunts, there may be a number of kennelmen. In hunts with a modest budget, the huntsman or even the Master cleans the kennels and feeds the hounds.

Lark. To jump fences unnecessarily when hounds aren't running. Masters frown on this, since it is often an invitation to an accident.

Lieu in. Norman term for "go in."

Lift. To take the hounds from a lost scent in the hopes of finding a better scent farther on.

Line. The scent trail of the fox.

Livery. The uniform worn by the professional members of the hunt staff. Usually it is scarlet, but blue, yellow, brown, and gray are also used. The recent dominance of scarlet has to do with people buying coats off the rack as opposed to having tailors cut them. (When anything is mass-produced, the choices usually dwindle, and such is the case with livery.)

Mask. The fox's head.

MB. Master of Beagles.

Meet. The site where the day's hunting begins.

MFH. The Master of Foxhounds; the individual in charge of the hunt: hiring, firing, landowner relations, opening territory (in large hunts this is the job of the hunt secretary), developing the pack of hounds, and determining the first cast of each meet. As in any leadership position, the Master is also the lightning rod for criticism. The Master may hunt the hounds, although this is usually done by a professional huntsman, who is also responsible for the hounds in the field and at the kennels. A long relationship between a master and a huntsman allows the hunt to develop and grow.

Nose. The scenting ability of a hound.

Override. To press hounds too closely.

Overrun. When hounds shoot past the line of a scent. Often the scent has been diverted or foiled by a clever fox.

Ratcatcher. Informal dress worn during cubbing season and bye days.

Stern. A hound's tail.

Stiff-necked fox. One that runs in a straight line.

Strike hounds. Those hounds that, through keenness, nose, and often higher intelligence, find the scent first and press it.

Tail hounds. Those hounds running at the rear of the pack. This is not necessarily because they aren't keen; they may be older hounds.

Tally-ho. The cheer when the fox is viewed. Derived from the Norman *ty a hillaut,* thus coming into the English language in 1066.

Tongue. To vocally pursue a fox.

View halloo (halloa). The cry given by a staff member who sees a fox. Staff may also say tally-ho or, should the fox turn back, tally-back. One reason a different cry may be used by staff, especially in territory where the huntsman can't see the staff, is that the field in their enthusiasm may cheer something other than a fox.

Vixen. The female fox.

Walk. Puppies are walked out in the summer and fall of their first year. It's part of their education and a delight for both puppies and staff.

Whippers-in. Also called whips, these are the staff members who assist the huntsman, who make sure the hounds "do right."

FOX AND FURIOUS

CHAPTER 1

October 13, 2024 Sunday

The cerulean blue sky, lavish, emphasized how beautiful was this fall day. A blur of red and a splash of orange interspersed with radiant yellow announced the true beginning of fall, late this year.

Leaves crunched underfoot as Jane Arnold, "Sister," walked briskly to keep up behind Marianne Casey, the Master of the Nantucket-Treweryn Beagles. The joint meet, blessed with long and fast runs, had worn out everyone but the beagles. Walking back was one of the few times Sister hoped hounds did not hit again. Accustomed to four legs, thanks to foxhunting, she felt the pace. The hunting had been so exciting she could have followed on horseback and not have been bored. Then again one was rarely bored with NTB.

The foot followers, a healthy forty-five in number this Sunday, showed signs of running hard. The group encompassed many ages, most being middle aged. The number was also fairly divided between men and women, women having a slight edge. There wasn't a woman out there who didn't want to hunt with men, for the simple reason that if you were stuck in a jam it was usually a man who pulled you up and out. It was amazing what could go wrong out there. The irritating thing about any quarry is they proved so much smarter than the humans.

For beagles, the quarry was rabbits. Anyone who ever said "dumb bunny" hadn't hunted them.

Sister made walking and running appear effortless thanks to her long legs, as she had been six-two since her youth. Now in her mid-seventies, she had shrunk maybe an inch. It didn't stop her, but she had to admit Marianne Casey could outdo any of them.

A good field master, Marianne kept a sharp eye on the hounds as well as the people. She had people in the field who could take care of those who were flagging. Today that was Susan Watkins. Good thing Susan was on duty. She was shepherding a number of red-faced followers, some surprisingly young. They had no idea that one needed to be fit to beagle or follow bassets, the other type of hound hunting rabbits. If you weren't fit at the beginning of the season, you sure were at the end of it.

Russell Wagner hunted the NTB pack while Winston Bradford, MB, hunted the Bradford pack. The two packs combined nicely. One could never take that for granted, but since the style of hunting proved similar it turned out to be a fabulous joint meet.

Peter Cook, the third MB for NTB and a tall, imposing man, followed with the field. Having a master mixed with the commons, to speak, is always a good idea. With him walked Andrew Bradford, Winston's brother and joint master.

On the right of the beagles Bill Getchell whipped-in. Knowing how tired most of the people were, Bill was particularly vigilant. If hounds found a line again, the masters would probably have to call up trucks and throw the people in to drive them back to the hunt breakfast, where all were heading.

As they crested a low ridge, the distinctive Georgian estate came into view. The late-afternoon sun intensified the contrast between the red brick and the white trim around the windows as it deepened to the color of the turning leaves.

Sister paused a moment to take it all in. Beautiful.

Andrew usually whipped-in but today he felt like being social. He sometimes hunted Bradford Beagles, not evidencing a hunter's flair. When people knew Andrew was carrying the horn they stayed home.

His second wife, the curvaceous, much younger Solange, dutifully supported him.

Andrew's first wife, still good-looking at forty-three, refused to shy away from hunting, at which she excelled. Georgia, ever polite to Solange and always admired by the followers, was even more admired now.

Solange also acted decently. The same could not be said for Andrew. If any man paid too much attention to his new wife he got in their face. He ignored his first wife unless it was to criticize some misdemeanor in the field. People began to like him less and less.

His mother, Olivia, forced "the boys" to keep the peace. She was bored with them, but as matriarch of the Bradfords, a lifetime of work had gone into Bradford Beagles. She had no intention of it failing now because of jealousy, sibling rivalry, who knows what. She had cooked, organized the breakfasts. Hunts at Bradford Hall drew a big crowd thanks to Olivia's warmth, as well as her cooking.

Others paused, too. The view, harmonious, carried one's thoughts to the people who had lived here, built it, passed it down. How many feet trod those green pastures, human, horse, hound? Some of the humans had been free, others not, but the beauty was there for anyone who had the proclivity to enjoy it.

Walking down the ridge with the hounds packing in, they turned left on an old farm road, winding their way to the Georgian estate, Bradford Hall.

Russ and Winston, along with the whippers-in, walked the hounds back to the wagons. As the field walked toward the house, the two masters secured the hounds in makeshift fencing, giving them water and plush beds for comfort. Once the breakfast was over each pack would be driven to their inviting kennels.

The food, so welcome, covered a long old walnut table. Betty, Sister's best friend and the whipper-in for the foxhounds, was chatting with Susan Watkins, comparing the difference in how you hunt rabbits versus foxes. Everyone was talking, laughing, happy to sit with their plate wherever there was room. You don't realize how glorious sitting is until you've run your butt off.

"Seeing as how you've inhaled your food, take a brownie," Susan teased Betty, who had disposed of her plate with unusual speed.

Taking a brownie in her hand, Betty blinked. "Susan, this thing has shot in it, the heaviest brownie I have ever felt."

"Olivia's," Susan mentioned, as Olivia had cooked most everything on the table, or supervised its creation. "Maybe she's found a new use for .28 shotgun shells."

They both laughed.

Betty scanned the room. "Good turnout. How often do you go out with NTB?"

"I try to make every meet. The season flies by so fast. Granted, on the days when the mercury hangs below freezing I question myself."

"Me too. And I find as I get older I mind the cold more."

Susan bit into a brownie. "What do you mind more, heat or cold?"

"Cold. Although summers have gotten so much hotter. It's the humidity that gets me. At least when it's cold I can throw on another sweater. There's no help in the heat."

"Climate change," Susan simply stated. "Although, do we

really know how much we contribute to it as individuals and corporations?" Susan was ever suspicious of easy explanations.

"You know, it doesn't matter. We have to do something." Betty then spotted Beryl. "Beryl looks sleek. She and Winston had their twenty-fifth wedding anniversary, right? It's been that long."

"Actually, they celebrated their twenty-ninth this June. Still in love." Susan grinned. "Me too. I got a goody."

"We both did. My husband is home. We received a last-minute Thanksgiving order. A specially printed dinner invitation, so he's home with the press." Betty's eyes shifted toward a beautiful woman. "I can understand how Andrew lost his composure. Had to have her."

"Yes." Susan murmured, voice low. "I'll give Solange credit. She doesn't rub people's noses in it."

Betty knew that Andrew divorced only to remarry in haste. The picture was quite clear.

"And who are those two wonderful-looking young people?"

"Andrew and Solange's gardener and wife, Scott and Ann Howlett. They were all at college together. The girls were on the girls' volleyball team. Scott was on the men's. He fell for Ann. That's about all I know."

Betty replied, "Andrew has surrounded himself with younger people."

"He has." Susan added, "It surprised me when Andrew hired the Howletts to work for him. I thought he'd be jealous of their friendship. Turns out they keep Solange steady. Apparently she can be emotional and demanding."

"No one wants hunting spoiled with human drama. Olivia has never said a bad word about Andrew's midlife crisis. Then again she hasn't said a good word either."

Betty laughed, which made Susan laugh.

From across the way, Sister, corn bread in hand, noticed her friends' laughter. She leaned toward Olivia, as they were sitting together, old friends. "People are having a grand old time. Great hunt and then you spoil us with this repast. All these years I have enjoyed your hospitality. You never do anything halfway."

"Thank you. Neither do you. But we were trained how to entertain by our mothers. Does that happen anymore? Not only did our mothers train us, they tolerated no complaining."

"Indeed." Sister remembered her mother, strict but fair.

"I follow the hounds from the car. I'm in my middle eighties now, Sister. I'll still go out on a trail ride but I can't hustle along like I used to. My legs get tired."

"I'll feel this tomorrow," Sister said.

Olivia smiled. "You will, but you're still out there."

"You know, I'm not sure I could live without hunting, on horseback, on foot, or even being a wheel whip. When hounds open up, something happens. I feel so alive. It's as though my life is being underlined."

"It's unique." Olivia looked from one son to the other. "I am a master emeritus, but I still have to resolve tiffs. Hunt members are one thing. My sons, another."

"Family." Sister nodded.

"They have always been competitive. Winston, being two years older, would torment Andrew. Just last week he teased Andrew about seeing Scott hug Solange."

"Bet that didn't go over well." Sister thought the statement added a new dimension to competitive.

"Sports bring people closer together. And Solange, Ann, and Scott earned their letters at Michigan State. Andrew, who slouched his way through the University of Virginia, doesn't have those feelings."

"Handsome young man, Scott. I doubt he'd be foolish enough to flirt with Solange. For one thing he could get fired. For another, Solange is his wife's teammate and dear friend."

"When you and I were in college we had a great time. Golf for me. We got all the old, used equipment from the men. We didn't know any different. Those girls are still my friends, those of us who are left."

"No Title IX for us." Sister envied young women at college yet was happy for them. "Think what we could have done."

"True." Olivia reached for Sister's hand, holding it for a minute. "I learned a sport that I still play. Could I have made money? I don't know. Is that the only value? Does anyone play golf, tennis, football, add whatever you want to the list, do they play for love anymore?"

Sister squeezed Olivia's hand. "I don't know. I hope so. I truly hope money isn't the only value."

"We married successful men. Money wasn't their only value but it was up there."

"It was a different time, Olivia. What were our choices?" She looked toward Solange. "She's so beautiful. She could have anyone. If not Andrew she would have married another rich man. What happens to those women who aren't beautiful?"

"Yes. A beautiful woman will always have power."

"You know what? Good. Yes, good. Whatever a woman has to do to get ahead I'm on her side. Patriarchy be damned."

They both laughed.

"How I adore talking to you. We can say anything to each other."

"Well, now that you bring that up, I don't know how Andrew found Solange. He's never discussed it," Sister remarked.

"TV," Olivia flatly stated. "The real estate ads from Washington. Saw her and had to have her and now he does. I felt best not to discuss it, the impulsivity of it."

"How is Beryl? Can she get along with her new sister-in-law?" Sister understood Olivia's point of view.

"She's been neutral. The boys, but not Beryl, and she and Winston are close to Andrew's ex. I'm in the middle. Winston keeps taking Georgia's part and I have told him to leave it. I loved and will always love Georgia. I spend time with Georgia. I have to work at it to spend time with Solange. Her interests are so different from mine. But she makes my son happy. So I do my duty. That's how I think of it."

"I'm sorry you have to go through this."

Olivia shifted in her seat. "We all have problems but I told Andrew: Work it out. Same thing I told Winston, who clearly does not like his new sister-in-law."

"You have your hands full," Sister commiserated.

"I do. I suppose I can be grateful that Andrew didn't buy a red Porsche to go along with his new bride."

Sister laughed. "I'd ask for a 1957 Bentley R."

"Does anyone remember them?"

"Just us old girls," Sister added.

"True. Forgive me. You are my guest and I'm sitting here complaining."

"I'm your friend, I will always listen, even if it's four in the morning."

"Do you think men are weak about getting older?"

"I think we go about it differently. Ray went through a period of endless infidelity. First it disgusted me then I didn't care. I considered most of it his reaction to our son dying," Sister responded.

Olivia thought about this. "You were strong."

"Thank you for thinking so. I thought about RayRay. I thought my son would have wanted me to stick with his father. Try to get him through. And he did eventually, only to drop dead of a heart attack twenty years after RayRay died. I wouldn't say we were in love but we were close finally. I think of them daily. Despite my first husband's ongoing crisis, I was lucky to have them both."

"Barry dropped like a stone. Sometimes I think God gave women a little extra," Olivia said.

"He gave you a lot of extra." Sister beamed at her friend, who was still attractive in her eighth decade.

"Thank you." Olivia plucked a brownie. "I think I overdid the brownies."

Sister picked up one, too. "I need two hands."

As they bit into the super-rich chocolate, Olivia wiped her mouth with a linen napkin. "The best thing I did was revamp my will last year." She paused. "After the remarriage, I didn't want my sons to be able to fight about the disposition of my estate. So I split it pretty much down the middle but I did reserve my jewelry for Beryl and Georgia." When Sister raised her eyebrows, Olivia continued. "I have no daughters. My sons have no daughters, and I still love Georgia. I did leave the sapphire and diamond necklace and bracelet to Solange. Will highlight her blue eyes. Also gave the sable to Solange. She doesn't wear it though. And my library stays intact. If they won't maintain it, it goes to my alma mater, Sweet Briar. Andrew was unhappy about the jewelry. Unfortunately, Winston told him to stuff it. I also left a chunk to Sweet Briar's beloved library. That won't be obvious until I pass."

"Prudent. Gray and I talk about this." Sister mentioned her husband, who was in New York City this weekend. "He reminds me that no matter how well we plan, God knows what will be happening in this country or the world."

"The best laid plans of mice and men," Olivia rejoined.

Both laughed.

CHAPTER 2

October 14, 2024 Monday

Laundry basket perched on one hip, Sister marched down the stairs to the basement laundry room. She divided whites from colors, tossed in the whites, bleach, got the machine rolling. Was there a chore more boring than laundry?

As she walked back up the last stairs she was certain there had to be more tedious chores but at this moment she couldn't think of any. Mucking stalls didn't bother her. Cleaning tack she found restful. Even doing the dishes could be relaxing, one's mind wandering. Doing them felt better than loading up a washing machine.

Sister shied away from machines. The washing machine truly made the chore easier, no hand-scrubbing, rinsing, scrubbing again then carting the clothing out to a wash line. She wondered how her female ancestors accomplished this without losing their minds. She knew her male ancestors didn't do it. Then again, they had their chores assigned by gender and surely some had to be miserable.

Do it and shut up about it was her motto. It had also been her mother's, so that settled that.

Back in the kitchen, she noticed clouds thinning in a blue sky as she glanced out the window over the sink. Most old farmhouses had a window over the sink once there was indoor plumbing. Windows were expensive. Still are. She sat for a moment to check her Monday list on the table. The cat, Golly, on the counter, observed. The dogs remained asleep.

It was eight A.M. Lots of daylight left.

Her cellphone, within a red cover, rested on the wooden table. For most people their cellphone is attached at the hip. Not so with Sister. She checked it periodically but rarely carried it on her person.

The kitchen phone rang. She rose and walked over to lift the receiver off the wall phone.

"Good morning, Glory," Betty's voice cheerfully greeted her.

"Clearing."

"It is. Cool, but given our summer, that's a relief. I'm calling you to give you some news. Ready?"

"Always."

"Olivia Bradford died of a stroke very early this morning. Susan Watkins just called me."

"Ah," Sister exhaled. "What a loss. She was generous and so good-humored. I'm glad we all got to see her yesterday. Had a wonderful talk with her. I'll miss her so much."

"Here's the strange part. No sooner was Olivia taken away in the ambulance than Andrew informed Winston he had to move the kennels because it was on his part of the land."

"What?"

"That's what everyone is saying. Five acres are dedicated to the kennels, but they are on Andrew's part of the land. As you know, she divided up her assets once Andrew got divorced, remarried. It certainly seems fair enough to me, the division I mean," Betty said.

"Those five acres are on the corner of the road. They're

fenced, set back, but it is on a potentially commercial corner or could even be sold as a house site, I suppose. Not that this makes sense."

"Well, I doubt Andrew is facing economic hardship." Betty then added, "Winston has a week to remove the hounds."

"You're kidding me." Sister was more shocked now.

"No."

"We're too far away to offer housing help. What a mess."

Betty cleared her throat. "When Andrew divorced, no one stood in his way, but Winston, shall I say, remonstrated. Maybe this is Andrew's revenge for Winston not supporting the divorce."

"I'd hate to think that. You know what, Betty, this really is disturbing. That is a great pack of hounds. Let me call Adrianna at Bull Run. They are close enough to Bradford Beagles, maybe they have an extra building stashed somewhere. That's the closest hunt I can think of with big territory."

"Right. Warrenton is a bit too far. You know, this dishonors Olivia."

Sister watched a cardinal perched on a branch by her window. "Yes, it does. How long before it winds up in court? Unless the will is clear that the pack has to move." She paused. "Olivia would never do that. She loved the hounds. Never. Never."

"My fear is we'll all be drawn into it."

"People feel compelled to take sides," Sister wisely noted.

"Who would? I can't imagine anyone taking up for Andrew. Especially anyone who hunts . . . be it beagles, bassets, or foxhounds. You don't just throw out hounds."

"No. Andrew is not a stupid man. Perhaps intemperate in his romantic life but not stupid. He has to know there's got to be backlash. A great sum of money might tempt him."

Betty thought about that. "For five acres?"

"Money's the only thing I can think of. Greed? Andrew proving he can make money? Actually, Betty, I have an idea. Will tell you later. In the meantime, let me see if I can reach Adrianna."

"Okay. Keep me posted."

Sister then dialed Adrianna Waddy, MFH of Bull Run. "Sorry to bother you. I don't know if you heard about Olivia Bradford's passing?"

"I did, and I also got an earful about Andrew demanding the beagles be removed from the kennels that are on his property. Heard she divided the land in half."

"Right. Winston has one week to remove the hounds."

"Don't fret. We have a small unused barn at one of our fixtures. It will do until he can build kennels."

Sister exhaled. "Thank the Lord. Bad enough this will blow up, but hounds shouldn't suffer."

"We should be grateful there are no young children." Adrianna then took a breath. "Although I guarantee you that Solange will get pregnant quickly."

"Why?"

"Should the marriage fail she'll still be secure."

"Oh, I never thought of that. They seem to be in love."

"It's new. She's younger. Great-looking. I'm neither for her nor against her; I'm for the beagles."

"Think we all feel that way," Sister replied. "Does anyone have any idea why this . . . upheaval . . . is unfolding?"

"I expect the seven deadly sins may be part of it."

Sister laughed. "Well, I suppose we are all in for a show."

"We are."

"How's cubbing been?"

"Slow. Still too warm. Hounds are focused. The youngsters are learning but until it cools we can only do so much. We've had short runs."

"I feel lucky to have that," Sister confessed.

"The weather will turn. It always does."

They agreed on that, Sister hung up the phone. She checked the clock. Not time to take the washing out yet.

Golly, her long-haired cat, strolled by, tail in the air.

"Good morning."

"Time for breakfast."

Sister recognized that distinctive "feed me" meow. She pulled out a can of expensive cat food, expensive food for the preening puss. The minute the can was opened, the dogs awakened. Putting the food in Golly's bowl on the counter, Sister looked down at two adoring dog faces; her Doberman, Raleigh, and the Harrier, Rooster. They received a half can of ground beef mixed with kibble.

Everyone chowed down. She gave her turtle, J. Edgar Hoover, vegetable bits.

What a happy household.

After making a cup of tea, she sat, not yet ready to cook breakfast. She needed the tea jolt first.

Sitting there she thought about what those five acres at the Bradford estate could be used to generate profit. The county code would need to be changed for a business. All of the central Virginia counties tried to manage development, since natural beauty was one of the draws to the area. So what could be worth the outrage this move would foster?

Depending on the number of division rights, it's possible to build a new look-old home or a fancy inn. That wouldn't generate a lot of traffic yet still bring some money into the county. If shops were part of the inn, it would bring in a bit more money if properly managed.

She took a deep sip of her black tea, which tasted marvelous. She knew she would forever miss Olivia. It was a terrible loss.

Then she considered a big stable. She dismissed that because Andrew probably couldn't tolerate a hack barn, one that rented out horses. They would need a full-time employee for that, as it was time-consuming, plus one had to deal with demanding customers. They would also need to rethink the pastures. Solange didn't seem like the kind of woman to run a hack barn. She didn't seem like the kind of woman to run a clothing store, any store either. But she did consider that Andrew had never truly worked in his life. Maybe he felt he had something to prove to his bride.

The footfall on the back stairway up to the second floor alerted her and the animals, even J. Edgar, that her husband was coming downstairs. His footfalls sounded heavier than hers.

"Good morning, honey," Sister greeted him.

He came over to kiss her on the cheek. "I know you are already industrious."

"Well, the laundry."

He walked over to grind coffee beans. "I love the smell."

"I can do that for you."

"You enjoy your tea. It's nice to see you sitting. In fact, how about eggs over easy?"

"Well, you're being nesty." She teased him.

"Want to keep you happy, as well as fed. You lose weight quickly."

She sighed. "I know and all those people out there are worried about putting on the pounds. Runs in my family."

He puttered around the kitchen.

Golly watched in case he might set butter aside. She could steal a lick. She loved butter, cream, milk, all meat, plus fishies, those crunchies in the shape of fish. Life was good for a cat at Roughneck Farm.

Gray, a good cook, put two plates on the table in no time plus napkins and cutlery.

They ate, happy in each other's company.

Sister told him about Betty's call.

"That's absurd." Gray, a former partner in a powerful accounting firm in Washington, D.C., shook his head.

Although retired, he was often called to counsel difficult cases. Gray understood that politics is a blood sport. He had a skill for uncovering financial malpractice, which his firm attacked with both barrels blazing. Gray was respected and feared. When he was a young man, few took him seriously because he was Black—light-skinned, but Black. He used it to his advantage, getting ahead before people actually noticed. He let the white guys puff up for one another. A few years had passed before the senior partners in the firm realized they had a resourceful, tough employee. Then he was put on the more difficult cases. He seemed to thrive in that environment, and soon even senators shook when he walked into their offices.

He and Sister had known each other most of their lives. Her husband died. He divorced his wife. Eventually they realized their friendship, formed in hunting when both were young, turned out to be more than that.

"Adrianna and Bull Run have found a temporary home for the hounds. Called her as soon as I got off the phone with Betty. Adrianna hunts so much territory I figured something had to be empty somewhere. She was on this even before we spoke."

"Any idea what's really going on?" He finished his coffee.

"Not really, although both Adrianna and I suspect some form of large profit may be involved."

"Or some form of revenge."

"Because of Georgia?" She raised her eyebrows.

"Whenever an older man marries a young woman with significant curves, there is always that possibility."

Sister laughed. "She certainly carries significant curves. Here's the thing about breasts: No one can miss them including other women but it has no effect on women. Or most women, I think."

"Well." How could he answer that? "They *are* just below eye level. You can't miss them."

"Keep going," she goaded him.

"Impressive but not so impressive a man should make decisions based on them. Between her figure and her age, Andrew dumped Georgia, married Solange."

Sister sighed. "I don't want to get pulled into this but I fear many of us will be, especially because of the hounds."

"Honey, it could be worse."

How right he was. It was about to get much worse.

CHAPTER 3

October 15, 2024 Tuesday

"Upsy-daisy." Sister carefully put her hand under an eight-week-old puppy's little bottom, placing the tricolor girl in the puppy wagon.

Two litters filled the wagon, their mothers in there, too. Sister had the last one.

As she scooted the adorable beagle into the wagon, Marianne Casey closed the door, latching it. The adult hounds waited in the larger hound trailer.

A rooster trail of dust appeared, and soon a brand-new GMC half-ton truck pulled to a halt. Andrew got out, slamming the door. His wife got out the other side. She took in the people there to help Winston move the hounds. Sister had driven fifty miles from the south and Marianne and Russ had driven about the same from the north.

Andrew looked at these people. He nodded to them. He had known Sister all his life, as she was one of his mother's good friends.

As to Marianne and Russ he had hunted with them over the years, usually at joint meets. His anger began to simmer, as these people had come to help his brother.

Solange came up to his side. "Would you like me to count the hounds?"

"No, but check the kennels, please. Is the power washer there?"

"Andrew, I took the meds, the collars, the leashes, I left even the brooms," Winston said.

"What did you do? Call everyone with a sob story or worse how—"

Solange interrupted him. "Honey, you might want to check the kennels. You know them better."

Andrew growled at his brother. "Don't you drive away until I check. Everything."

As Andrew walked into the practical kennels, Solange did not follow him.

"I'm sorry," she softly said. "He's devastated by Olivia's death."

Winston couldn't help himself as he shot back, "So am I. Why take it out on me?"

She held up her hands imploringly as Andrew returned, asking, "Where are you going?"

"Adrianna is lending Bradford Beagles a small barn," said Winston.

"Boy, you didn't waste any time, did you?"

"Andrew, you told me to get the beagles out of here. This is your half of the farm. People have been helpful. I'm leaving now before I lose my temper. Mother loved the beagles."

"Don't bring her into it. I'm a joint master."

"No you're not. You threw the pack out of the kennels. God knows what you're going to do to these five acres, but I don't give a damn. You aren't hunting with Bradford Beagles ever again."

"I'll do what I want. I need to get the beagles off my land."

"And you have succeeded. We're going. But don't you ever come near our hounds."

At that, Andrew lunged for his brother, a smaller man. Winston, wiry, let loose a blow to Andrew's stomach. Andrew wasn't in as good shape as Winston, a little soft. He bent over.

"Honey!" Solange cried, then yelled at Winston, "Don't hurt him."

Winston ignored her, landing another punch, which made contact with an audible crunch.

Sister, taller than either man, wondered if she should try to separate them. She looked at Beryl, Winston's surprised wife. She shook her head.

A few teeth flew out of Andrew's mouth as Winston landed a right, a hard right, to his brother's jaw. Sputtering, tears appearing in his eyes, Andrew began flailing, kicking. He bent down to pick up a small rock by the side of the farm road. Finally, Russ—having seen enough—grabbed Andrew's right hand.

"Drop it."

Andrew twisted to hit Russ. With a rock in his hand a landed punch would hurt more. Russ, in great shape, a former CIA man, twisted Andrew's arm. Winston took the opportunity to hit his brother with a left hook, then blasted him with an uppercut with his right hand as Russ held Andrew's hand. This was not what Russ had intended but neither brother had one ounce of self-control.

Solange, stricken, as her husband was getting the worst of it, pleaded, "Honey, please. You'll get hurt. It's two against one."

What a sop to his ego.

Andrew dropped the rock, and Russ let go of his hand. He figured they could fight it out but no weapons. A rock can do a lot of damage. He joined Sister, Beryl, and Marianne.

Andrew, head down, ran at his brother. Winston turned to let him pass, planning to knock him flat from behind. Instead of ramming Winston Andrew stopped, kicked his brother right in the crotch. Winston howled, going down to one knee.

Andrew launched at him. Feeling the effects of the hard kick to the testicles, Winston fell over on his side. Andrew kicked him in the back, kicked him in the head. Winston struggled to get up, swaying a bit. Andrew gave a roundhouse swing. His brother caught his arm, twisted him around, and it was his turn to blast his brother's nether region.

Screaming in pain, Andrew went down. Solange rushed to him. He blinked up at her hazily.

"Stop, honey. I need to take you to the emergency room. You're bleeding, you've lost teeth. God knows what else he's done."

Using that as their cue, Winston hobbled to the large hound trailer, firing it up as Beryl jumped in the passenger side; Marianne and Russ got in the puppy trailer; and Sister hurriedly slid behind the wheel of her SUV.

Andrew, now on his feet, supported by his wife, shook his fist at Winston. "I'll kill you! I'll kill you."

"Honey, he's not worth going to jail over. Come on, baby, you're bleeding."

Andrew allowed himself to be led to the truck by his wife. She opened the door for him. He realized as he climbed up that his legs were shaky and his testicles still hurt.

Solange made sure he buckled up. She got behind the wheel of the expensive truck to head to Warrenton. She figured she could get there in twenty minutes. She wanted him to get to the emergency room.

"I need some painkillers."

"We'll be there as fast as I can get you there. Let a doctor look at you first. I'm sure one will prescribe serious painkillers. You'll need more than aspirin. That was so unfair that they ganged up on you. You would have taken him down."

Oh, how good that sounded.

"I'll sue his ass."

Soothingly, she reassured him, "We can think about that later. Why waste money on him?"

"I'll win. And if I don't win it'll cost him time and money. Or I'll kill him."

"Don't say that. Think about how this looks, Andrew. Your wonderful mother has just died of a stroke. Your brother attacked you." He didn't, but Solange knew just how to handle Andrew. "If you let it go, you are much the bigger man. Let people take your side."

He rooted around in the glove compartment, for handkerchiefs.

She pulled to the side of the road. Got out, opened the back door, and grabbed a towel. She kept towels there as well as a bag of extra cloths. This big-ass truck was another gift from her besotted husband. Back in the driver's seat she handed him the towel. "Hold it on your mouth, keep it a bit firm."

"Right," he mumbled. "Hurts."

"Another ten minutes."

As Solange was tending to Andrew, Sister followed the two vehicles in front of her. She had no idea what had provoked Andrew's attack. Winston came and got the hounds. Well, Andrew being told he was no longer a joint master enraged him but what did he think? He threw them out. She had known Olivia through foxhunting, also a shared interest in architecture once they got to know each other. Olivia introduced Sister to beagling, which she learned to enjoy. Their last conversation hinted at troubles, but knowing

Olivia as she did, Sister figured that was why her friend divided the farm when Andrew dumped Georgia and married a much younger, beautiful woman. Thinking as she drove, admiring the fall color, she was realizing Olivia felt there would be trouble. If only she had asked a few more questions, but then there was no way they could have talked about what Olivia suspected or hoped to avoid once she could no longer be a calming force between her sons.

Sister pulled into the barn at Bull Run on the back acres. She didn't need directions as she had hunted with Bull Run for decades. Loved the territory and the people.

Winston and Beryl were talking to Adrianna. Russ and Marianne just pulled in, Sister behind them.

Adrianna noticed the blood all over Winston.

By the time Sister reached them, Adrianna had the basics of the story.

Winston said to someone he much admired, "Let's get these hounds settled. Adrianna, don't worry about me. It looks worse than it is."

"We put straw in the stalls. We haven't had any frost yet but it will get into the forties. They can snuggle up and the straw will help keep them warm. You can do whatever you need to do. I know you'll have to fence the pastures to divide the males from females. On the other side you can fix that for the puppies. I have two puppy doors in the tack room. Stopped in Orange on the way home from work, so actually you have five doors."

"Adrianna, thank you. And anything we can do to make these beagles safe . . . you know we'll remove it once I build a new kennel. I can't thank you enough."

Adrianna smiled at him. "We're all hound people, Winston. Hounds, first."

Russ and Marianne, already in the barn, thought it would work just fine.

Marianne said, "Just popped into my head. You don't think Andrew would come down here and make trouble, do you?"

"He can't be that stupid."

"I'd hate to bet on that," she replied.

It took six people to get the hounds settled, food put in the tack room, blankets also put down in stall corners. The blankets were from their old kennel, so they smelled a bit like home. Adrianna stayed to help. With six of them all was done in an hour.

Winston, feeling where he'd been hit, would not sit down, even though the others tried to get him to rest just a minute.

Beryl looked around. "This is one of those wonderful old, well-built barns."

"Our ancestors didn't believe in waste or shoddy construction," Adrianna replied. "Would you all like something to eat? We can run up to Mike's. He's out of town but Betty's there." Adrianna mentioned her joint master's wife. "She'd be happy to see you."

Beryl said, "Thank you, but we've got to get back."

"Come on and hunt with us. Despite the drought we're having a good year. If you need horses, I'll have them," Adrianna said.

"Some hunts, foxhunts are getting runs, others not much, we've had just enough moisture to hang in there." Sister was glad for every drop.

"We'll be back, as you know. I'll be here every day to walk them out, feed, clean. Beryl, too, and we have a few members who will help. And if you need hands for anything, we'll do it. I can never repay you for this. Coming through for us on short notice." Winston was so grateful.

"Winston, I haven't had time to tell you how sorry I am that Olivia passed. She was a mentor to me. Sister and your mother helped me. Well, they never stopped helping me, not just when I became a master. This is a small thank-you to a wonderful woman and good hounds." Adrianna took a breath. "I'm glad she . . . well, this is a painful time. I don't understand what's happened."

"Neither do we," Beryl honestly said. "He's changed."

"I'm sorry."

As she drove home, Sister felt some of that sorrow. Two brothers who should have been a support to each other were now enemies, with Andrew screaming he would kill Winston.

The sun was setting as she drove up to her house. Sunrises and sunsets were magical for Sister. She opened the door to two rapturous dogs, a thrilled cat, and her turtle, who may not have been rapturous or thrilled but knew Sister was home. Gray would be home late. She'd fill him in then.

She fed everyone. She made herself a cup of herbal tea. Morning tea would keep her awake. Sitting there, she was exhausted. Seeing that uproar had affected her. Moving the hounds kept her mind off the worst of it, but sitting in her kitchen the ugliness of it hit her. Losing Olivia hit her, too. Another good friend gone.

She wanted to reflect. What happens to people?

CHAPTER 4

October 17, 2024 Thursday

The seven-thirty A.M. start, 48 degrees Fahrenheit gave hounds a chance to pick up scent. Sister and staff knew it wouldn't last for long, as October was proving warm. Then again, fall everywhere was warmer. By this time in her youth even up to her fifties she could depend on frosts by mid-October, the beginning of enough bracing runs to give her young entry confidence.

Young entry were hounds hunting for the first time. They'd been walked with the pack once physically mature. Before that they were walked with one another, learning horn calls and human voices. Every hound knew his or her name and every staff member knew each hound's name. For the youngsters, hearing their name taught them they were being watched. When back in the kennels it meant a treat or affection. If a youngster heard his or her name while hunting, it was usually from a whipper-in and it meant "pay attention."

Because she had two couple young hounds out (hounds are counted in couples), Sister wanted to hunt close to the kennels. If anyone got lost, the hound could find its way back. All those hound walks in the warm weather on Roughneck Farm, After All, her adjoining neighbors, or even across the road at Cindy Chandler's Foxglove would pay off should a hound get lost or go off on illegitimate game.

The whipper-in usually took care of that, guiding the animal back to the pack. Sometimes in heavy woods young entry could get lost or slip off.

Fifteen couple of hounds, noses down, moved across Sister's wildflower field, the huntsman's cottage in the background. They'd been cast from the kennels, which also gave the youngsters a bit of confidence. They would be taken to farther fixtures as each week progressed, and they learned to disembark from the hound trailer, known as the party wagon. Again over the summer they had been taken on short rides with a few older hounds over to Cindy's or even to Tattenhall Station ten miles away or twelve depending on your route.

Today the fours were in the middle of the pack, surrounded by the older hounds. Excited as they were, they kept their noses to the ground.

The tall milkweed bent as the hounds brushed by. Sunflowers, seeds dropped courtesy of birds, also swayed when hounds moved close. The large plants were not trampled. Even the smaller plants, blooms almost gone although the black-eyed Susans were hanging on, bounced right back up if a hound stepped on one.

Sister, leading the field of six, small during cubbing's early hours, inhaled the morning air carrying a touch of refreshing chill.

Weevil, her huntsman, slowly walked along. He took the hog's back jump up ahead, landing in the Bancrofts' land. Betty, whipping in on his right, cleared a jump down the line; while Tootie, whipping in on the left, took a new hastily constructed coop. Her horse, Iota, had a moment then decided all was well.

Tootie, early twenties, so graceful on a horse, attracted attention. Many people were good, strong riders but some have that something extra that makes them elegant. Tootie had it, plus great beauty. She looked like her mother, a Black model who broke into modeling. Her mother, Yvonne, had moved from Chicago to be closer to her daughter, who she loved but didn't exactly mother. Yvonne had divorced her husband, Tootie's father, and dramatically changed her life a few years ago. She'd learned to ride, finding the courage to jump. She loved it.

Sister had Yvonne behind her, as well as Kasmir Barbhaiya and his wife, Alida. Walter Lungren, MD, her joint master, was back there as well as Ben Sidell, the sheriff. Behind them rode Bobby Franklin, Betty's husband, with two new riders. They didn't take the jumps, so Bobby rode a little faster to reach a gate.

Once on After All, hounds picked up their pace. Hopeful. Soon their sterns began to flip, and then Diane, a wonderful hound, opened up.

Everyone joined in, the magical sound of hounds speaking as one, filled the air with excitement. Everyone tightened their leg a bit as they were off.

The run lasted an invigorating fifteen minutes taking the group through the covered bridge, then heading north on the farm road. Scent sputtered, hounds cast about, but not much luck as the temperature was rising.

Not disappointed, Sister patiently waited as Weevil cast again. The run would give all the hounds a bit of reward, promise for more bracing runs in the future. The killer was excessive heat, drought, or torrential rains day after day. Hounds can't find scent in those conditions. Their spirits can flag even though their work ethic does not. Sister wanted them to experience that primal thrill of the chase.

Weevil waited then called the hounds back. "Come along."

He rode toward a house down the farm road from After All's impressive estate. This was called the Home Place, belonging to Gray Lorillard and Sam, his brother.

Gray was not in the field today, home working. Sister thought he worked harder in retirement than when he was in Washington. Sam rode alongside Yvonne. He'd been her coach, fallen in love with her as most men did, but she responded to him to everyone's shock for he hadn't much by way of material possessions except the Home Place. He had blown a scholarship at Harvard thanks to drink. Stayed an alcoholic for years, finally going into rehab in a clinic in Greensboro, North Carolina, paid for by his brother. He was kind, helpful, incredibly smart. Beautiful though Yvonne was, Sam loved her for herself, a new experience for her.

This crossed Sister's mind for a second. She liked seeing people come into their own but at that moment one of the youngsters was coming into his own. A weedy fellow, still filling out, Arnie, stopped.

"A *red*." His voice, deep for one so young, ran out. Diana walked over, sniffed the line, calling, "*He's right.*"

Sister watched all the hounds honor the youngster's find, roaring onward, singing as one.

They barreled down the road, reached the white clapboard home, jumped into the graveyard, jumped out, ran in a big circle around the house, finally stopping at a large tree stump in the back. It was a den but not occupied. However, the fox, Uncle Yancy, used it to foil the pack. Running about ten minutes ahead, hounds closing to seven minutes, he had blasted through the graveyard, jumped in the stump den, jumped out, then ran around again, doubling back on his tracks, slipping into a den in the graveyard as hounds followed his original line. Yancy loved fooling hounds, having dens, cubby holes, even large round bales he used for that exact purpose. His real den was in the mudroom of the house itself. He cleverly had chewed open a hole under the mudroom large enough for him to jump up into the room where he, years ago, learned to pull a pile of old towels over his entrance. Then he'd jump from the tack trunk up to a shelf, finally to a shelf over the door, where more old towels and coats had been folded. Heat from the kitchen warmed the mudroom to a perfect temperature for a fox. After all, he wore a permanent coat, a double coat in winter.

Hounds circled the large stump, digging.

Weevil did not blow "Gone to Ground," for he knew the fox may have been there but he wasn't now. So he praised his hounds, called out Arnie by name, then turned to go back down the road.

Heat was coming up. Hounds' tongues weren't hanging out yet, but another hard run even if only fifteen minutes would do it.

Sister smiled as she watched the young hounds learn their trade. She also wished she hadn't put on a silk undershirt this morning. As the mercury shot up fast, the silk was sticking to her, her regular shirt also sticking to her.

Following Weevil back, she looked up overhead.

Large, white cumulus clouds against a perfectly blue sky announced a beautiful fall morning, even though it didn't feel like fall at the moment.

How tempting it would be to loosen one's tie. Always a stickler for protocol, she wouldn't do it. She would the minute the hunt was over, but mounted never.

They reached the bridge. She let out a low whistle, a signal to Weevil that she was riding up to him.

"Madam." He smiled at her.

"A good start, don't you think?" she asked.

"I do. We've been hunting now since mid-September, the heat has been relentless. We got a bit of a break this morning."

"Let's pick them up on a high note."

"Yes, Madam. If you don't mind, I'll let them play in the creek for a moment. The water will feel good."

"I wouldn't mind it myself." She smiled.

After the hounds drank, plopping down in the water, they rode back to the kennels. Weevil and Tootie put up the hounds, checking everyone's paws. They'd feed them after the breakfast, laid outside the back of the house.

Sitting outside when weather permitted was always a pleasure. Everyone brought a dish. Sister supplied the coffee, tea, and cold drinks.

Horses were given water, tied to trailers. Sister quickly pulled the tack off her Matador, wiped him down enough, put him in the stall. He'd enjoy a good bath after breakfast.

Once everyone was there, they caught up with one another.

The two new members in the back with Bobby happily recounted how much they enjoyed the ride. As they usually rose early the seven-thirty start time was no problem.

One of the women, new to the area, had bought the old farm next to Cindy Chandler's Foxglove. She and her husband and three children were restoring it. She would be starting a hack barn, and being in hunt territory should help business. The barns were in better condition than the house.

"Lorraine, any hunt club can use a barn filled with good horses people can rent."

"I hope to be useful." Lorraine Shoemaker smiled.

The other new member was Dinah Jamison, not quite as talkative but happy, too.

Once everyone was eating, Kasmir and Alida, his wife, sat next to Sister. Betty was on the other side of Alida, Sam and Yvonne across the table. Weevil and Tootie were walking up from the kennels.

"Sister, I'm so sorry you lost a good friend." The Indian gentleman, a hard rider, commiserated with her.

"Thank you. Olivia was a dear friend. Decades of living through each other's ups and downs."

Yvonne, who didn't know Olivia, asked, "Was it expected?"

"No. Stroke," said Sister.

"Olivia started Bradford Beagles back in the early sixties. She still followed, usually in a car. Her two sons ran the club. Except now there is a crisis between them." Betty filled her in, as Sister had told her of events.

"That doesn't sound good," Alida commented. "Right after their mother's passing."

"Fortunately Olivia divided up her estate last year so no one is going to contest the will. She divided it in half. I suppose we should all attend to our wills."

"Sister, no one wants to think about that." Sam smiled.

"No one has ever lived forever, but I'm willing to try." Sister laughed.

"Lorraine and Dinah, you haven't met my aunt yet. She's in her mid-nineties and we know she's lying about that, so I think if anyone lives forever it will be Aunt Daniella," Sam informed them.

"Well, we'd never be bored." Yvonne smiled.

"That's the truth." Betty laughed. "Sister, are Bradford Beagles going out Sunday?"

"I think so. Olivia wouldn't have wanted hunting to stop just because she did." Sister rightly understood her friend.

"Is it true Andrew threatened to kill his brother?" Alida asked.

"News travels fast," Betty commented.

"It does," Alida agreed. "Thanks to you I have gone out with the Bradfords from time to time. I quite like them. I can't believe Andrew threatened to kill Winston."

"Things happen when people lose their tempers," Kasmir,

who barely knew them, remarked. "And with one's mother dying, who knows what got stirred up."

"That's true." Yvonne nodded. "But do you think he'd do it?"

"Perhaps it's best not to speculate. I was there and I attributed it to the passion of the moment, Winston was moving his hounds off what is now Andrew's property. It seems foolish to me, and unnecessary, the five acres on which the kennels sat. Nice kennels," Sister answered.

"How much did he inherit?" Lorraine was enthralled.

"Financially, I have no idea, but he inherits about six hundred acres and Winston also six hundred acres. She divided everything in half."

"Twelve hundred acres?" Lorraine was impressed.

"Beautiful acres." Betty knew the place fairly well having hunted there for years.

"Let's hope it all blows over." Sister changed the subject. "Saturday I thought we could hunt at Tattenhall Station. Kasmir has kindly agreed to it."

"Great idea." Yvonne lived nearby, so she could sleep an extra half hour.

"When do we get a fixture card?" Lorraine asked.

"You should get it in the mail this week. Some hunts put out a card for cubbing but we don't, as so many of our landowners are harvesting their crops. We don't know when they will cut hay, cut corn, wheat. And what I am finding out is climate change is changing that quite a bit. By now in the past almost all the corn would have been cut. Plenty still standing here and in the Valley." She mentioned the Shenandoah Valley, right over the mountains.

"That makes sense." The newcomer was realizing she had a lot to learn.

"All hunting depends on the generosity of landowners," Betty filled in. "We aren't allowed to pay to hunt land. When the Master of Foxhounds Association started in 1907 they were quite clear about that, as they knew if renting land or paying for privilege of hunting were the order of the day, poor hunts would be squeezed out of territory."

"I see." Lorraine nodded.

"Imagine trying to think ahead in 1907." Dinah figured she needed to read some hunting history books.

"Imagine doing it in 1776." Sister laughed.

They all smiled. Those men and their wives, rarely given credit, did indeed create something that was firm enough to last, flexible enough to change.

"And many of those men were foxhunters," Betty added.

"I think our forefathers and -mothers knew how to have a good time," Bobby, swallowing a deviled egg, said.

"We need more good times," Kasmir wisely said.

Later, horses washed, tack cleaned, Sister walked into the house and sat, happy with the hound work. She thought about the foxhunting history, protocol, and she thought about the beagle hunt Sunday, a joint meet with Nantucket-Treweryn Beagles in their territory. She hoped it would be an event. Surely Andrew wouldn't show up to harass his brother. She thought a minute about the young wife.

"That woman will earn every penny." She mused. "A man owes his success to his first wife and his second wife to his success." She said that out loud to her animals sitting around her. "Well, I guess not, as Andrew inherited his money. Maybe rich men buy their young wives like commodities."

Golly avidly listening replied, *"I'd like some catnip."*

CHAPTER 5

October 18, 2024 Friday

"What do you think?" Sister asked her handsome husband standing next to her in the main room at Wolverhampton.

Kasmir, Alida, and Ronnie Haslip, the club treasurer, were with them.

"We're almost there." Gray felt relief.

This was a big project.

"Need to make sure the third-floor fireplaces are serviceable," Ronnie said. The third floor had been the servants' quarters.

"What we need to do is test the propane wall heater up there," Alida, also an accountant but retired, said.

"I thought that was in," Kasmir replied.

"It is but we haven't really tested it," she answered.

"How do you intend to do that?" Ronnie wondered.

"I'll have to spend the night in one of those rooms. That's a test. I'm cold-blooded by nature." She laughed. "That's why I married Kasmir."

Kasmir laughed, too. "All those flues are cleaned. Well, it's two major flues, but every fireplace is cleaned, in order. And right now propane is reasonably priced. Tiger Fuel sensibly prices gas, diesel, propane."

"Yes, they do. All should be well but remember this is an old house and doesn't have the kind of insulation we now have. It's horsehair," Gray reminded them. "We put new insulation in the attic, all the ceilings. We needed to repair most of them without destroying the woodwork where the walls meet the ceiling."

"That is art. All that woodwork, chair rails, staircase carved by Czechs in the nineteenth century is really art." Alida looked dazzled by the work.

"When Wolverhampton was constructed in the 1880s all that carving was done by new immigrants." Sister grinned, as she loved it, too.

"Works." Ronnie shrugged. "Isn't that what you and Sam have at the Home Place?"

"We do. But a high-grade insulation would work better," Gray replied.

"We'd have to take down all the walls, put insulation up, put drywall back up and paint. There are a lot of rooms up here." Kasmir was figuring in his head.

"Do you think people will use these servants' quarters? If we get people who come for hunting, they'll sleep on the second floor. I can't imagine anyone would bring enough people to fill all the servants' quarters," Ronnie noted.

"Who knows how many people will come?"

Alida hoped it would be a lot.

"Staff members, it could add up," Gray thought out loud.

"If that happens we'll deal with it. It will be colder up here but with wall heaters and a fire in the fireplace it ought to be reasonably pleasant. And the bathrooms down the hall will be warm.

Again, we'll cross that bridge when we come to it." Alida was positive.

"I wish we could have gotten this place finished by cubbing season." Ronnie worried about rentals during formal hunting, when it was colder.

"We did the best we could. Look how long it took for Sheila to agree to sell the place," Sister remarked of the owner, in jail for being an accomplice to murder.

She might have been the murderer herself but no one could prove it, so Sheila pinned it on her deceased sister, Veronica. A terrific lawyer made her a good deal. So she was in jail for seventeen years instead of life. The Jefferson Hunt Club, once they had a number willing to form a syndicate, kept at her. She finally agreed to sell the impressive place built in 1880, along with the 750 acres. The price was three and a half million, cheap for the desirable area, especially with all that land and outbuildings, including a good barn with a small cottage. What convinced Sheila was the fact that if the place sat, it would be a snowball on a hill. Get what you can, have your broker invest it. No law against earning money while you're in jail. She finally agreed.

The syndicate included Sister, Gray, Kasmir, Alida, Ronnie, Crawford and Marty Howard, and Yvonne, who also bought ten shares for Sam. Crawford, restoring Old Paradise, down the road in this Chapel Cross area, put up money to secure the well-being of his own huge investment. Plus he wanted to show good faith with Jefferson Hunt, as he had not always done so.

Sister bought ten shares for Betty and Bobby.

Ronnie surprised everyone by volunteering to be in charge of weekly rentals, or weekends. Of course, they would accept a longer tenant, but no one expected that immediately.

Kasmir shrewdly put an ad in *The Wall Street Journal* with a photograph of the impressive house.

Sister put an ad in Horse Country's newspaper. It was a start.

They walked through the rooms, slowly being furnished as everyone ransacked their belongings. Kathleen Sixt Dunbar, an antiques dealer, had been invaluable. Right now the place looked spare, but the furniture was of the period. The rugs added color. The beds upstairs were modern. A huge, stacked pile of firewood was near each fireplace in the house, far enough away to be safe but close enough so one didn't have to go outside. The third floor had an enormous pile of firewood stacked in both large shared social rooms, one for men and one for women. They were quite proper in those days, at least on the surface.

The Sherwood sisters had accomplished a great deal with a crew of women contractors. They took women from halfway houses, even those released from jail, and taught them a trade: glazier, cabinetry, carpentry, floor sander, everything needed for housing restoration. The business boomed and the women seemed to stay out of trouble.

Three murders put this to an end, with Veronica dead and Sheila in jail but everyone had to admit that the work was terrific. The paint matched original colors, curtains also matched old photographs from the 1880s, curtains helped keep the place warm.

It was a risky investment but if renting it out didn't cover some of the expenses, sooner or later the place could be sold, probably at a handsome profit. No risk. No gain.

The library beckoned. "Isn't this the perfect space?" Sister admired it.

"There's not really a bad room in the house. Keeping that woodburning stove in the kitchen was a masterstroke." Alida turned to Ronnie, who argued for it. "We also put an Aga in there. If someone wants to cook they'll have their opportunity. My grandmother used a woodburning stove."

Alida learned a lot by watching her grandmother.

"Bet she was a good cook." Gray remembered his grandmother using the woodburning stove at the Home Place he shared with his brother. He stayed there two days a week, the rest of the time with Sister. It was a wonderful arrangement, giving each of them time apart but most of their life together. Now that Sam and Yvonne were in love even Yvonne stayed there and she, too, owned an impressive historic place, Beveridge Hundred.

Pleased with themselves they returned to the front hall. A knock on the door surprised everyone.

Gray opened it. "Crawford, Marty, please come in."

"Smoke coming from one of the chimneys," Crawford explained.

"You're part of the syndicate. You can come and go as you please." Sister meant that even though they could and did cross swords over time.

"Thank you," Marty, his wife, demurred.

"Please, sit. We started a fire in the living room just to see how it felt and it warms the room. Pulls it together." The wealthy Indian, who had made a fortune in pharmaceuticals, led the Howards to the living room, everyone in tow.

"You know, there's tea in the kitchen. Can I convince any of you to have a sip?" Sister loved her tea.

"Well, it is cold out there today." Marty smiled.

Alida put her arm through Sister's.

"We'll be back with a tray. You all will smell that delicious Assam tea. You'll have to have it."

As the two women reached the kitchen, Sister looked at Alida. "Assam?"

"Bought a can at the tea store. Let me pop out to the car and I'll be right back. Bought a bottle of Blade and Bow bourbon, too. There are ice cubes in the fridges."

The two organized everything while the pot boiled, catching

up on other hunt seasons so far. Hunters are bound to talk about hunting, horses, and hounds when together. With others they'll make a stab at well-rounded conversation.

Within ten minutes a tray was in front of everyone, as well as that bottle of bourbon, glasses, ice cubes, and rather delicate teacups.

"Where did you get this stuff?" Ronnie loved the cups, being a china aficionado, rare for most men.

"Actually, it was a gift from Kathleen, who brought it over last Friday," Alida informed him.

"How's her business going?" Crawford always wanted to know about business.

"A slow summer, a brisk fall." Sister kept up with Kathleen, a road whip along with Aunt Daniella.

"New people?" Alida filled him in then realized essentially she was a new person. "They want fine furniture. Of course, no one has done the research and restoration that you two have. You might think about teaching a college course." Alida's voice was extra warm.

"You flatter us," Marty replied. "But my husband, ever so smart, hired Professor Abruzza as a researcher, and she really has been critical to our project. Of course, Wolverhampton has to deal with people coming and going, which is why we are here."

"Oh." Ronnie's eyebrows shot up.

"We've been contacted by old friends in England who can't stand it anymore. They'd like to come here for hunt season and see how they like it. Labor, now running the show, will make life difficult."

"Well, of course." Kasmir, who had studied at Oxford, immediately answered.

"May we video the place? The rooms. The grounds. The stables," Marty continued.

"Of course," Alida replied echoed by Ronnie, who was thrilled at the thought of receiving a consistent rent for at least four months, if not more.

"You know they know protocol." Crawford sighed. "They are dear friends. We've tried to tell them it's different here."

Sister, as a master, took this one up. "Because our soils, forests were still quite wild compared to England, and we need a different kind of hound. I do hope once they get used to it, they'll like it. And you have your pack of Dumfriesshire hounds. That will seem similar."

"We've had no enclosure laws; but still, our fields tend to be squares and some are even defined by brush. I bet they'll learn to like it." Alida, having visited Oxford with her husband, so hoped this would work.

"Crawford, as you know, I hunted in England throughout my days at Winchester and then Oxford. I would be more than happy to help them. It is a bit of an adjustment, but once you do it, the hunting here is thrilling. Virginia is perfect. Perfect." Kasmir glowed.

"Thank you, I'll put you all in touch." Crawford knew he didn't know enough, not that he wanted to admit it.

"Any children?" Sister asked.

"Grown. Mid-twenties. Unmarried."

Yvonne laughed. "Oh, we can take care of that. This is a university town."

Everyone laughed. Charlottesville and the adjoining counties were filled with youth, good-looking, energetic young people, and the university itself was smashing.

Crawford savored his bourbon. "What is this? I thought I could identify all bourbon, but I don't recognize this one."

"Al Stitzel-Weller Distilling Company, it's put in old Pappy Van Winkle casks." Kasmir, although from India, had learned the joys of American bourbon, being especially fond of Woodford Reserve.

"Really? Where can I get this?" Crawford inquired.

"At the ABC store," Alida told him. "I bought it for Kasmir, but now I have an excuse to buy more. I'll get you a bottle."

"You know I have paid far too much for Pappy Van Winkle," Crawford admitted. "This doesn't taste like it, but there is a lingering velvet on the tongue."

"You men can get poetic about your bourbon." Sister laughed. "For Gray, it's scotch."

"Well—" Gray reached over to his wife's hand.

"So it's settled?" Crawford usually stuck to the subject at hand.

"It is. If they like this, Crawford, you will have made our worries about bills fade away."

"That's the idea."

On the way home, Gray, driving his old Land Cruiser, the toughest car he'd ever owned, murmured, "Remarkable."

"It is. I'll say my prayers that it works, especially since the mortgage is due the first of every month."

"Thinking about protocol," Gray said, "I guess if you're raised with a queen and now king, it's natural."

"Never thought about it, but I'm sure you're right."

"Speaking of being proper. We're going up to White Post to the joint meet. What do we do if Andrew and Winston are there? Didn't Winston tell Andrew he's no longer a joint master?"

"Yes. We ignore it. We concentrate on the hunt and hope Russ is hunting the joint packs. I mean, really hunting them."

"Yes." Gray thought about it. "When you told me over the phone, it sounded absurd to me. I mean, why would Andrew come and act like a joint master if he threw the pack off his land?"

"Honey, I have no idea, but I wouldn't put it past him. Best we don't expect the Bradfords to be reasonable."

C H A P T E R   6

October 18, 2024 Friday
Late Afternoon

Andrew, novocaine wearing off from caps put on his teeth, sat at his desk placed opposite of his wife's desk. She also sat at her desk.

Using a silver letter opener, with a thin blade, the handle topped with a horseshoe containing a horse's head facing left, she flicked open envelopes.

"Bills." She sighed.

"Sympathy cards." He sighed.

Ann Howlett, tall, good-looking, although not as smashing as Solange, walked into the room. She turned to leave.

"What?" Solange asked.

"The miniature crepe myrtles are here. When you get a minute, Scott would like you to look at them before he plants them."

"Five minutes."

"Okay." Ann left.

"Bet it's boring being married to a gardener." Andrew rubbed his chin.

"She loves him. Says he's creative."

Andrew opened a bill addressed to the farm. "Creative? I guess. This bill is for the Leyland cypress he is planting on the border between my land and Winston's."

"That was me," she said. "I knew the land was divided. Of course I had no idea all this . . . well, I had no idea your mother would die. But Leyland cypress grows fast. We won't have to look at Winston's place."

"For forty-two thousand dollars, I guess not." He raised his voice.

"It's only a half mile off the border."

"You could have asked me first!"

"Honey, I did. I don't think you paid attention."

Voice louder, Andrew bellowed, "I wouldn't forget that."

"I didn't really know the price." She worried.

Andrew snatched the letter opener from Solange and threw it on the floor. It rattled. He pushed his chair from the desk to advance on her.

Ann appeared. Too quickly, so she had to have been in the next room, listening.

"Andrew, it's my fault, I told Scott to block that view."

Andrew stopped, stared at Ann, then stared at Solange. "I'll be damned if you two can spend money! I need to know."

"It's my fault." Ann stood her ground.

"Hell!" He kicked the letter opener and stormed out.

Ann walked over, picked up the silver, expensive letter opener. "Here."

Absentmindedly, Solange took it. "He has a filthy temper."

Ann put her hand on Solange's tense shoulder. "I know."

Solange examined the letter opener, pulled a file out of her drawer.

"I'll make this sharper. I'll keep it in here. No point destroying good silver." She paused. "I'm glad you were in the next room."

"I don't trust him." Solange inhaled. "Don't worry. He's easy to manage. Olivia's death has him on edge."

"Yeah, well, I'll make sure he doesn't run out of his Viagra prescription."

They both laughed, as Solange ran her thumb along the edge of the distinctive letter opener.

CHAPTER 7

October 19, 2024 Saturday

Still no frosts, but temperatures were cooling. At five-thirty this morning the mercury was fifty-two. Now, at nine-twenty, give or take, it had climbed to sixty. Getting too warm, but the hunt had been okay, two decent runs.

The hounds, sniffing behind Beveridge Hundred, found traces of scent. Usually they picked up good lines at Yvonne's place. She had built a sturdy doghouse for foxes with two entrances, a plush rug, doors that could be pushed open. This kept the cold air out. The doors accommodated foxes, but not hounds. The best part was, she put down treats, leftovers. She liked watching them. Ribbon, her Norfolk terrier, liked watching them, too. He declared he was protecting her when he barked.

The lines hounds were following headed away from the east back toward Tattenhall Station, the old Norfolk Southern train stop. As this was where they'd started, folks felt they were heading back. Not bad. They'd been out for two hours.

Giorgio, in his prime, walked slowly. *"Coyote."*

The others flocked to check. Coyote it was, legitimate game.

The chatter heated up until it was full cry. Coyotes run mostly straight and fast. Their scent is heavier than fox, easier to follow on a spotty day.

Hounds charged toward the old train station not yet visible, thanks to the rise in the land. They turned sharply left, climbed over a coop jump or under the fence. No stopping them.

A sturdy jump made out of railroad ties loomed up ahead. Weevil cleared it. Tootie and Betty took jumps farther down the fence line. Next came Sister on DeSoto, a horse she bought at the end of last season. He was bombproof, made. Her horses, all wonderful, but a few aging prompted her to buy this good animal she had seen at Bull Run Hunt. It was becoming a marriage made in heaven.

Not only did DeSoto soar over the railroad ties, his landing was so soft. The older she got, the more Sister appreciated those soft landings. A field of fifteen people made it over. Bobby Franklin had to gallop to the gate, open it. But mostly people were getting over, touching the Chapel Hill South Road, only to face another jump, this one beautifully laid stone. Over.

Sister, tight in the tack, was nonetheless relaxed. DeSoto knew his job, which was to stay behind the roaring hounds. What a sound rising heavenward. Most of the people thought that they were in heaven; hard-running quarry, a fine pack of hounds, horses that loved what they did, being with other horses outside, people they liked.

Giorgio, not the fastest hound in the pack, surrendered his first place to Taz, a hound of three years. All the T's moved up. The pack ran flat out over land at Old Paradise, Crawford Howard's restored estate that he opened to the public. He spent time there but didn't live there.

The stables in the distance, shadows still sliding on them, told Sister they had covered about a mile and a half in surprising time.

An old farm road curled around where other farm buildings once stood. These were not rebuilt for accuracy's sake.

If a barn or hay shed had fallen down but was built after the original proprietor's death, Crawford didn't rebuild it. Sophie Marquette had made a fortune stealing from British pay wagons and supply trains during the War of 1812. She was beautiful, clever, and when she would visit their encampments along the James River, the redcoats never suspected her. The men were thrilled to see her. She'd leave with fond goodbyes. A day or two later as they moved toward Maryland or farther toward the ocean, they were besieged by marauders.

She loved it. She grew wildly rich, acquiring thousands of acres in newer territory as opposed to the Tidewater. Chapel Cross, the Wild West at the time, bedazzled her with its beauty. One of those people with a good business head, she kept making money. Born in 1788, she passed in 1851, a good long life.

Sister could never gallop over the rolling land without wishing she had known the courageous, brilliant woman. Beauty is its own power. Sophie used hers well, weakening the invader.

Hounds ran toward the base of the mountain, turned sharp right, blasted through the large graveyards, only to drop down from that slight ridge into cut hay fields, heading east.

Hounds had been out for a bit more than two hours and this was one hell of a finish. Again a stone fence, up and over. Then the road. Another zigzag fence made of railroad ties, and they were back in Tattenhall Station land.

Up over a meadow then a ridge, down, slippery toward the strong creek alongside the old railroad tracks. Boom. Scent vanished. If a coyote dumps you, that's frustrating, it was a hot line. Nothing.

Hounds circled, tired.

"Get 'em up. Get 'em up," Weevil encouraged.

Dasher, a reliable hound, older now, grumbled. *"When did coyotes learn to fly?"*

Hounds laughed, sounding like they were blowing some air out of their noses.

Many higher vertebrates have a sense of humor. Humans miss it. Sister did not. She admired animals, knowing they had abilities she did not and vice versa. She sat there glad for the rest, as the mercury, low sixties, was up enough to sweat during a hard run.

Betty moved along with the hounds as they tried for scent. Tootie did the same on the other side.

Sister stayed back. Those behind her, breathing hard, were grateful.

After ten minutes that seemed longer, nothing, Sister rode up to Weevil. "Good day. Let's call it."

"Yes, Madam."

She grinned at him, adored him. "Coyotes can be a bitch."

He grinned back. "Yes, Madam."

He would never swear in front of his master, though she could swear in front of him.

They walked back to the station looking as it did in the 1920s up to the sixties. It had fallen into disrepair; Kasmir, who bought everything across from Old Paradise, brought it all back to life. One almost expected to hear, "All Aboard."

Finally back at the large parking lot, people dismounted, many removed their tack, put on a halter, and wiped down their horses. Then they put on thin fly sheets. Although some didn't use any type of covering.

Horses can take a chill after a hard run if it's cool. But the mercury continued to climb. No one would take a chill today. Hay bales tied to the side of the trailers, large buckets of water underneath, kept the horses happy.

The people shed their coats, put on a tweed, repaired to the station itself. Inside, tables awaited them, the smell alone drew everyone right to the tables. Kasmir also always hired a bartender. At the other end of the waiting room, two fireplaces, one at each end of the room. A young lady served hot teas and coffee for those desiring that. As the room was large, the fireplaces kept it comfortable since sitting wasn't as warming as galloping.

Gray brought Sister a plate and she sat. People usually peppered her with questions, forgetting she was starved. Sister, like many a foxhunter, didn't eat breakfast before going out. Gray also brought her a hot tea.

Somewhat restored, she answered what was thrown at her, mostly stuff about Bradford Beagles.

Betty, across from her dear friend, jumped in, answered hunting questions so the Master could swallow her food.

A new member, Pete Jensen, sat next to Betty. He could ride, would get better on uneven ground as he came out of the show ring. Granted, he rode in the show ring years ago, for he was in his forties, but he could ride.

"How did the Bradfords make their money? Have heard some of the gossip."

"Roland Bradford, four generations ago, started North Carolina Atlantic Timber," Sister replied. "Over the years they acquired other timber companies and successive generations of Bradfords proved to be good businessmen. Usual, but for me the best part is Olivia ran the company when her husband died in 2002. She increased the profits. She was a wonderful woman, generous to a fault."

Alida, hostess, walked by. "Anyone need anything?"

"It's perfect." All replied.

"Well, Sister, where do you think that coyote went?" Alida asked.

"He's in his den, getting ready for college football."

Gray came back. "Oklahoma."

Sister looked at Pete. "Next comes the betting. If you're a betting man with a favorite team, you're at the right hunt."

Ronnie, plate in hand, found a seat down the table. "I spoke to the English couple, the people Crawford suggested."

"Did you call them?" the Master asked.

"Did." He picked up a piece of warm corn bread. "The man's first name is Prosper. I love it."

"Since you're an accountant, I'd think you would," she teased him. "Remember Prosper Merimee."

It was a normal Jefferson Hunt breakfast. Welcoming new people or guests from another hunt, laughing with old friends, realizing how lucky you were to be healthy enough to hunt, bold enough to do so, and lucky enough to ride in the midst of some of the country's most beautiful land.

Finally, driving home with Betty, the two of them usually hauled the horses in the three-horse trailer, caught up on the hunt, what youngsters were getting it, where the hell did the coyote go, and hadn't Yvonne enhanced the gardening at Beveridge Hundred.

Gray and his brother often rode together, which they did today. Football proved contentious. Different teams. Then they both considered the upcoming election for maybe two minutes. Too much drama for them. They returned to football.

The two old girlfriends chatted.

"I'll pick you up at nine," Sister told Betty.

"Good. Gives us a lot of time to get up to White Post. This is a big state."

"Yes, it is. Gray wanted to go, but he said he could use the quiet time to go over figures. He's working on a consulting job in Richmond. It will be quiet."

"Won't be quiet with Nantucket-Treweryn and Bradford. Should be a rousing hunt." Betty loved watching pack work.

"Should."

"Thank you for giving me a share in the Wolverhampton Syndicate. What a wonderful birthday present. Business has been erratic, picking up for Thanksgiving and Christmas, but I am happy to be part of the syndicate."

"Betty, I can never give you enough. Your friendship has carried me through decades."

They drove in silence, then Betty said, "I think friendship is love made bearable."

CHAPTER 8

October 19, 2024 Saturday Afternoon

Winston directed twenty-two people at his farm. Not only was he paying them, he was paying them overtime. A six-stall barn, ready-made, had been hauled and placed one hundred yards below his beautiful house, the original Bradford House. Yesterday he paid a dozen men to smooth out the places for the stable and yet another group to lay down an inch of concrete for the base.

Slowly the stable was lowered onto the base. Fit perfectly. After that was accomplished, men drilled a hole in which to place four telephone poles at each corner of the ready-made stable. Winston felt this could keep the structure from being blown off its base or even over.

Beryl watched, keeping her mouth shut. The minute the stable was secured, a crew went inside, creating places for male beagles on one side of the stable, females on the other. Flaps were cut into the outside stall doors so the animals could come and go at will. As that was happening, the the fence crew put up heavy chain link. This covered an acre on one side, divided into three large outside areas.

The stable had six stalls. Winston thought everything out. This way young hounds could be separated from older hounds.

The one thing he had not created was a birthing room and a place for a mother and newborn pups. That would come in time. Given the uproar, he didn't want to breed until spring. By that time he would have everything accomplished.

The men worked nonstop.

Fortunately, Winston had a deep checkbook. He happily paid the price because he wanted to get his hounds back home as soon as possible. Grateful as he was to Bull Run, he didn't want to prevail on Adrianna's generosity.

He believed he could move the beagles back Monday at the latest. Painting the new quarters would take a bit longer. Best to get the living quarters, the food storage, the plumbing done now.

As the stable was near the house, all he had to do was run a line from the house well to the kennels. He wanted to dig a new well, but that took county approval, which always took time. The more people who moved into the county, the more rules. He absolutely hated it; but then, he grew up in the country, knew how to properly do things.

Beryl walked back into the house just as she heard a shot, which made her jump.

"Goddammit," Winston cursed.

The workers stopped, then nervously returned to their tasks.

Winston slammed the door of his kitchen. Grabbed his cellphone, which he had left on the table.

Beryl, thinking fast, picked up the phone. "What's happened?"

"Andrew shot at the stable kennels or me or both."

"Calling the sheriff?"

"You damn well bet I am." He dialed. He knew the number by heart, as did many residents of the county.

The sheriff was respected. Like most county law enforcement people the department needed more people, more money. Yet even with reduced circumstances, they proved reliable, being as neutral as possible.

After hearing Winston's complaint, Sheriff Wolf called to his deputy, a younger woman named Kate Fortesque. Originally, he was not in favor of women on the force. As an older fellow, he felt women shouldn't be subjected to danger. In time, he learned how valuable a woman can be. Kate could see things he couldn't when it came to people.

"Okay. Let's go."

On the way, he explained what had happened.

"Has anything like this happened before? If so, I've not heard about it."

"No. Olivia, whom you met, kept the peace. The minute she was gone, all hell broke loose."

Pulling up to the stable being worked on and the chain link going up, the sheriff cut the motor.

"Chain link costs a fortune," Kate exclaimed.

"It sure does. The county could sure use it for the animal shelter. You ready?"

They disembarked, walking to the area where Winston and Beryl supervised.

"Sheriff, thank you for driving out." Winston shook his hand then Kate's.

Beryl remained silent.

Winston reviewed what had happened. Beryl added that she heard the shot as she opened the kitchen door.

"He's threatened to kill me," Winston calmly reported.

Winston then explained moving the beagles, the fight, his brother's threats, as well as the severity of the violence.

"You didn't feel it was serious enough to report?" Sheriff Wolf asked.

"No, not really. Andrew has a short fuse."

Beryl added, "Their mother could keep the peace."

Sheriff Wolf smiled. "Olivia was a wonder. Can you show me the direction from which the shot came?"

"There." Winston pointed in the direction of Andrew's house. "I want to file a complaint."

"Of course. I do need to check with your brother. It's possible there's another explanation."

"He can lie with the best of them," Winston said.

Sheriff Wolf let that pass. Kate meanwhile checked the grounds. Sharp-eyed, she found a casing by one of the telephone poles. She put on her gloves, picked it up, fished a Ziploc bag out of her pocket. She walked back, handing the bag to her boss.

"Good range." He put it in his pocket.

"He's a good shot," Winston simply said. "Bet he was hiding behind that pole. I never saw him."

While the paperwork was filled out, Kate doing that, the two men walked around the stable. Winston again explained what had transpired, why all this activity was going on.

"Any hint that something like this could happen?"

Drawing in a deep breath, Winston replied, "No, not with the beagles but once he divorced and remarried, well, he changed. Anyone who remained close to Georgia became his enemy."

"I see." Sheriff Wolf scribbled a note in his notepad.

"She hunts with us, we all socialize."

"And the new wife?"

"She's quiet. Hasn't made trouble. Avoids Georgia, but isn't rude. She and her gardener and his wife, the Howletts, seem to keep busy at the house, new gardens, all ride, trail riding. They are close to Solange. But I can't fault her. He, on the other hand, seems to have to impress her constantly. God knows how much money he's spent on her. He'll complain about it, but he'll do it." Winston quietly but forcefully said, "I actually believe he wants to kill me."

"Winston, I hope not, but it certainly seems to be serious. I'll go over there now. If you think of anything else, you know where to find me. And I assume you will contact Sharpie?"

"Yes."

Sharpie was Winston and Beryl's lawyer.

As Sheriff Wolf and Kate drove off, she remarked to her boss, "This is a family feud squared."

"Seems like it."

They drove down the long, winding driveway to the old state road, turned left only to turn left onto the long winding driveway up to Ashton Hall, the name of the newer estate.

Sheriff Wolf stopped the car in front of Ashton Hall, built in 1830, whereas Bradford Hall was built immediately after 1781, the end of the war.

Before he could even get out of the car, Andrew was right there.

"Did that son of a bitch call you?"

"He did." Sheriff Wolf got out.

Kate rolled down her window but stayed in the car, noticing Solange standing at the front door, along with Ann and Scott, Scott's arm around his wife's waist.

"He's right. I did shoot. He's putting that right there in my sightline. Sightline!"

The sheriff turned to look. "Yes, it is but it's far enough away."

"The hell it is." Andrew shook his finger in the sheriff's face. "I'll kill that bastard. I swear I will."

Hearing the threat, Solange, Ann, and Scott stepped out.

She stood next to him to calm him down as only she could do. "Andrew, Scott will be planting Leyland cypress. You won't see his kennels. They grow fast."

"I will remove his miserable face from the earth."

"Andrew, please don't say that to Sheriff Wolf. You're upset. Winston isn't worth it."

Ann stood next to Solange, picked up her hand to support her, then dropped it.

Andrew scowled.

Scott moved to stand next to his wife. He didn't want to cross his boss, but he knew he might have to help calm Andrew along with Solange and Ann.

"She's right, Andrew. I must make note of what you say. Should anything happen to your brother, you will be a person of interest," Kate Fortesque warned him.

He blew air out of his nostrils. "I hate his guts."

"You might, but he isn't worth going to jail over. Reconsider, dear." Solange tried to soothe him.

"She's right, boss. She doesn't want to lose you." Ann said exactly the right thing.

Andrew calmed a bit.

"How about I leave you and you forget all this," the sheriff soothingly said as he got back into the squad car.

Kate had never gotten out of it but she sat there scribbling.

As they drove off, the sheriff shook his head.

Kate remarked, "She's drop-dead gorgeous."

He nodded. "If he's lucky, she loves him. If he's willing to pay for this and she doesn't love him, he'll join the ranks of many an older man with a younger woman."

"I often wonder why older women don't marry younger men. You know, older rich women."

"I don't know. Maybe they have more sense." He smiled.

"Better you say that than I do," she came back at him.

CHAPTER 9

October 20, 2024 Sunday

Early-afternoon light bathed White Post in the middle of the crossroads, almost a small square. White Post really was a white post.

Sister drove around it, turning left.

"We made good time," Betty noted. "Not much traffic."

"Lucky." Sister checked the speedometer. "Sometimes I forget to slow down once we're off the main roads. It's beautiful up here."

"Northern Virginia is beautiful. Its weather system is different than ours." Betty leaned back in the comfortable seat.

"I read that somewhere, but mostly I've known it by living it. Think of some hunts we've had with Piedmont, Warrenton, Blue Ridge, Old Dominion, Orange, the list. It's often colder than home by as much as ten degrees. My feet tell me. Ah, think this is where we turn in."

She turned onto Farnley's estate's well-tended land, ponies out in paddocks, where she parked amongst a row of cars. This would be a big day. Joint meets usually were. This one started early because

Bradford Beagles had miles to travel to get here. They would be moved into their new quarters in two days. Winston worked non-stop.

Nantucket-Treweryn bumped casting time up to one o'clock. The light was good. The air coolish, still warmer than normal for this time of year but at least not shooting into the seventies.

Both women emerged from the SUV. Sister had borrowed Gray's Land Cruiser should Bradford need help moving the hounds later.

Marianne saw them. "Welcome. So glad to see you."

Sister and Betty hugged the Master.

Russ and his whipper-in were about to uncork the beagles from their party wagon, which was the perfect size for up to twelve couple hounds. Today Russ pulled six couple. A joint meet demanded careful selection of one's hounds. Too many youngsters could lead to some wandering off but usually it was a touch overwhelming for them. Like any good huntsman, Russ wanted his young entry to develop confidence, to blend into the made pack. He also knew Winston would be bringing his made hounds, also six couple. He'd heard about Andrew's shot when he called last night to check on the number of hounds.

Thirty-five people, in tweeds, good shoes because they'd be running in them, waited. This was a time of catching up with friends, meeting new people. There were always people who had never beagled before. Susan Watkins made sure a member or two who knew the drill was near them to help. She herself would bring up the tail today, a responsibility she happily fulfilled.

Sister greeted everyone she knew, maybe ten people. She hugged Susan, whose husband, Jim Rose, was sitting in the car waiting for latecomers. This was a nice touch on NTB's part. People would be fussed up. Jim, naturally laid-back, could calm them and guide them to the field. Otherwise, a newcomer could blunder right into the middle of a hunted fixture. Never good.

It's possible that if Russ and Winston had a gun, they might fire it in the air if hounds rioted, but that would scare people, too. Neither master feared a riot. They looked forward to a bracing go.

Some people parked on the side of the road, having passed the hunt on their Sunday drive. Susan would wave to them, and if they rolled down a window she'd tell them what was going on and make them feel welcome. NTB left little to chance. Hunting being hunting, no one could ever control what happened, but a good team weeded out what they could control. The rabbit was truly in charge.

Checking his watch, Russ nodded to Winston. They let their hounds out of the hound wagons. The whippers-in surrounded them. At that moment, the hounds were more interested in going to the bathroom than anything else.

A shiny new Mercedes roared down the driveway, parked with a lurch. Andrew got out, as well as Ann and Scott. Solange emerged as Andrew ran around to open the door for her. She had a pile of mail, which she grabbed from the mailbox as they left. She was frustrated with herself, as she should have thought to have a bag in which to put the mail. She had thrown the silver letter opener on the floor.

"What the hell." Marianne couldn't help herself. It did escape her lips.

Sister, being invited up front along with Betty, said under her breath, "Act like a Virginia lady. Pretend everything is just fine."

This made Marianne laugh. Born in Needham, Massachusetts, she had learned Virginia ways, which generally meant a smooth repression of anything uncomfortable. One could always rake it over the coals later with dear friends. The point was: Don't react.

Well, no one did, but they certainly noticed.

Winston's face reddened.

Russ knew enough to just start hunting, which he did. Winston had to stay up with him.

"That son of a bitch," Winston cursed.

"Bella is veering a bit off. But her head is down." Russ cleverly focused Winston on his favorite female hound, who was in fact feathering.

Her tail was rocking.

Bill Getchell, an experienced whip, moved slightly closer. He, too, noticed Andrew, but his job was to keep the hounds on their path. As a Navy man, he was good at discipline.

Andrew hurried up to Bill as he, too, was whipping in, according to him.

Bill didn't say a word, except for, "Dry day but we should get scent."

Solange ran to the field, catching up with Susan, who was watching with Georgia, who was in good shape from running with beagles.

Dear God, why me? Susan thought. "Get a little in front of me, Solange. You'll be bored all the way in the back."

Georgia ignored Solange. The gardener and wife, being younger, were already up in the middle of the field.

"Oh, thank you." The gorgeous blonde gushed and did indeed run, which she could do, up to the middle of the large group, catching up with her two dear friends, who instantly fell in step together.

Outrageous as this was, it was pushed into the background because the joint pack opened at once, flying down the farm road heading south. The hay field, cut, helped hounds move along. Scent was hot. Peter Cook, NTB joint master, was whipping in at a far southeast corner. They ran right for him. He turned to run with them. Tall, long-legged, even he was outpaced. Hounds were flying.

"Tally-ho," a field member yelled as the rabbit broke cover, crossed the farm road only to quickly disappear in thick hedges. Hounds barreled into the hedge, scent began to fade. Rabbit scent is notoriously faint and that fellow knew just how to foil it.

The field caught up as the pack worked to pick up the line. Nothing doing.

"We could push them a bit to the north, half circle," Andrew, hoping to impress Bill, suggested.

"That's up to the masters."

"I'm a master."

Bill, not missing a beat, replied, "Yes, but you aren't hunting the hounds today. Russ is part hound. He'll find scent. Bet you ten bucks."

"Alright." Andrew liked to bet.

Standing on a slight rise, Marianne waited for people to catch up. They were like a beaded necklace when the string has broken, rolling everywhere. She observed Solange run up, noticing what good shape the young woman was in, a good athlete. She also noticed Susan with Georgia bringing up the rear. As Andrew and Bill passed by, fifty yards from them, Solange blew a big kiss at Andrew. Georgia was grossed out. Susan was, too. Her job was to keep the field together. Her reaction was a slight flicker of her eyes.

As everyone gratefully stopped to catch their breath, Russ and Winston walked alongside the shrubs. Finally, they turned and headed back toward the main house, through fields a good quarter mile to the west of the house.

Hounds dutifully, noses down, moved along. Once the pack reached the hay bales in the open field, they let out another roar, moving in a big circle around the bales. Marianne stopped. If they took off straight, she'd follow but running in circles, while the field could do it, could make problems if the rabbit turned back on its own tracks. Then again, who wants to run in a circle?

Hounds sounded glorious. Then Gilly, an NTB stalwart, moved away from the hay bales. Bill and Andrew stayed to the side, slightly behind this run. Hounds picked up speed.

No one could keep up. Fast as they were, Russ and Winston could keep them in sight but not get right behind them. As if on cue, for people were about to drop, the rabbit showed himself, turned, retraced his steps. Now the hounds ran right for the people.

"Hold hard," Marianne ordered.

Sister, thrilled at the hound work, happily stayed still to watch and also watch the rabbit put on the afterburners, only to disappear over a slope. Did he disappear into a den? Who knew, but that fellow saved himself.

Bill turned, realizing Andrew wasn't with him. It wasn't his job to shepherd another whipper-in if the man couldn't keep up, so be it. Andrew may have been thirty years younger than Bill, but Bill possessed an uncanny sense of what hounds would do.

He also knew the territory. Andrew should have known the territory better, but he rarely hunted Bradford Beagles.

Marianne, walking back, picked up field members as she did. Susan, bringing up the rear, stopped when she saw the Master and field master turn back. Susan wished she had brought amyl nitrate. Some of the people looked as though they would pass out. She noticed Solange putting her arm under an older lady's arm. Step by step they walked back, the older woman clearly exhausted. Ann quickly got on the older lady's other side. Scott followed closely in case one of the ladies needed reprieve.

Finally, everyone reached the parking spaces. Hounds were allowed to cool off a bit then walked into two round wire pens, which Jim Rose had put up for both packs. Hounds eagerly walked in, drank some water, laid down. They were well trained. This saved them being put in their trailer, so much less room. The running could raise emotions. This way hounds cooled down. No one wanted a trailer fight.

Winston, noticing Beryl, who had pulled up in the car, left to greet her.

"Perfect timing." He then told her about Andrew.

"It's hard to believe." She kissed him on the cheek.

"Let's go inside." Marianne was on her way to the big house, passing Winston and Beryl.

"Be there in a minute." Winston nodded. "Honey, there's only that one downstairs bathroom. I'll nip over there to the rows of hay bales by the equipment shed. Won't be a minute."

She waited. He ran over. She lost sight of him. He passed Georgia on the way. She briskly walked by the front of the equipment shed to the rear of the house. She wanted to take off her muddy shoes, brush her stockinged feet, and go in the back door.

The tea was perfect but then Mrs. Charles Abeles, elegant and gracious, never failed to delight people. Her selection of tea was highly anticipated and the silver accoutrements were worth the trip along with the artwork. Her daughter, Damaris Abeles Brown, chatted with people, putting them at ease.

Another group of beaglers a bit late, eleven, walked up the stairs, Solange joined them. No one mistreated her. People were polite. For one thing, no one wanted a scene in front of Mrs. Abeles. For another, everyone took off their shoes and when leaving it was easy to confuse, lose shoes, which is why Georgia wisely went in the back door.

The food was wonderful. The tea exactly what one needed. A few gentlemen with flasks offered stronger fare. Everyone was reliving the hunt.

Solange, after twenty minutes, continued to glance at the door.

Finally, she said to Bill Getchell, "Have you seen Andrew? I went back to the car to get a towel, left it with my shoes by the front door. I lost sight of my husband, so I just came up to the breakfast."

"No. I lost him once the hounds tore away from the shed and hay bales. I'm sure he'll show up," Bill replied.

She then walked up to Russ, who was speaking with Peter. "Excuse me. Are there any hounds out?"

Russ replied, "No. All in."

"Have either of you seen my husband?"

Peter said, "No. We haven't."

Concern rising, she asked others had they seen Andrew. No one had.

As the group broke up, Sister and Betty walking out together, Betty remarked, "Can you believe we hunted for over two hours. It felt like fifteen minutes."

"Good hunts always flash by, don't they?"

As the two walked out, Solange caught up with them. "Excuse me. Have you seen Andrew?"

Sister stopped walking. "No. He was whipping in. Maybe Bill knows."

"Bill says he lost him as he passed the shed and the hay bales."

"Maybe he left to go home," Betty volunteered.

"If he did the car would be gone," Solange sensibly answered. "I've called his cell. No answer. Maybe he's so tired he's sitting down."

Betty spoke up. "He's got to be around somewhere. He can't be far. Maybe someone pinned him into a long conversation."

"As long as it isn't Winston." She grimaced.

"Ah, here comes Susan. She was shepherding the rear." Betty wanted nothing to do with this.

Solange left Sister and Betty. Susan, not inclined to like her, wasn't unpleasant.

"Susan, have you seen Andrew? Did he join the tail end of the field?"

"No."

Solange then went on with her worries. Ann and Scott joined, having left the breakfast. She told them she couldn't find Andrew. She was worried.

Scott looked around. "He can't be far. Ann and I will drive the car down the road. It's chilly enough that he would be close, walking back, if he got separated, and we wouldn't see him. It was a hard hunt. Andrew's a bit out of shape."

Solange replied, "He was close to the big hay bales. Not quite at the shed."

Susan feeling she should offer some counsel, said, "You're right, Scott. I'll bet he is tired."

"Give me your keys." Scott held out his hand to Solange. "Andrew has his set. Don't worry. He could have turned back for a minute."

"It's been too many minutes." Her voice registered worry. "And Winston can be hateful."

Ann nodded. "He could but he's at the breakfast now. Really, Solange. Don't worry. Scott and I will take a look. Why don't you go back to the breakfast?"

Susan seconded this suggestion. "A drink will perk you right up."

"No." Solange put her hand in her pocket. "Put these back with my mail. It's all over the seat."

"Sure." Ann and Scott walked toward the Mercedes.

Susan, thinking of NTB first and their hostess, made a good decision much as she didn't want to.

"How about we look a bit, too?" She smiled at Solange.

Sister and Betty watched Susan and Solange go off, as Marianne joined them. Betty told her she well understood how important it was not to create problems for one of their favorite landowners, a lady deep in hunting tradition. The last thing they wanted was Solange asking Mrs. Abeles about Andrew.

"I'll go help." Marianne pulled out her phone, called Russ and told him what she would be doing. "Take the hounds back. I'll get a ride home."

"We'll take you home," Sister offered. "Will give us time to catch up. Maybe he had the sense to be too embarrassed to go inside."

"I doubt it." Marianne lifted her eyebrows.

Deciding to help Susan, who had Solange on her hands alone, they followed twenty paces behind them heading to the equipment shed, where Bill said he'd lost sight of Andrew as he passed that shed. Andrew had fallen behind.

The two reached the round hay bales. Susan stopped to peer down the middle, too tight for a hound. She inhaled the distinct scent of fox. Someone made a good living.

Sister, Marianne, and Betty caught up as Susan and Solange circled the hay bales.

Farm equipment, an older tractor, and a spider wheel tedder stood deep in the shed out of the weather.

Solange and Susan walked inside the shed.

"Andrew!" Solange screamed, running to him.

Her husband had been dumped on the spider wheel tedder, the spikes passing though his body, not all the way but halfway. Susan, stunned, got ahold of herself and ran over to Solange. She gently put her hands on the screaming woman's shoulders. "Solange, best not to keep looking."

"My husband. Someone has killed my husband!"

Sister, Betty, and Marianne rushed up, saw the body, the blood, to their shock. Andrew was jammed on a lower wheel perhaps four feet off the ground, the wheels at different heights.

Marianne called Russ, told him to get everyone out. Then call 911.

Solange screamed, "Winston's killed my husband. I know it! I know it! Get him off of that! Get him off of that!" Solange broke free of Susan, then tried to pull her husband off the lower spider wheel tedder, where he was impaled.

Sister, the tallest, literally picked her up and set her down. "You can't do that. The sheriff needs to see it. You'll destroy evidence."

"I don't care. He can't be like that."

Marianne and Susan looked at each other. Both were strong enough to subdue Solange if need be.

Marianne, voice firm, said, "Let's step away from here. This is a terrible sight. I can hear sirens now."

She couldn't, but it did give Solange pause.

Both NTB women kept Solange away. It was a horrific sight.

Sister studied the body. "Betty, I can't really see, thanks to his coat, but some blood is oozing through his coat."

Betty got close, close enough to smell the metallic smell of fresh blood. "You're right."

"He had to have been dead or dying before he was jammed onto the tedder." Sister's mind was trying to take it all in. "And he didn't scream. Someone would have heard him."

"Well, whoever did it wasn't super tall. It's a lower wheel." Betty, too, was thinking.

Solange sobbed.

Sister and Betty joined Marianne and Susan. Sister reached in her pocket, she always kept linen handkerchiefs. She gave one to Solange, who clutched it in her hand.

Now they did hear sirens.

When the sheriff arrived, he stepped out, Kate stepped out on the other side. They walked to the shed, as Marianne directed. The sight stunned them, too.

The young deputy blurted out, "Someone really wanted him dead."

CHAPTER 10

October 21, 2024 Monday

Overcast skies, an eight-mile-an-hour breeze, the temperature was 52 degrees Fahrenheit but felt cooler. The breeze gave hope that the usually long fall warmth would disappear.

Walking hounds, Sister, Betty, Weevil, and Tootie each wore a sturdy work jacket. Weevil wore an old Carhartt jacket, which cut the wind, a sweater underneath. The girls, as they thought of themselves—well, Sister and Betty did—wore their old trusty Carhartt Detroit jackets, too. These farm canvas jackets proved light enough, so one could move while still having lining for warmth.

Walking through the wildflower field, now shorn of flowers, they reached the hog's back jump into After All, the Bancroft estate. Everyone swung a leg over the jump, which had slumped down from three foot six inches to three foot three inches over the years.

"*Uncle Yancy.*" Trooper sniffed up the fox's scent.

"*Well, we aren't hunting and it's cold,*" Pansy, one of the younger P lines, noted.

The P line, now in their third year of hunting, had improved into steady, reliable workers. Hound lines, like human lines, could be flighty, brilliant, steady, slow to learn or quick. Personalities could range widely, too. Although often hounds from a litter thought more alike than not. And as with people, some animals were outstanding: great noses, strong work ethic, and marvelous problem solvers. One of the hounds, Diana, still close to her prime, noticed all the raptors in the air.

Her littermate, Dreamboat, also looked skyward. *"Storm?"*

"Everyone wants to eat before the rains come." Giorgio could smell the moisture.

"Let's hope it really does come," Zorro declared. *"I'm tired of sniffing up dust. Then I cough."*

"Me too," came the chorus.

"Why don't we walk up to the gate, double-check it. Bobby said it needs WD-40. He also said he'd do it, but I took the precaution, if it is a precaution, of sticking the oil in my pocket in a small Ziploc bag," Betty answered.

"How smart you are." Sister meant it.

They reached the gate.

"Hold up, Weevil, Tootie." Betty unlatched the gate, swinging it on its hinges. "Needs a shot."

She applied the useful oil, swung the gate a few times, squeezed another application. "There. That should hold us until spring."

"Hopeful." Tootie leaned against the three-board fence.

"Well, nothing will help when the hard frosts come. That's why my husband wears his gloves, expensive gloves. They're supple but lined. He usually has to touch the metal," Betty declared. "I don't."

"I suppose the day will come when I can't jump much anymore. I'm not there yet but I do notice the landings more." Sister grimaced.

"Sister, I'm in my early thirties and I notice the landings. The drier the ground, or more frozen, the more I feel it," Weevil kindly said.

"*A raindrop,*" Tatoo crowed. "*Really.*"

Sister held out her palm. "Drops from heaven."

Betty sang "Pennies from Heaven," to everyone's delight.

"Master?" Weevil asked.

"Sure. Let's go back just in case it really does pick up. It's almost worth getting soaked if it does. What a drought this has been. I don't remember anything like this and I've been on earth longer than you all."

"Oh, what's a decade or two?" Betty teased her.

They turned briskly back to the kennels. The rain was now light. The shoulders of their jackets shone with small beads of water.

"*Feels good to be inside.*" Dasher would hunt through anything but he never liked rain.

Huntsman and one whipper-in touched heads, said a few words, putting the hounds back into their kennels or outside runs with the luxurious condos. Weevil then mixed up kibble, a touch of corn oil, and some mash, keeping weight on hounds during the season especially when the mercury fell, proved so important. Lost weight during the season proved very hard to replace. Given that some of the older hounds still had a pound or two to lose, one of Weevil's jobs was to determine what to feed to whom. Most of the hounds could eat from a trough, but a few needed special rations. They needed to be fed separately. A designated small room fulfilled that function.

As the two young people removed collars, fed the boys first, Sister and Betty ducked into the hunt office.

"You know, I think I'll start a fire. The first of the season." Sister started folding up newspapers from the pile of *Wall Street Jour-*

nals she kept in a box. Another large box alongside it held the stacked split wood. Betty joined her in crunching paper.

Sister, on her knees, stuffed the papers in the large fireplace. Betty handed her what she had done. Betty then selected logs from the firewood box.

"Good and heavy." Sister set them in a square.

"Dry. The wood you cut and split over the summer will be dry, too, but what's left from last year's is good as starter logs. Fatback helps." She grabbed a few fatback sticks.

Wood, a higher layer, crossed the square. Sister then took another light piece from Betty, setting it in the middle. She struck a kitchen match. Vroom.

"That's quick." Betty stepped back, as did Sister.

"Don't you love the smell?"

"I do. I have that cherry and pear wood, which Bobby and I save for special occasions. If it smells that good to us, think how it smells to the hounds."

"True. Gray and Sam cut up old apple wood for here, some old peach, too. I'm sure Aunt Daniella has a good supply. Let's sit in front of the fire. Come on, pull up Methuselah's chair."

They sat in the deep old leather-covered cushions. The chairs had been used since the 1920s when Sister's first husband's uncle built the kennels and furnished the office. The kennels were the most recent buildings on the property. Simple brick, as was the main house, it withstood the elements.

When Uncle Arnold died and Ray inherited his property, both he and Sister revamped what needed a bit of restoration. Not much. In the early seventies they replaced most of the interior wall with heavy insulation, covered it with wood panels, and painted. The handblown windows remained untouched, as they did in the main house, which meant you didn't sit near them when it turned cold. If you did, you threw a shawl over your shoulders.

As to painting, Sister tried to keep up with it every ten years. She hated painting.

The office quickly warmed, the aroma of wood filling the room.

"Now that we're alone, what did the sheriff ask you? He spoke to us together then separated us." Betty stretched out her legs.

"Did I see anyone go to the shed? No. Did I hear any noise? No. How long had I known the deceased? Close to forty-two years." Sister paused. "He didn't ask who I thought might have killed him. I actually think that was wise."

"I got the same questions. Although I've only known Andrew for fifteen years. Grisly as the murder was, the sheriff was quite calm."

"With me, too, but then that's his job." Sister also stretched out her legs.

Sister got up and pulled over a hassock for Betty and one for herself. They, too, were ancient vintage. They'd been recovered with thick leather two times since Sister and Big Ray inherited the property.

"Do you have any ideas?" Sister asked her friend, who watched way too many mysteries on TV.

"The obvious suspect would be Winston. Of course, they'd have to prove it. But I'm sure he's been grilled as to his whereabouts." Betty sniffed.

"I'll call Marianne, maybe tomorrow. I'm sure she and the NTB gang have been questioned. Can't be easy, too close to home."

"Boy, that's the truth." Betty folded her hands over her chest. "My hands ache. I don't know why."

"Arthritis." Sister's mouth curved upward.

"I don't have arthritis."

Sister's eyebrows raised. "Well, then I have enough for both of us. Not so much in my hands though. But I tell you, Betty, getting out of bed in the morning and straightening up has become an adventure."

Betty laughed. "I feel it after a hard hunt or too much gardening. Actually, I don't think there's ever too much gardening, but my back says otherwise." She paused, rubbing her hands. "Do you think Winston could have killed his brother?"

"I'd hate to think he would, but we heard Andrew scream he'd kill Winston. A lot of anger between those two," Sister replied.

"I believe Andrew could, but Winston? He doesn't seem like the type."

"No, he really doesn't, and to do something like that literally a few days after your mother's passing, no."

Betty considered this. "Did you ever feel she favored one over the other?"

"That's a tough question." Sister straightened a leg, lifted it up, set it back down. "Olivia was a strict mother. Loving but she was not a mother you sassed. Andrew had a bit of sass. Did she favor Winston over his brother? Not that I could see."

"He'll be the prime suspect. So will Andrew's ex-wife, Georgia."

"Oh dear." Sister was beginning to imagine a large cloud scudding over Bradford Beagles, edges of it would touch NTB, too.

Sister's cell rang. It was in the pocket of her Carhartt. She got up, retrieving it as the coat was hanging on the wall. "Hello."

Betty's ears picked up.

"She's right here with me." Sister then spoke to Betty. "It's Marianne."

Marianne informed her, "We went down to Bull Run today to move hounds back. Winston and Beryl are shaken. Both were really grilled."

"We thought they would be. Winston is a prime suspect. And Georgia."

"Fortunately, she was seen at the tea. No one saw her go out. She said she came into the house through the back door."

"Let's hope others saw her come in."

"I hope so. As for Solange, she was too out of it. God bless Susan. Ann and Scott drove her home. She was hysterical. Threw her mail on the ground. Took off her shoes and threw them. Threw a letter opener. Ann knelt to pick her shoes up. Susan and Jim had to help Ann get Solange in the car. Scott stayed behind the wheel. I think they were afraid Solange might try to drive the car. Everyone was shook up, but Scott and Ann could hold it together."

Sister nodded. "Susan thinks ahead. I guess Ann and Scott will have to keep close to Solange."

"Probably." Marianne confessed. "Susan said they were great, they promised her they'd stay in the house with Solange. They wouldn't leave her alone. They called her doctor. The doctor put Solange to bed. He had given her a powerful sedative. They called Susan to give her that report."

Sister murmured, "It was a shocking sight. How did Georgia take it?"

"Again, *shock* is the only word I can think of, but no tears. No seeming sense of revenge. You know, he got what he deserved kind of thing. He treated her shabbily. It certainly upset his mother, for Olivia loved Georgia. I think she was good to Solange, but they could never be close. This is a terrible thing to say, but I'm glad Olivia didn't live to see this."

"Yes," Sister agreed. "The deaths are so close together. Is there anything we can do for you or for the Bradford Beagles?"

"Thank you. No. Winston will carry on. He'll get a good lawyer. He's going to need one."

"I fear you're right." Sister sighed. "If you need anything, let me know."

"I will."

After Sister clicked off the phone, she and Betty again considered what had happened.

"People are unfair. This will hang over Winston's head." Betty frowned.

"People are so perverse it will make him more interesting." Sister shrugged. "People will want to meet him. Hunt with him."

"Do you think Winston is capable of murder?"

"I guess we are all capable but I don't think he would do it, even outraged as he was by Andrew throwing the pack off those damned five acres. The firing at the new quarters. How stupid! I suppose if Winston were to kill someone it would be in blind rage. Maybe that murder was in a blind rage. Who knows?"

Betty sat up straight then lapsed back into the club chair. "It was grisly."

"He was in the tool shed. Nothing amiss happened even though he was arrogant enough to show up at the hunt. Whoever killed him got close to him, so I figure he knew them."

"Winston. He knew Winston."

"True but given Andrew's threat to kill Winston, I think he would be a bit leery of being alone with his brother in that shed."

"You think someone could have been lurking in the shed?"

"Betty, well, yes in the sense that if skinny they could have hidden between those big hay bales. But again, I think there's more to this than a temper explosion. Maybe Andrew's stupid move gave someone the opportunity to do it to him. Who knows who else he has enraged? He was off the rails: fistfights, threats, moving hounds."

"I, well, let me put it this way. I don't know him that well but I never thought he had a lot of enemies."

"Not that I know of either," Sister agreed. "But maybe he was part of a volatile business deal. Maybe he cost someone a lot of money. Anything is possible."

"Like selling part of the farm, his inheritance." Betty's mind was racing.

"Could be. He didn't have time yet to meddle with his inheritance. If there were a significant financial loss or undoing Olivia would have known. She was a solid businesswoman. She ran North Carolina Atlantic. That's a big operation."

"Right." Betty cupped her chin in her hand.

"Maybe we'll know more when the medical examiner goes over the body. Who is to say he wasn't given drugs before the hunt? Slowed him down. He was led to the shed? Or he could have promised to meet someone there."

"Possible." Betty sank deeper into the chair. "I suppose we'll find out in time."

"Usually the truth comes out."

"Thought of something." Betty's voice rose. "Did Georgia get a good divorce settlement?"

"Yes. He was so in the wrong that Olivia told him to pay up or shut up. Also the last thing she wanted was for the family's finances to be public. Olivia was shrewd, North Carolina is privately held. Even Andrew in the throes of major lust was smart enough to figure that out. And you know Georgia is not a big spender. She reinvested most everything. Georgia didn't get on a plane to go to Paris or Vienna. Buy a new house, you know. She did have to buy a new house, but it's that simple, charming Virginia farmhouse. Okay, six hundred acres. But that's it. But after all that, did Andrew make Solange sign a prenup? No one has even said a word. Andrew lost a lot of money in that divorce. He deserved to pay out millions but he was stupid. I think it hurt Olivia what he did to Georgia and I think that he was so stupid."

"The more we talk about this, the more confusing it gets."

"I expect that is the killer's intent," Sister quietly said.

CHAPTER 11

October 22, 2024 Tuesday

A low ridge, three hundred and forty-five feet, paralleled the Moormans River. Hounds worked the inviting flatland alongside the river. Sister on Keepsake, a dependable Appendix horse, Thoroughbred and Quarter horse, looked below. Tuesday rarely had big fields. As field master, she liked to get her people close to hounds, but today she wanted to watch, a broad view. Behind her rode Yvonne, Sam, Ronnie, and Alida. That was it. Everyone else was either tied down with business, had repairmen coming to the house, or was out of town for a few days. New England was in the middle of the peak of fall color, so a few members had traveled there to see the fabulous reds of all the maples. Color was only just beginning in Virginia by the Blue Ridge. While there were sugar maples, nothing like New England. The oaks began to blush, the sycamores, top of trees, glowed yellow, as did some of the oaks, which ranged from yellow to orange. She looked around, figuring another ten days before the color really hit.

So far, the temperatures remained pleasant. The drought had

caused havoc with crops. Made for horrible footing. Like brick. Well, nothing she or anyone could do about the weather, but it was maddening.

Hounds fanned out. There should have been some scent by the river. Water underground hugged the river's edges. One couldn't see that, but the moisture extended on either bank. Helped pick up scent but nothing today.

She watched. The youngsters, noses down, were learning.

Young Diesel, working next to Pookah, stopped. *"Is this fox?"*

Pookah, older, inhaled a deep breath. *"Turkeys."*

"I thought they left big scratch marks." The youngster was learning, remembering.

"This group was traveling. They scratch when they're looking for food. And don't chase them. Turkeys can get nasty. If there's a flock of them they'll fly right for you."

"Okay." Diesel moved on.

Weevil walked with the pack while Betty and Tootie whipped-in. He knew the day would be difficult, but hounds needed to be encouraged for trying.

An arrow whizzed right by him, flying over the river, sticking in the bank.

Sister, seeing this from above, looked around. A bow hunter, hidden behind a big tree, had no game in sight. This was uncalled for.

She rode down. Her small field followed. Riding up to the bowman, decked out in camouflage, he stepped out.

"The Richardsons did not tell us there would be bow hunting today."

"I paid for this hunting privilege." He was smart enough to be accommodating.

"I'm sure you did." Sister called Weevil. "Pick them up."

"You drove off my game."

"I never saw your game but we are leaving."

He so wanted to be important and right. After all, these were rich assholes in his book. "Bet you never drew a bow."

"How much would you like to bet?" She smiled broadly.

Behind her, Sam smiled. Yvonne noticed, so she drew a bit closer.

"I'll bet you twenty dollars."

She reached into her tweed pocket, drew out two ten-dollar bills; she always carried some cash when riding. "Sam, will you hold my horse? And will you hold his money?"

The man, fortyish, dug into his camo pants, pulling out a twenty, which he handed up to Sam.

Sister dismounted, shook her arms a bit, then asked, "Pick the target."

He pointed to a large oak thirty yards distant.

"You first," she said.

He looked at her, then the target, took his stance, and let fly an arrow. It grazed the side of the tree.

"May I?" She took the bow from his hand, reached into his quiver, pulled out an arrow. She took the stance. It wasn't until she was on the ground that the bowman realized how tall she was. In her prime, Sister was six feet two inches. She'd lost an inch, but she remained often the tallest woman in the room. She flexed the bow. She looked at the arrow, from feathers down to the point. Then she drew and let fly. The arrow hit dead center with a thunk.

She handed his bow back; Sam, now down, gave her a leg up and handed her the money.

"Easiest twenty dollars I ever made." Then she turned and left the bowman fuming.

He, of course, had assumed she would be too weak to pull his bow. Nor did he factor in that she might have good hand-eye coordination. Then again, he'd never jumped a horse, so he had no idea how accurate one had to be to hit your spot.

The small field turned. They wisely refrained from laughing but when they got back to the trailers everyone enjoyed his discomfort.

He, meanwhile, sulked back to his tree.

A few sandwiches filled them up. A small group, so not a lot of food, but enough. Betty had made her chicken salad sandwiches. Yvonne made deviled eggs and Sam brought a chocolate cake. The cooler, as usual, was full of drinks.

Weevil, having seen the arrow hit its mark from the distance, couldn't help but laugh. "He'll think twice before making a bet again."

"Maybe. My experience is people like that don't think. Life is emotion. Needing to be important. They are cannon fodder, if you think about it." Sam shrugged.

"Well, if not cannon fodder, they don't get too far in life." Yvonne cut the cake, saying, "Somone has to cut it."

She then put pieces on plastic plates.

"Mom, you didn't bake this," Tootie teased her.

"I did not. But I could have."

They chatted, enjoying one another's company.

Back at the kennels, the hounds, wishing they could have gotten a tiny run, ate their food, eagerly drank water, then returned to their runs and condos.

Once back in her house, tack cleaned, Sister called Elaine Richardson, a woman she had known for years and liked.

"Sister. How good to hear your voice. How did the hunt go?"

Sister proceeded to tell her.

"Jerry and I have made clear what parts of our farm can be

hunted when. The deer club knows you were hunting the river part of the farm. Jerry will take care of it."

"He was fortyish, scraggly beard, all decked out in camo and the bow was expensive. A traditional bow, I'll give him credit for that."

"Ames Dewey. No one, wait, let me put it this way. He knows the rules. No excuses. Jerry will be more than direct." She paused. "Usually we have no trouble with the hunt club. You know a lot of those fellows. But there were new people. The deer club needs money and so do we, insofar as we rent our land during the season. Have you seen our soybeans? I thought they would make it, but Jerry is leaving them in the field. I suppose it will bring in your foxes."

"Probably. They are omnivores. I think we are all struggling with this weather. I got one decent hay cutting. The second, so-so. I did hear though that crops in the Valley are better because they have had more rain than we have on this side of the mountain. The weather difficulties seem to be endless, no matter where you are in the world."

"Yes. I avoid those discussions. Not with you, but people get so emotional. Solves nothing."

"No, Elaine, it never does."

She hung up her wall phone, which she still used and liked, mostly because the cellphone's service could come and go. She was close to the base of the Blue Ridge.

"You have cat Greenies." Golly reminded her by brushing against her leg.

Hearing the word *Greenies,* both Raleigh and Rooster left their plush beds to join the cat at Sister's feet.

"Beggars." Sister did go to the cabinet to give out the desired treats. Then she opened the fridge, broke off some lettuce, picked up little carrots, which she put in J. Edgar's living quarters, which now had an addition.

The phone rang again.

"Betty, I was going to call you. Spoke to Elaine. She was fine. The fellow was in the wrong."

"Did you tell her about the bet?"

"No." Sister smiled thinking about it.

"I called to tell you Susan Watkins called me. She said during more questioning, that Beryl admitted Winston left her for a moment to go to the hay bales."

"Oh, that's not good."

"When Winston was questioned he said that was true. He went over there to go to the bathroom. He also reported Andrew was not there. Or that he didn't see him because he stayed by the hay bales."

"No sheriff wants an unsolved murder. They double down."

"I'm afraid so. Susan also told me that Solange is still sedated somewhat. Her gardener and his wife are in the house, watching over her."

"That's prudent."

"I wonder if once she comes to her senses will she be revengeful?"

"That will be the second bet I'll take today. I bet she will."

CHAPTER 1 2

October 26, 2024 Saturday

The drought slowed growth. Corn reached only to one's eye. The hay, too, was stunted. Even soybeans began to brown out. The Mitchells, who owned Skidby, cut their hay hoping it would be good enough for the cattle, as it wasn't nutritious enough for their few horses. The fall frustrated everyone. The summer drought lasting for over two months gave way to days of hard rain. Again there was no relief as the ground was so hard that the rain tore up roads, damaged bridges, flowed into creeks and rivers, which then flooded the lowlands. Then the drought returned with a vengeance.

The field, hoping for a bit of action, walked slowly behind the hounds, making good the ground in the front pastures of the old Virginia estate. The Fishers built the frame house in 1840. Additions had been well done. Diana Fisher, pretty as most Fisher women proved to be over the decades, married Dr. Mitchell in the 1970s. So the place was still in the family although the last name had changed.

Diana was a good farmer. Knew the hay was going to be poor. Same with the corn. She didn't make her living farming, thanks to her husband. Had she farmed exclusively she would have invested in an irrigation system but that, too, could prove dicey when creeks were drying up.

The crowd, nearing the mid-forties in number today, gave Sister hope the weather wouldn't keep people away. The ground might be brick, but one could have a lovely day outside no matter what.

People wore salt sack jackets, a light beige jacket often made out of linen, thinking it would warm up. Many wore their lightest tweed. No one thought it would cool off, so they dressed to minimize the warmth. As it was, their heads would sweat in their helmets.

Weevil walked toward the west, hoping the slight breeze would carry a hint of scent into those famed foxhound noses.

Sister, who couldn't personally greet everyone at the beginning, nodded to all. She noticed that Solange Bradford was in the group, flanked by her gardener and his wife. Andrew, a decent rider, knew men would be dazzled by his wife, so he had rarely missed a hunt that she attended. Ann and Scott were solicitous of Solange. Sister knew after the hunt she would have to welcome the widowed woman. It wasn't that she didn't want to be polite, but she wondered what was Solange doing here so shortly after her husband's murder.

The thoughts whisked right out of her head when Barmaid opened as the hounds crossed into a wildflower field even bigger than the one between Sister's farm and Cindy Chandler's.

Hounds opened at once. If anyone was loose in the tack they would regret it.

One could feel the three-beat canter up one's spine thanks to the hard ground. Sister rose into her two point. It somewhat eased the pounding.

A stout new painted coop sat in the fence line up ahead. She cleared it. Rickyroo, her bay Thoroughbred in his prime, a smooth jumper, couldn't do much about the landing.

Bobby galloped to the gate at the corner of the field. By the time Second Flight was all clear, Sister had jumped another coop at the other end of the field into an uncut hay field.

Hounds fanned out then fell back together, running closely together. Betty and Tootie rode ahead. They quickly came to a fork in the creek on their right. Hounds stopped, trying to find the scent. The fox easily foiled his line by jumping in the shallow creek, coming out on one side, jumping back in going to the other side. He or she did this enough so that as the waters widened, hounds had to work harder to cross the creek.

Finally scent vanished. A series of logs, one crossing the creek, possibly gave the animal his way out. Hounds, smart about this, got on the logs, noses down. Nothing. Scent disappeared.

Weevil called the pack to him, paused, allowing everyone to drink and submerge themselves in the creek if they desired. They did. Heat was coming up fast.

Sister watched as deer, stock-still, watched them. The graceful animals stood perhaps a football field away. As a kid she would imagine what it would be to ride a deer. Riding one might be exciting. The jumping would dump humans into the dirt. A deer could walk right up to an obstacle, three and a half feet, four. From a standstill they would rock back slightly and soar over. The sight never failed to amaze her.

"Come along," Weevil told his charges, all of whom got out of the water, shook, and prepared to go wherever he pleased.

He continued to head west. The breeze, four miles an hour, could be helpful, but there wasn't any scent. Those Jefferson hounds would pick up even a hint.

As mercury climbed, Weevil slowed a bit. No point trotting.

After an hour of viewing undulating country but no scent, Sister rode up to him. After a short conference, he nodded, she turned back to the field noticing everyone looked a bit damp, a few patted their foreheads with handkerchiefs. Turning back as she noticed raptors flying low over the mounted people. Very intelligent, keen-eyed, the birds hoped the horses would dislodge some mice; however, even the mice were sitting tight.

Finally back at the trailers, people tied up their horses. A few took off saddles, sponged their horses as their horses drank out of their buckets.

Sister, who usually left the saddle on, removed it. The saddle could keep a horse's back warm when it was cold, but in this heat she wanted to give Rickyroo a chance to cool off. Then she threw his fly sheet over Rickyroo.

She couldn't wait to get out of her coat. She loosened her tie just a bit, slipped on her breakfast tweed, and walked to the group along with Betty, Tootie, and Weevil, who had finished walking and loading up hounds.

The hounds also had water buckets in the trailer. They drank then laid down, soon fast asleep.

Kasmir, Alida, Freddie, Ronnie, Yvonne, Sam, and Gray helped put out the food with Kathleen, who came in early. Aunt Daniella, her wheel whip partner, sat in a chair, bourbon in hand.

People dragged over their folding chairs, got food, and sat.

Sister would often eat last, for she greeted everyone.

Solange quietly said, "Thank you for allowing me to hunt. I needed to have a change of scene. Your hounds did so well on a difficult day."

"Thank you." Sister smiled. "I hope despite the heat this has helped you a bit."

"It's hard to be home. I keep waiting for him to come through the door, then I burst into tears. I can't control myself. Forgive me.

You've known the Bradfords for so long. I'm not asking anyone to take sides. I think the law will sort it out. Of course, I think Winston killed his brother, but there's nothing to gain by obsessing about it with other people."

"That's a wise decision." Sister complimented her.

"When things calm down, please come up and see what Scott and Ann have done for the gardens. All the old trees, huge bushes, are there. Most of the changes we made were annuals, some perennials. A bit more color. Olivia used to tell me you liked gardening. She was an avid gardener, as you know. And I'm putting up Leyland Cypress to obscure the view of Winston's house. Leyland Cypress is so graceful. I think Olivia would have approved."

"She studied gardens in England and France. She stretched her studies to Wales, Ireland then she discovered the Baltic States. We don't think of them, but she said some of the gardens there were spectacular. You two must have had exciting talks." Sister missed Olivia, thinking of her often.

"We did. She was gracious to me. I know I wasn't what she expected."

"These things happen. Divorce rattles everyone, but it all turned out."

Solange almost whispered, eyes now moist, "We loved each other."

She'd started to turn back to the table when Sister asked her, "Have you read Gertrude Jekyll?"

"I have."

"Good." Sister smiled then also asked about her good friends who nodded they, too, had read the great lady's work. After making the rounds, she hit the table, plate with deviled eggs and Alida's ham and cheese sandwiches. Once seated, she realized she was starving.

"Honey," she called to her husband, who was on his feet. "Will you move my chair next to Aunt Daniella?"

"Of course."

When at last she was seated next to one of her favorite people, Sister asked, "Did you see anything in the car?"

"No. A few deer but not much moving about today. Got too hot too fast."

"Yes, it did."

"Who's the raving beauty?" Aunt Daniella nodded toward Solange, who was talking with people, mostly men.

"Solange Bradford. Her husband was—"

"Yes, sorry to cut you off. Gray told me. She's moving about with unseemly haste."

"She said she had to get out of the house." Sister repeated what Solange had said.

"Yes, but that doesn't mean one has to be out in public. I stick to the old ways."

"I do, too, but people grieve differently," Sister agreed. "How are you feeling?"

"Fine. As long as I can take my daily walk, I'm good. I need to move about in fresh air. Always did."

"Me too."

They caught up on each other's activities. Kathleen joined them. How relaxing it was to talk to friends.

Once home, horses put up, house animals fed, showers taken, Sister and Gray sat in the library, where he nursed a scotch.

"The house is cool, not too cool, not too hot."

"I set the thermostat at seventy-four. This house seems to handle whatever the season is."

"The new heat pump helps."

He grimaced. "Cost over ten thousand dollars. The old heat pump lasted thirty years."

"Stuff is built to disintegrate but like you, I nearly passed out when we got the bill. Still, well, I could get through the summer.

After all this house is protected by huge trees, but I couldn't get through the winter. I don't know how our ancestors did it."

"Lots of wood. Lots of fireplaces. Sam has the thermostat at the Home Place set at sixty-five. He keeps the fire going in the living room and the kitchen. He doesn't mind a cold bedroom. Once you're under the covers, it heats up fast enough."

"Heats up faster if I'm under the covers," Golly, sprawled on the sofa, announced.

Sister absentmindedly petted the long-haired calico.

"Given all that's transpired, Andrew's wife appeared to be stable."

"I told you what she said to me. She was calm. One can be calm yet be suffering. I called Marianne while you were showering. She said Solange has also been hunting up there. She's been out with Old Dominion and Warrenton. She doesn't want to be home."

"The great thing about hunting is while you're out there, you can't think about much else."

She agreed with her husband. "You can't. I believe that's why we are so renewed. We are alive in the moment. Sometimes a sliver of fear shoots through your veins."

He laughed. "Whenever anyone tells me they've never been frightened in the hunt field, I know I'm in the company of a liar."

"Me too. What did you think of her gardener and his wife?"

"A stunning pair. Thought that when I saw them at White Post. They seem close."

"I told Marianne that Solange invited me to see the gardens. They've been somewhat changed since Georgia was there. Georgia built on what Olivia started. Oh, Marianne said some people are suspicious about Georgia. Others Winston. People should shut up."

"Honey, that will never happen. People think their reproductive organs are the most seductive part of the human body but it's the tongue."

This set them both laughing.

He sipped his good scotch then asked, "Do you think either Georgia or Winston could kill?"

She thought about this. "If someone they loved was threatened, yes. Andrew screamed he would kill Winston. Rage. Winston knew that. He's seen his brother blow his top plenty of times. But no. Winston wouldn't kill. As for Georgia, she would have nothing to gain."

"Revenge," Gray replied.

"Andrew and Solange have been married one year. I'd think the satisfaction of revenge would fade with time. And I really don't see Georgia as a killer."

"Me neither but I wondered what you thought. You've known them longer than I have."

"It certainly was a dramatic death." She put her feet up on the coffee table. "Feels good."

"Like the death in *The List of Adrian Messenger*, remember with Burt Lancaster hung up on the farm equipment?"

"Yes. He was too clever by half." She loved the movie. "Maybe that will happen to our killer."

CHAPTER 13

October 27, 2024 Sunday

A winter sky hovered over the Episcopalian church. Sister left the service with Betty and Bobby. Gray had gone to the African Methodist church, taking his aunt Daniella. Sam attended mass with Yvonne. Usually he accompanied his aunt but lately he'd found himself enraptured by the theater and color of the Catholic service. Yvonne, wisely, said little although she eagerly answered his questions.

Sitting in Bobby's car, a low-slung older BMW, Sister sighed lightly as the heat came on.

"Do you think it will snow?" Betty asked her friend.

"Looks like it. How odd that it was so warm even two days ago. I can't figure out the weather." She peered out the window as they pulled out from the parking lot. "I do love snow. Cleansing somehow."

"It is. That pure white." Bobby drove westward toward the Lorillard home, which would take twenty minutes or more depending on traffic.

"I love looking at it but my hands and feet suffer. Do you know there are now knee-length electric socks, well, they aren't really electric, but you plug them in and when charged the warmth lasts twenty hours. I am tempted." Betty stared at the big orthopedic hospital, University of Virginia, on 250 West. "Dear God."

"Is that a prayer's beginning or an exclamation?"

"Oh, me. Medicine is such a big business and with so many old people will only get bigger."

"Careful," Sister warned.

"You know what I mean," Betty replied.

"Honey, we are all candidates, sooner or later, for shoulder, hip, knee replacements. Those operations are a cash cow for any hospital." Bobby didn't mind the stream of traffic as the churches had let out.

"Before I forget it, November is almost upon us. Any suggestions for Thanksgiving hunt? Anything different?" Sister asked. "That's our second high holy day."

"No. Having it at Mill Ruins makes it special. Walter opens up the house. How he has time, being a cardiologist, I don't know. Love being in the old place."

"Okay. I love Thanksgiving. It isn't commercialized. Another thing before I forget. Betty, we need to silently raise money for Weevil and Tootie for their club Christmas gift."

"I've already started. Talking, I mean. People are good about it. It's been a spotty season so far, even for the beaglers, too."

"Yes, well, they have more to deal with right now than we do. The Bradford crisis has cast a pall over clubs. Not in a sense that anyone thinks a master will be impaled but in the sense that it's horrible publicity."

"I bet. Think of what it means about a club's kennel location." Bobby nodded, finally able to pick up speed to fifty-five miles an hour. "If kennels are on private property they can be lost if the property changes hands for any reason. That's why it's important for clubs foxhunting, beagling, bassets, to own the kennels."

"I own ours."

"You do." Bobby smiled in the rearview mirror. "What happens when you're gone?"

"Oh, on the surface it looks like we have rich people who can take it over. But no one is but so young. We need someone in his or her thirties or forties or we need, say, the Barbhaiyas to run it until younger people can be found. There would be no point in abandoning or destroying those serviceable and actually quite pretty kennels. Pretty to my eye anyway." She sighed. "In my heart of hearts, I dream Tootie and Weevil will marry and they'll carry on."

"Maybe we should sit down with a few friends and talk this out," Betty suggested.

"Let's get Wolverhampton rented first. Haven't heard a peep."

"Sister, Ronnie has to be on it. You know how persistent he is. He has to be wooing those English people here to see it and hunt, which means we'd better have some good mounts for them. Why would they want to rent a big place in the middle of a lackluster hunt?" Betty had given all this much thought.

"Well, this season has been lackluster. We've had a few good runs but nothing really long and those runs have been early before mercury climbs." Sister looked out the window. "Looks as though it won't climb today."

"Let us pray." Betty grinned.

"I thought we did that," Bobby teased her as he drove over the covered bridge and on back to the Home Place.

Sam, who had prepared the meat, cut the vegetables and potatoes before church, was in the kitchen with Yvonne. They both enjoyed cooking and the rest of the group, in the living room, could hear the occasional pot bang on the stove.

Aunt Daniella, wrapped in a shawl, sitting beside the fireplace, listened. "Sam is a lot like his mother. Cooking, gardening, he takes pride in it. I never did."

Gray, sitting next to his aunt, praised her. "You're a good cook."

"Thank you, but I'm not imaginative."

They caught up with one another, compared sermons, a bell rang.

"Dinner." Sam's voice rang out.

Gray escorted his aunt, Sister behind him, while Bobby and Betty brought up the rear.

As they sat at the table, Aunt Daniella said grace.

Dishes were passed. Gray cut the fabulous roast beef, wine was poured. They talked, laughed, seasoned the dinner with enough gossip.

Everyone agreed if the decent snow came early, they would celebrate with a gathering at Roughneck Farm. An impromptu supper and drinks.

After dinner they sat in the living room.

Uncle Yancy swooned as the aroma drifted into the mudroom from the kitchen. He could barely wait until the garbage was put out.

The humans didn't know he was there, but he could have given them a weather report. His senses proved better than radar. It would snow slightly tonight.

A jingle bell ringing irritated Sister. She'd forgotten to turn off her cellphone, leaving it in her deep skirt pocket. "Damn thing." She fished it out. "I'm sorry. I need to take this." She rose, walked into the kitchen, where Yvonne and Sam were stacking the dishwasher. She opened the door, stepping out into the mudroom, which was much cooler. She could smell Uncle Yancy but had no idea he was above her.

"Marianne."

"Had to call you. Bradford was hunting today at the home fixture. The sheriff arrived with reinforcement. When Winston came in with the beagles after hunting he was arrested in front of everyone on suspicion of murder."

"Good Lord. That's awful." She paused. "Was Solange there?"

"No."

"I am so sorry to hear it's come to this."

"My fear is it's only going to get worse."

CHAPTER 14

October 28, 2024 Monday

"Good girl." Sister patted a shiny beagle as she walked the tricolor into her new quarters.

"She is a good girl." Beryl, in the next stall, standing, echoed Sister's thoughts.

Sister and Betty had driven up in Sister's SUV, lots of miles on that odometer.

Marianne and Susan Watkins came from Clark County.

Georgia brought in another fresh hay bale. "This should do it."

The women were making the stalls warm, comfortable. Each stall had a run attached to it, chain-link fencing. That run could be closed in the back, fifty yards, by a gate. All the runs opened onto a two-acre playground. The boys were on one side of the stable, the girls on another.

"These dog doors close pretty good," Susan noted. "New. Doors will soon need to be replaced, all that coming and going."

"Good for them to be able to go in and out. We have it for the foxhounds. The doors are bigger and we need to replace ours, too. They wear out fast." Sister sat in the straw to pet the girls, most from ages three to six.

"Sister, you could have asked for a chair. I've got a folding chair in the back of the truck," Susan offered.

"Why? You think I'll struggle to get up again?" Sister teased her.

"If you don't, I would."

"Susan, don't pay attention to her. She will get up easily enough. She likes to show off." Betty pretended to grumble.

"How do you know I just don't have better drugs than you all." Sister teased them right back.

They chatted, made light of things but there was an undercurrent of darkness for it had been a troublesome day. Winston, allowed a phone call, had called Beryl last night, begging her to bring the hounds up from Bull Run. He felt Adrianna Waddy and her joint master Mike Long had been very helpful, but having a pack of hounds in a barn was a lot to ask. And this would ultimately be easier on the Bradford Beagles people. Running back and forth to Bull Run territory was a hike. He wanted the hounds close to Beryl, Georgia, whippers-in.

The women met there at nine in the morning, loading up the hounds. Georgia stayed behind to clean the stables, not a lot to do, then she joined everyone at the new stable/kennels.

Winston, paying everyone fortunately before he was arrested, saw all the work accomplished except for painting. That would be done next spring when he felt they could shift the hounds around so those excellent noses wouldn't be full of paint smell. Like all huntsmen, Winston wished to protect his hounds' noses. He also gave Beryl strict instructions about walking, puppy work, and so forth.

She knew it all but it made him feel better as he waited in the county jail. The jail, simple, would have been easy to break into or out of but Winston harbored no such ideas. He prayed the legal team from McGuire Woods would spring him soon enough. His father used McGuire Woods, knew all the partners. The company now had depth throughout the Mid-Atlantic. Large though it was, clients were not lost in the numbers and a Bradford would never be lost.

Then again, with a last name of Bradford one would not be forgotten. The Bradfords came to Virginia in 1607, survived the starving time and eventually flourished. They felt we had to separate from England, worked to do so and fought in a war that so many felt was never to be won. The men who survived never forgot their commanders or the men under them. It was a Bradford trait to be loyal to anyone who helped the family, free or not free.

Winston wasn't worried. Beryl was. She knew Andrew had inherited a huge sum of money, which was now for all purposes in Solange's hands. Solange would pursue conviction, she was sure.

But Beryl dutifully listened, filled the other women in as they worked. Their work was almost done. Georgia had called for pizza. No time to cook anything and Beryl and Georgia wanted to at least feed the dear friends who helped them.

Sister was now kissing the stout girl with a wiggly tail.

"If that hound is missing, I'll know where to look." Beryl smiled.

"I can't help it." Sister kissed the hound again.

"She's the biggest softie. I veer away anytime we are near an animal shelter." Betty put down an old blanket.

Some hounds like to get in beds in heavy straw and hay. Others want to snuggle in a blanket. So every stall had deep straw and a handful of old blankets.

Hounds had been fed in the center aisle with troughs. Water was clipped to the side of every stall so hounds could drink at will.

Beryl walked up and down the aisle, checking the hounds. "Girls, I think we're done."

The pizza truck pulled up at the right time. Georgia went out to pay as Beryl shushed Sister, Betty, and Susan into the tack room. A table was in there and some foldout chairs. A big wing chair was also there. Winston had instructed two of the male workers to have the space ready for someone to sit. There was also a refrigerator and a hot plate. Beryl had filled the fridge with water, sodas, and beer.

The ladies sat, realizing they were more tired than they'd thought. Georgia cut the pizza, took the drink orders. They eagerly ate the pizza.

"You know what? I forgot bread." Beryl rose up.

"Sit down," Sister ordered her. "We are fine. You don't need to run up to the house. You've had enough to do."

Slowly Beryl sat. She felt her shoulders relax a little.

Georgia held up her soda. "Here's to a good day's work."

They clinked glasses.

"Nothing was hard. Mostly it was time commitment. Oh, I put some of the meds in the fridge. The others are in the cabinet." Susan pointed to the cabinets along one wall.

"Thanks." Beryl polished off her slice. "Vet prices have gone up."

Sister agreed. "They have but then so has everything else. I'm grateful I'm not on any medication. Expensive. My friends with diabetes are paying more. I doubt we will ever see drug prices drop despite what the government says about controlling costs."

"Costs usually don't come down but then again look at the price of computers and TVs over the years," Georgia remarked.

"True." Betty thought about it. "I guess I still believe in competition. If there's competition prices will at least stabilize and there will be times when they do drop. But mostly I think, say, like surging inflation, when people get accustomed to paying a spiked price it rarely falls and if it does, slowly."

"Corrupt," Susan simply replied. "We are living through a period of almost complete corruption."

"I want to argue that but I can't." Sister wiped her hands on her napkin.

"That's what worries me. Can Winston get a fair trial?" Beryl softly said.

"In essence it's Bradford versus Bradford. A rich man is accused of killing his rich brother by his rich wife." Susan looked at Beryl. "Sorry to be so blunt. I think the judge will be level."

"You have good people here." Sister wanted to bolster Beryl.

Georgia picked it up. "We do. My hope is that he gets out on bail."

"They'll set it high," Susan correctly noted.

"Pretty much the county has to do that. Otherwise it doesn't look fair," Susan added.

"I just want him home. Until then I'll go down after hound walk and show him pictures of the hounds. Show him what we've all done. I'm hoping he'll be out on bail next week."

"Me too," the others replied in unison.

Georgia murmured, "I bet Solange's lawyers will argue she's in danger."

"Then you'll have a psychological evaluation. More time. But he'll be out. I don't for one minute think Winston killed his brother but I also don't think this will be an easy case." Susan was forthright. "Starting with the beagles being thrown out of the kennels, after Olivia died there isn't much that makes sense."

Sister, leaning back a bit, sighed. "Something will make sense in time."

"Does anyone have any idea what really is happening?" Beryl, voice a bit shaky, asked.

"No," came the chorus.

"No," Georgia again reiterated. "But I bet I'll be on the griddle, too."

"Why?" Susan wondered.

"Because I came in the back door for the hunt breakfast. I passed the hay bales and the shed. It's a matter of time."

"Georgia, what do you have to do with this?" Betty's eyebrows shot up.

"Why wouldn't Solange accuse me of killing her husband out of revenge?"

"I thought you more or less got along." Susan felt uncomfortable, as Georgia could be right.

"On the surface. We did."

"Do you think she was afraid he'd go back to you? I mean, she is expensive. Most young wives are." Susan exhaled.

"God no, she had him under her thumb. But she knew, she knows, I belong in this community. She doesn't. Few people have been nasty to her, but few have made her part of the group. Yes, if there was a dinner invitation, she went, beautifully dressed, was treated well, but she can't be so stupid as to think she's part of this. I think she's only relaxed with the Howletts, her friends. She has none here."

"Yes. Yes, I can see that." Sister was getting the picture. "If he ever divorced her she'd be out, with a bundle but really out."

"Well, he wouldn't divorce her. Then he'd have to admit he was snookered." Georgia couldn't help that remark.

Many would have said worse.

Sister paused then said, "If only Olivia were alive. She would have more insight than the rest of us."

"She never said a bad word." Beryl's voice rose. "But one knew, knowing Olivia, that she worried about what he had done."

"Like male menopause?" Betty asked.

"Female is bad enough." Beryl cracked a smile. "But anything is possible."

"Do you think he gave her cash? Gave her a separate bank account?" Susan was really thinking now. "I mean, she could have been socking away money since dating."

"Yes, she could have done that. He spent plenty on her even when dating, but most of it was to show off his hot babe to other men. At least that's what I think and that's what Winston thought." Beryl had pondered this, of course.

Susan nodded. "True."

"Well, yes, but what if she's in love with someone else?" Betty piped up.

"We'd know. I think we'd know by now." Beryl folded her hands on the table.

"Maybe we couldn't. You mean, someone like Scott?" Betty said.

"Good Lord. I never thought of him." Beryl's eyes widened.

"They are close. Granted they've known each other since Michigan State. And you'd think Ann would fight back. I doubt there's another person."

"It's possible but not probable." Susan shrugged.

"While I think that's far-fetched, I don't think it's far-fetched that I won't be questioned again. I'll be grilled." Georgia held her hands out, palms upward. "If you think about it, I did have time to kill him. Was there a time when I could have killed him if I could? You bet. But I began to understand I was better off. I could be my own person and that person is a middle-aged woman who has a few of her own passions like opera. Things he loathed. Yes, it is painful, public, you all know. But I really am my own woman."

CHAPTER 15

October 29, 2024 Tuesday

Hounds flew over the still somewhat green pasture. Jefferson Hunt, at its easternmost fixture, was close to running out of territory. The fox scent got made good on his innate business. If he should reach the wide, strong-running creek, which feeds into the Mechums River, he'd be fine.

Sister and Midshipman, a young fellow coming along, soared over three fat logs tied together. This formidable jump backed off a few horses in the field. Sister tried to introduce her horses and hounds to everything, and luckily she had some heavy logs to jump at the farm. That only worked if someone in the field had hunted at Roughneck Farm. Today a handful of people had not.

A steady wind, six miles an hour, blew scent right into hounds' noses until the fox veered sharply left. Scent now blew at an angle, so the hounds faltered for a moment then had to adjust. The fox made good on the delay.

He reached the creek, swam across, sped alongside of it, then disappeared into the thick woods and into his den.

Hounds nosed along the creek until Yancy swam across. *"Found it."*

The hounds jumped in as Sister looked for a decent crossing. She got on the other side, water splashing on her britches, as Twist, the last hound over, scurried in front of her. Hounds roared, blasted into the woods then held up at the mouth of the den, which was under an upturned tree trunk. He, of course, had other entrances. Taz dug at the opening, his butt in the air. Dirt flew from his paws.

Weevil quickly dismounted. Betty came over to be closer to the hounds. As Kilowatt ground-tied she didn't need to hold his reins.

"Good hounds. Well done, Taz. Trooper, Twist. Good boy, Dreamboat." He called each hound by name, blew "Gone to Ground," then mounted up.

Sister rode up to him. "Weevil, we're out of territory and in Farmington's."

His face froze a moment. "I shall head back."

"Yes. According to the Master of Foxhound Rules, if a fox enters an adjoining hunt's territory, your hounds are on, you have the right to follow your hounds. Regardless of the rule I'll call Pat Butterfield when I get home. No need for someone to babble on about how we were in Farmington territory. People love to report anything that might be, oh, out of bounds. And I doubt anyone but hunt staff knows the rules. Anyway, he's easygoing. He knows I wouldn't willingly barge into Farmington's territory. But don't hunt the hounds back. Don't cast them until we go a mile toward the west."

"Yes, Madam. All right, come along."

She turned to rejoin the field. Tempted as she was to recite the rule she resisted. It would eat time. If there was a chance to pick up another fox let's go for it. Sister always wanted to get on terms with her quarry.

Given the run, no one complained about walking for a mile. By the time the pack reached the old outbuildings, some of them stone, people had regained their breath.

Tootie moved ahead on the left. Betty stayed even with the pack as Weevil cast around those old outbuildings, which had been constructed in the late 1700s. Our forebearers wasted little. They picked up the field to create good pastures for their stock, using the stones to build sheds, small stables. Depending on how full of stones the fields were, they could create structures. Sweat, not money, cash is hard to come by, whether it's the eighteenth century or the twenty-first.

Dreamboat's tail flipped. He walked with determination.

Diana joined him. *"Old?"*

Dasher sniffed loudly. *"Warming up."*

Soon the whole pack worked with the three D hounds. Tinkle, a youngster, not the best name, followed the leaders closely. Young, though she possessed great drive.

Tinkle veered off toward the second stone outbuilding, roof sagging. *"She's right."*

Off they ran. If anyone needed to tighten their girth, it was too late now. The gray ran a huge figure eight. Sister liked starting her youngsters on grays, not that you could determine red or gray. Grays, a bit smaller, gave young hounds a good test while keeping the hunted area easier to manage. A red, again depending, often shot off to keep hounds moving, swerving, running hard then changing pace. They were damnably clever.

"Didn't we just pass this old tractor?" Taz complained.

"Did," Tatoo tersely answered.

"If you two don't shut up and keep to business, that gray will sit in the driver's seat of the tractor and you'll miss it," Diana chided them.

Everyone on, they trotted. A turn around the small stone stable and the trot burst into a gallop. This fox was having fun with them. He zigged and zagged, slowed and speeded up and now sat on a mid-level branch of a sturdy pin oak tree. A female downy woodpecker, in her nest in the trunk, sat at the edge.

"*You'd think they'd get tired of it,*" the pretty bird remarked.

"*They will eventually. I fouled my scent back by the chicken coop. That should take care of this unless they backtrack.*"

"*Do you get tired of it?*" the black and white bird asked.

"*No, because I can dump them when I've had enough, need a breather. It's only worrisome if they're close.*"

"*I'm lucky. All I have to do is spread my wings.*"

"*Yes, you are.*" He smiled as hounds turned back to the chicken coop baffled by the mixture of odors.

Weevil pulled them away from the chicken coop, a large one with good fencing including a turkey foot fencing over the top so the owls couldn't carry off chicks.

Heading back toward the house, still not visible, Weevil encouraged the pack. "Get 'em up."

They tried. The day, warming, still held some scent on the ground, but it wasn't fox scent. The hounds picked up deer, turkeys, bear, even bobcat, but no fox.

Finally all reached the trailers. People dismounted. A few discovered their legs wobbled. The run had been longer than they'd thought and not everyone was hunting-fit yet.

Before joining the group at the breakfast Sister immediately called Pat Butterfield, who couldn't have been more gracious. Life is much easier if one has good relationships with adjoining hunt masters. In this case the two truly liked each other, always saving a dance together for any hunt ball.

———

While Sister drank her hot tea, chatted with field members, Beryl Bradford, who was sitting with Georgia Bradford, heard Miss Priss, a retired beagle, making a hell of a racket.

"She's vigilant." Beryl rose.

"Is that a nice way of saying big mouthed?"

Laughing, Beryl walked to the window, where the now chubby hound was carrying on.

"What the hell?" Beryl exclaimed.

Georgia now by her side said, "What the hell is right."

The two women hurried to the mudroom, grabbed jackets, then walked briskly toward the kennels.

Solange, Ann, and Scott were inside, the big SUV parked in front.

"To what do I owe the pleasure?" Beryl's face reddened. "And get your ass out of the hot bitch's stall. No hot bitches right now but I'm sure you can find your own," she said to Scott, whose wife's jaws tightened.

He nearly walked out.

"What are you doing, Solange?" Beryl was within walking distance.

"Well, half this pack is mine," Solange said.

"You're out of your mind!"

"Now, this can be amicably settled," Scott said, while Ann nodded in agreement hoping to lower the hostilities. "She loves the beagles."

"That doesn't mean half the pack is yours," Beryl fired back.

"Andrew threw this pack off our land. I didn't. He was a master. He didn't resign his position. As his wife, I inherit it." Solange stuck her forefinger in Beryl's face.

"You inherit nothing. A master must be elected if it's a subscription pack, which this is," Beryl said.

"Olivia Bradford wanted those paid members to feel involved, hence a subscription pack. We have a board of directors and positions, like being in charge of our little library, being in charge of membership. The only way you can be a master is to be elected," Georgia filled in more details.

"Then call a special election." Solange didn't ignore Georgia, but she wasn't agreeing to anything.

"I bet you never talked to Andrew like this." Georgia hit the nail on the head.

"Why would I? We were in perfect agreement about everything. Ah, but you missed that boat."

That fast, Georgia unleashed a slap, the sound of which bounced off the walls.

Solange lunged for Georgia, but Scott grabbed her. As he was quite strong he easily held her.

"Let me go."

"No. If you smack her around it may not go well for you when all this winds up in court. The murder, I mean."

"He's right." Beryl allowed herself a sly moment. "You need to continue to be a grieving widow."

"I am the grieving widow!" Solange shouted.

"You don't look like it." Georgia was now thrilled to be able to bedevil a woman she considered a gold digger, a marriage wrecker, although in truth she was glad to be out of the marriage.

"I want half the beagles." She turned, looking up into Scott's face. "Let me go."

"No. You're too angry." He himself did not sound angry.

She realized this. "I have a right to be angry."

"There is nothing to prevent you from forming your own pack, but you aren't getting any of the Bradford hounds. You know nothing about taking care of a pack of hounds." Beryl was right.

"Go," Georgia simply ordered.

"Why are you here all the time?" Ann challenged her, surprising the others, as she was usually quiet.

"Because my best friend's husband is in jail, accused of murder. Her mother-in-law has died and you all are ever so eager to put Winston away. You've got the farm and his money, Solange. I should think that would be enough." A drip of venom slipped into Georgia's voice.

Solange raised her arm again but Scott grabbed it, again.

"Boss, let's go. We aren't getting anywhere." His voice, deep, was consoling.

"Call the National Beagle Club of America, Solange. They'll tell you the rules. You have not inherited a mastership and have no claim to the beagles." Beryl, calm now, added, "You can google the number. And if you want a pack of beagles, don't make trouble. You need the national club."

Unsure as how to absorb this, Solange stilled.

"Come on," Ann echoed her husband. "It is probably worth calling. Let's go."

As the three walked out, the hounds remained quiet.

Solange turned. "I wish it was you that stabbed Andrew. Then I could watch you hang."

Beryl half smiled. "Be careful what you wish for. The gods have an odd sense of humor."

Once back at home, showered, relaxing, Sister picked up the phone in the library as Gray watched the news. As it was her cell she walked into the hall as not to disturb him.

Marianne Casey, whom Beryl had called, was now relating what happened to Sister.

"Is she nuts?" Sister wondered.

"I don't know but it makes me think there's a screw loose. She tried to slap Georgia."

"That was a mistake."

"Beryl said if Scott and Ann hadn't been with Solange, restrained her, she has no idea what would have happened. They are doing their best to keep her somewhat calm. Andrew's death seems to have unhinged her."

"Before I forget, has the medical examiner determined cause of death yet?"

Marianne answered, "No. There's a backlog. Seems to be an uptick in murders, but Beryl says the autopsy should be complete by this week. As to funeral arrangements, no one knows. Will Solange turn it into a drama, a large gathering? My God, could it get any worse?"

"Marianne, don't say that," Sister half whispered.

CHAPTER 16

October 30, 2024 Wednesday

"1914. The start of the battle of Ypres." Sister pulled on her gloves as she and Yvonne walked around Wolverhampton.

"You remember dates." The gorgeous woman could remember birthdays, that was it.

"My grandfather fought in World War I. Granted, we wouldn't get over there for a few more years, well, we ended it really, but he said what he saw."

"I can't imagine it. The noise alone." She stopped to inspect a massive holly bush. "This has to have been planted in the early 1800s, when this area was being discovered."

"Holly can grow forever. Tough. Can you imagine seeing all this for the first time? Seeing Sophie's work down the road? Once the tribes left people came."

"Driven off."

"It's an odd thing, Yvonne. Some were yet others had the fore-sight to see the wave of Europeans wasn't going to stop. Then again, we were breeding. We'd just defeated the English. People's hopes shot up thanks to the victory."

"Crawford has done an incredible job restoring the slave graveyards. I bet there's one here, too. He's been respectful of everyone's dead."

"Maybe in time we'll find it. Will we ever know how many souls toiled? I think even the people knew then slavery had to stop."

Yvonne shrugged. "Knowing and doing are two different things."

"That's the truth." Sister walked to the old barn, stepping inside the center aisle.

Inhaling, Yvonne smiled. "A hint of old leather."

Sister inhaled deeply. "Don't you love that smell?"

"I do. Well, should we rehabilitate this now or wait until springtime?"

"Good question." Sister moved along to the old tack room in the middle of the barn.

A woodburning stove, sitting on a heavy slab of slate, pipe going up through the roof, could still provide warmth if filled with wood. The saddle racks covered one wall, the vertical rows precise. The adjoining wall held the bridle half circles. The well-thought-out place proved once again that running a stable hasn't changed for centuries.

"What I was thinking was, why don't we wait to see what the English family decides. Should they rent this place for say even just a season then we can spiff up the stable. There's electric here. We could put baseboard heat by the pipes, then wrap stall pipes, the faucet for drinking water. Easy enough. Wouldn't disturb the building at all."

"Anything's better than a burst pipe. We don't know what kind of stables these people are accustomed to. They might have a long list but you're right, I think we should do it. If for nothing else than this place would be as we wish should we need another renter."

"Maybe we should expand our advertising. We've only put one ad in *The Wall Street Journal.*" Yvonne worried about the large place sitting empty, especially with winter coming on.

"If the others agree to it, I'm for it. You're the businesswoman, I'm not. Crawford and Kasmir certainly know how to make money, and you know how to reach people."

Yvonne pulled her coat tighter. "You're kind to consider my business background, but Sister, when I started I had no idea."

"Maybe not, but you could see flashes of the future. I admire that ability. Well, let's go into the kitchen and get the fireplace going. We can warm up. I've brought a notebook. Whatever is left to do if we do get a longer-term renter, if I write it down I'll remember."

They left the stable. The sky above looked like a true winter sky, dark gray, lowering clouds. The wind had a bite.

Once inside the kitchen, Sister crumpled newspapers stacked by the back door for this purpose. Filling the big old fireplace with paper, she then took the cut wood Yvonne handed her and made a base, then crisscrossed other logs. She liked building a fire.

"Here." Yvonne handed her a long kitchen match. Sister scratched the side of the brick fireplace with it, flame spurting out, touched it to the paper. Soon a much-appreciated fire warmed them.

"Okay." Sister sat with her notebook open. "Since we were just there start with the stable."

Yvonne enumerated what they'd discussed, plus added a few touches of her own, like curtains for the windows in the tack room. "You know if we do bring the stable back, I think I'll build a small one at the same time. If workers are out here, might as well use them."

"Right. As it is, the stable is serviceable. But I'm with you, a bit of modernization is in order. Okay, when we all visited the house, things seemed to be in order. The third floor needs better heat and there's no air-conditioning at all."

"Expensive. Air-conditioning, I mean. The fireplaces up there work. One would need to get up in the middle of the night, but until we know how and if that floor will be used, we can wait that one out."

"Well, if no air-conditioning we can put up fans. I don't think the third floor needs to be but so beautiful."

They batted ideas back and forth.

A car pulled up. A door slammed and Ronnie appeared at the back kitchen door. They waved him in.

"Cold out there." He pulled off his gloves. "Stopped by your house, Yvonne, and Sam, back from Crawford's, said you might be here. Good to see you, too, Master."

"Sit down. We can make coffee or tea if you're interested," Sister offered.

"No." He sat on the offered chair as he unbuttoned his coat. "This cold hit us all at once. You never know. The reason I wanted to find you is the English people aren't coming over. They've decided to stick it out another year. Crawford called to tell me. Labour may not prove as bad as people thought, plus they've only been in power since January 2024. Plus they have less than a third of members in the House of Commons."

"Meaning it might not be so bad for rural people?" Yvonne asked.

"Well, a lot of people think of the Conservative Party as rich people. And foxhunting is perceived as a rich sport even though that has changed. But then again rural people here have been ignored. Whether here or there."

Sister smiled. "Seeing as how the Conservatives have been in power for fourteen years it's different for them, well, it's a different system."

"You know more about politics than I do." Yvonne felt the heat from the fireplace fill the room.

"I've always had an interest but I don't know how much I know," Sister replied.

"Don't you think all these differences including here are a way to divert your attention that the parties, many of the people are corrupt. If I learned anything in media it's everyone truly has a price. My husband was an expert at figuring out who to pay for what." Yvonne then changed the subject. "Well, enough of that. I am obviously cynical. So what do we do now?"

"Put ads in or on equine sites, trail sites. Maybe we'll get some weekend rentals," Ronnie suggested.

"Then we'd better get to work, spruce up the stable. Put sheets on the beds and heavy blankets. Stack firewood. If anyone should rent this out soon, after all formal hunting is around the corner, all we'll have to do is get the fireplace going so they come into a warm, pretty place." Yvonne felt tired just thinking about it.

"There's no baseboard heat in the stable," Sister reminded Ronnie. "We can put in an electric stove, there's electricity and we can stack wood for the woodburning stove in the tack room. Or we can put the electric stove in the tack room. The stove is well situated but I worry, you know if someone leaves the door to the stove open and sparks fly."

"It's hard to believe people would be that dumb." Yvonne, accustomed to Chicago winters, grimaced.

"Best not to take a chance until we can rehab the stable. It's decent. No holes in the roof. Well, you know all this." Sister faced Ronnie. "It has to be good enough for a groom or two to sleep there if a horse needs attention."

"Well, I'll call the syndicate to see if we can schedule a workday. If everyone can't show up on the same day, I'll assign chores, carefully." He smiled.

"Do you think we can get weekend rentals?" Yvonne stood to throw another log in the large fireplace.

"I do. It's a start. Nothing would be better than a long-term rental but a weekend's stay could turn into one. Worth a try." Ronnie looked up at the ceiling, freshly painted.

"Well, let's get on it, then. I'll call the girls. You can call the boys." Sister thought practically.

"Women." He smiled devilishly.

"Oh, Ronnie, for God's sake I'm in my middle seventies. Everyone's a girl to me."

"Oh, Sister, who would know?"

"You two," she looked at Ronnie, "are giving me the business."

"Nah." Ronnie smiled his toothy grin.

"While we're sitting here in the warmth have you all heard the latest about Bradford Beagles?" Sister asked.

"I did. Russ called me," Ronnie answered.

"I haven't," Yvonne replied.

They both took turns filling her in on the crazy details.

"Maybe we could consult an astrologer. It's been crazy, out of control, nuts. And this news about the English people deciding to stay in England isn't such good news either."

"Well, at least no one is dead." Ronnie lifted his eyes heavenward.

"At this point, nothing would surprise me." Sister's voice lifted a bit as she enjoyed Ronnie's sense of humor.

"Do you all think it's easy to kill?" Ronnie thought out loud.

Yvonne came right back. "Depends on the circumstances. If anyone touched Tootie I'd kill them. In a minute."

"I suppose we would all defend those we love." Ronnie grew suddenly thoughtful. "I'd kill if anyone hurt my little Atlas, the world's perfect Chihuahua."

"True for most people, I think. What provokes murder? Self-defense or defense of those you love as you all said. But there are people who kill for money, for social status, for political power. For thousands of years empires have been built on the bones of the dead. Not just Greece versus Persia but think about the Crusades or Genghis Khan. If you give people a reason to kill, tell them it's for the good of the tribe or the nation, you know they'll do it."

A silence followed this.

"Do you think Andrew was killed for any of those reasons?" Yvonne stood to put another piece of wood in the fireplace. "I'm taking a chill."

"It's raw," Ronnie agreed with her.

"Andrew?" Sister's eyebrows raised. "Winston killing him would make the most sense, but as we've known him, especially me, I don't think he did it. I come back to something we don't yet know. A bad business deal. A nutcase in love with Solange. Crazy stuff."

"Love? Money? Power? Weren't those the reasons?" Yvonne repeated them in reduced form.

"I'd rather concentrate on getting this place ready. I have no other ideas." Sister exhaled. "Murder is beyond my powers. Bringing in firewood is not."

CHAPTER 17

October 31, 2024 Thursday

Hanging on took precedence over looking good as the Jefferson Hunt field encountered jumps in difficult territory.

Sister had just cleared a new three-foot six coop, pressed her left leg hard on Keepsake to make a two-stride ninety-degree turn to the right. The Appendix horse, so balanced, easily cleared it but she was reminded of why a rider needs a tight leg.

Behind her, she could hear an "oof" "oof" when people parted from their mounts.

As it was Halloween, a larger number turned out even though it was a workday. A few put orange and black yarn in their horses' manes. She steered clear from festive colors in manes, bridles, and such, but she didn't mind if other people wanted to celebrate a holiday. She did mind listening to those people parting company.

Walter, bringing up the rear of First Flight, had his work cut out for him. His mount, Clemson, a bit older, rock solid, still very fit, could take most anything—which meant after everyone leapt back on their horses, assuming no injury to man or beast, he'd have to lead them over yet again.

It was a formidable jump, but given the territory, there was no alternative, as the adjoining pastures needed to be separated, one full of cattle, the other for four horses, and all of it near the base of the Blue Ridge Mountains so there really wasn't wiggle room.

Hounds flew. Sister needed to stay with the hounds. If they roared up the mountainside, there was nothing to do. The club had no trails up the steep side. That would come in time yet never be desired. A hard climb up meant you wore out your horse, most times, and if not, you sure as hell wore yourself out.

This newer fixture, Frogmore, was nestled up the northern end of North Chapel Cross Road. People were coming in. Out this far, they truly wanted land, old houses or houses that looked old. The builders, the Lattimores, proved easy to work with. They promised they would sharpen their riding skills and eventually ride with the field.

Sister hoped they would. Having an owner ride is always an advantage to a hunt, just like having a vet or an MD in the field. But a landowner often knew quirks and shortcuts that even a field master could miss. Good as Sister was at reading territory, she never deluded herself that she knew it all.

Right now Weevil, her whippers-in, and herself depended on the wind. The sky, overcast, was perfect. The mercury hung about 48 degrees Fahrenheit, also good. Scent was lifting a bit, but close to the ground. A hot line would stay hot for a good long run, which they were having.

Given the pace and the direct line, although no sighting, Sister felt they were on a coyote. A surprised coyote, as they were now learning to hunt Frogmore, so the game needed to adjust.

The wind hitting her face, stronger due to the galloping, tingled. Despite that, she was sweating in her English fabric coat and her vest, both purchased at Horse Country over forty years ago. Good stuff lasts, whether clothing, friends, or hounds. Longevity is the mark of a good business as well as hunt leadership.

She wasn't thinking of leadership. Those people behind her, including Walter, looked at their master in front of them, mid-seventies, still pushing it. Motrin helped, but Sister never thought of age. She only thought of what she could do and how much she was willing to endure to do it.

Fortunately, her aches and pains usually came from stiff muscles. She could stretch for an hour but when she got up in the morning or mounted up, she felt a stiffness, and then it worked itself out.

Right now there wasn't a hint of stiffness but there was a hint of running out of territory. Damn, this fellow had blinding speed.

Hounds screamed. What the aging master felt was joy, passion, and gratefulness to still be able to hang in there. She didn't know how people could live without passion. Even bridge. You've got to love something. Someday, one hopes, something will keep you young.

Weevil, forty yards ahead, cleared another simple three-log fence. But there was really nowhere to go after the landing. Hounds tore up a mountainside growing steeper the higher they climbed. There was no way he or his whippers-in could call them off a hot line. And as huntsman, he felt guilty doing so. These beautiful creatures live for a hot line, a hard run. They are born to it just as people are truly born to hunt. It's either there or it isn't. Often people don't know until their first hunt, when they feel that extraordinary exhilaration for the first time realizing they are one animal among others.

Weevil pulled up, Gunpowder unhappy with it as he heard the

hounds. His job was to stay behind the hounds. Weevil waved to both Betty and Tootie. No point in them climbing.

Sister stopped shy of the jump. The people behind her breathed sighs of relief.

The music enticed her. No go.

Weevil jumped back. Tootie and Betty stayed on the other side of the fence, new and therefore stout.

"Madam?"

"Let's sit for a bit. You can blow. My hunch is the coyote will turn. Whether he comes back or not, who knows. But if you blow and he's lost them for a short time, maybe they'll come down."

"Hot line."

"I know." She half smiled. "Why don't you call the girls back. Sometimes Betty has had no sense when the hounds are roaring."

He smiled, put the horn to his lips, and blew for his whippers-in to come back. Betty cleared the logs first, followed by Tootie, who was close behind. The two rode up to Weevil.

They did not report what they saw or what they felt. One doesn't do that unless asked by the huntsman or the Master.

"Well done," Sister praised them, as they'd had to hustle plus negotiate newer territory, as well as newer jumps. "Weevil and I have decided to sit briefly. They might lose the line. If not, it will be a long day."

They both smiled because it meant they'd take their horses home, drive back, having left the party wagon, praying they could pick up hounds.

Walter double-checked his people. Ronnie, Kasmir, Sam, Alida, and Freddie, winded but fine, used the occasion for a hit from their flasks. Yvonne, who stayed on Buster, breathed hard, catching her breath.

"Tough jump." Alida smiled at her.

"I am learning the necessity of prayer." Yvonne laughed at her-self.

Pete Jensen, Lorraine, the newer members, were still wide-eyed. Reverend Taliaferro and Father Mancusco rode to them.

"Would you like a prayer?" Reverend Taliaferro beamed at them.

"I'll take anything," Lorraine replied.

"Me too. That two-stride jump is one of the toughest things I've seen. High jumps in the show ring, but nothing like that, and I thought our corners were tough."

Father Mancusco told him, "You took it like a champ."

"You two gave us the lead." Lorraine was thankful.

"We figure we have help." The good father laughed.

They could hear the hounds turning back, now running half-way up the mountain but coming down.

Weevil continued to blow his three long blasts.

After about seven minutes, the wind having its effect on the standing people, Diana first took the three-log jump, followed by Giorgio then the rest. Hounds, too, were a bit winded. Climbing a steep grade takes it out of you.

Giorgio looked at Weevil. *"Slipped us."*

"Yeah. We were right behind. We could have accounted for him if he didn't disappear," Tatoo bragged.

Dasher, now among them, shook his head. *"Tatoo, for all we know he headed to his pack. Coyote usually have a pack. Don't ever be alone scouting for a coyote. Not that I don't want to get them. They do a lot of dam-age."*

"Do you think if they had a lot of food put out for them, they wouldn't kill human pets?" Pookah wondered.

"I don't know," Dasher said. *"Most animals with a full stomach just sleep, you know."*

"Good hounds." Weevil praised them, calling each hound out by name.

Sister glowed. She loved her hounds, knowing some of the bloodlines over the fifty years and studying beyond that. Blood tells. Her uncle-in-law had repeated that many times over. She had occasion to learn the truth of the statement.

"Huntsman, I do think we've had enough and we have to take that right-angle jump. I expect a few more people will part company from their mounts," Betty, sharp eyes, noted. "If you're willing to go out of your way, we can head toward the road. There's a coop there and we'll be in another field. Give or take ten minutes longer, but some of those people are beat."

"Horses, too, I figure," Tootie, who said little, chimed in.

"Go ahead," Sister ordered. "Betty, that's a good suggestion."

Weevil called his hounds with a simple, "Come along." Betty took the right side, Tootie took the left. The wind picked up. They were heading straight into it but Weevil trotted, which helped cover the distance faster. He took the jump, hounds followed, as not being on a scent they fell behind instead of charging ahead. Betty went next then Tootie. There were no further jumps down the line, so they needed to take the same one, then quickly go to their places with the hounds happily trotting alongside.

Sister easily cleared it, as did most of the field. Walter urged those in the rear, "Head up, heels down. Give a good hard squeeze. There you go."

Everyone made the jump. As they crossed the fields, a halfway parked-out woods to their right drew the hounds to it. Weevil followed. Hounds walked briskly in stopping at a tree, the bottom of which had rotted out.

Weevil instantly dismounted; the whippers-in rode up.

"Leave it. Leave it. Good hounds."

He knelt down to find three fox cubs, frightened.

"Betty, get down here with me."

She hopped off Aztec, who stood like the good boy he was.

"Oh dear." She looked at the young handsome huntsman. "You think the mother's been trapped?"

"Probably. Foxes have few enemies. These little guys will need milk, and a warm bed." He stood. "Sister."

She rode over, immediately grasped the situation. "If you hand them to me, I'll put them in my coat. The warmth will keep them quiet."

Weevil picked up a beautiful red little fellow. The cub didn't even squirm.

Handing it up to Sister, he then knelt for the next little one. Betty stood by, ready to take one if Sister couldn't carry all three.

"Upsy-daisy." Weevil handed up the third, a little girl.

Sister felt them wiggle in her coat, snuggling together. "I'll walk back. Betty, stay with me. Weevil, lead the rest of them and the pack to the trailers."

Once at the trailers, everyone was filled with curiosity, which Sister did not satisfy. She needed to save these three little ones, not answer people.

Weevil rode to her trailer as did Betty. They loaded up.

"Tootie," Sister called to the young woman. "Tell the people to enjoy their breakfast, potluck. I need to get these cubs to the house, fed, secure, whatever they need. And tell them to shut up about it. Nicely, of course. We don't need some government agency inspecting these babies and determining where they should go. Give someone a little power and a little person has to use it. You hope for an official who knows when to turn a blind eye. Okay. Thank you for whipping in on a tough day."

While Betty cleaned the horses and tack, Sister, the foxes still in her coat, walked to the house. The large dog crate was rarely used.

She pulled it out of the backroom closet, taking it into the kitchen. She placed an old blanket in there, then gently lifted the three red babies into the crate.

She put out a small dish of water. Then she walked out to the kennels, grabbed some Esbilac, the plastic shooters, and hurried back to the house.

Raleigh and Rooster, curious, sniffed at the large crate, which had ample slats for air, but nothing big enough for even a baby to crawl through.

Sister warmed some milk, low, poured it into a deep bowl then mixed in the Esbilac. The kennels always had a good supply should any litter of puppies need addition to the mother's milk. Mother's milk contained antibiotics to protect puppies in their earliest stages. Same with cats.

Sister sat on the floor after removing her bye day coat. "Rooster, Raleigh, lie down."

"Can't we get closer?" Raleigh politely asked.

"No. Now lie down."

"Do you think she understood what you said?" Rooster asked the Doberman.

"Up to a point. She's afraid we'd harm these cubs."

"I don't care about them one way or the other." The Harrier put his head on his front paws.

"Well, I do," Golly complained. *"We had to adjust to a turtle who makes turtle noises and now we'll have to adjust to fox cubs. You know they'll start yapping once they feel better."*

"They won't yap as much as you do," Rooster crabbed.

"At least I say interesting things. All you do is ask for long walks and food," the calico shot back.

The first fox cub, wrapped in a towel and held by Sister, opened his mouth for milk. Little by little she pushed the stopper and he drank the amount. She then rubbed his head. She didn't want to overfeed him, such a little stomach. She dipped the plunger into the milk, pulled up a small amount, putting the plunger back in his mouth. She squeezed a tiny bit out. He had enough. She petted him again, then unwrapped him, putting him back in the cozy crate. Out came the little girl. Same process, and lastly the other boy. Fed, warm, safe, she closed the front, leaving the crate near the kitchen table. Over the night, the fire would die down and the flue being open would allow colder air to come down. Better to be away from the fireplace.

She knew these cubs needed food and warmth. In time they'd adjust to where they were as well as to her.

"You were good dogs," she praised Raleigh and Rooster.

"Good? All they did was lie down." Golly found this false praise. *"I could have jumped down and helped you while you fed the cubs."*

"All right everybody, time for suppers."

This was met with enthusiasm as Betty came through the mudroom door.

"How did it go?"

"Pretty good. They're too weak to fight back but I think they have a chance."

"With you, even a praying mantis has a chance," Betty teased her.

"All things bright and beautiful." Sister quoted the famous line. "I am still cold. Tea?"

"Sure. And since we missed the breakfast, what's in your refrigerator?"

"Eggs, cheese, parsley. I love fresh parsley, as you know. And I have some hamburger left from last night. I'll make an omelet if you toast the bread and butter it."

"That's a deal."

The two old friends worked, Betty humming. She hummed to

herself or with Sister. Show tunes. Sometimes Sister would sing the words. They both loved old show tunes.

"Close," Sister advised her.

"Me too. Let's get the food on the table and I'll pour the tea. You grab the tea bags."

"Let's make a true pot of tea. I was sent this wonderful tea from Marianne and Russ. Never had it before. Hu-Kwa."

"Me neither. Is it dark?"

"It is. Supposed to have a terrific, unique flavor. Here, you guard the omelets, this will take two seconds." Sister opened the large can, scooped out two tablespoons of the fragrant leaves, putting them in two large tea balls, which she dropped in an old beloved china teapot that had belonged to her mother.

They sat, instantly digging in. One is hungry after hunting, especially in the cold.

"Oh, this cheese is, well, what is it?" Betty asked.

"Muenster. Nothing special."

"Maybe it's the parsley making it so good."

"Mayonnaise. Duke's." Sister grinned.

"You have your secrets."

"Betty, it's not a secret. How many years have you watched me put mayo in an omelet?"

"Well, I didn't see you do it today."

"Your back was turned."

They nattered on, teasing, asking questions about how the hounds were doing, about people they knew, about books they were reading. Both were avid readers. Betty loved mysteries. Sister inclined toward history and the occasional novel. Two old friends who dearly loved each other, listened to each other and told the truth to each other. What could be better?

"That was good."

"Thank you. I'll expect deviled eggs next time we're together. Betty, I can never match your deviled eggs."

Betty smiled. "You know exactly what I put in them."

"As my mother would say, 'The cook's hand.'"

"I believe that. Well, I think the babies are sound asleep. No whimpers."

"They are so beautiful. I pray I can pull them through. And then I have to figure out what to do with them."

"Oh please." Betty rose, taking their plates to the sink as Sister poured more of the remarkable tea. "I'm pulling out cookies."

"Okay."

"As to figuring out what to do with them, you haven't figured out what to do with the turtle or tortoise. I get the nomenclature confused."

"He has a large cage. He chirps, you know, and when I let him out for exercise, you can't believe how fast he goes. I'm looking for a little skateboard for him."

"Jane Arnold, are you looney tunes?"

"Of course I am. That's why you love me."

They both laughed as Betty sat with an unopened bag of Pepperidge Farm chocolate chip cookies, dark chocolate. Sinful but wonderful on a cold day. So wonderful on any day.

"Do you want me to call Frogmore about the cubs? Obviously there was probably a trapper. They're my old friends. Scratches the call off your list."

"Thank you. The older I get the more I hate trappers. I expect Roland should investigate his land."

Betty's eyebrows raised. "God help anyone if he finds them. I've known Roland since my junior year in college. A quick and ferocious temper."

"I can see you with your Kappa Kappa Gamma pin." Sister grabbed another cookie.

"You didn't have sororities at your college or you would have pledged. It was a wonderful way to have a group of friends. My college wasn't enormous, no Ohio State, but it was big enough. When I first got there, I was overwhelmed."

"It was fun, wasn't it? Being on your own for the first time. Luckily, we both had discipline, thanks to our parents. I never minded studying, but I sure hated finals."

"Me too. The essays got me. I'm not good at expressing myself. William and Mary had such a good English department. I struggled. I really can't express myself."

"Betty, how can you say that?"

"I can express myself with you. I trust you, but I can pop off and then I regret what I've said."

"You tell the truth."

"Honey, I could certainly tell it more diplomatically."

"Well—"

"I try. Bobby gets after me but I blurt things out."

"You're too hard on yourself. I've only heard you blurt things out once or twice but you are direct in your statements and what's wrong with that?"

"If I were a man, it wouldn't be so disconcerting."

"Oh, hell, Betty, if we were men a lot wouldn't be disconcerting. Think of the times you blew by a bloviating egotist visiting from another hunt, cleared a four-foot fence while he had to veer toward the lower one. Drives them nuts when a woman outperforms them."

"I'm a whipper-in. I should outperform most everybody. Which reminds me, has Tootie heard from vet schools yet?"

"I don't think she will until the new year, and that's early, but you know she'll get early acceptance."

"She will."

Sister's cell rang. It was on the table. She so often misplaced it. She was trying to remember to carry it around.

"Hello. Oh Marianne, Betty and I are drinking the Hu-Kwa."

"Verdict?" Marianne asked.

"Fabulous." Betty leaned toward the phone.

"I agree," Sister added.

"Calling because Winston was released on bail today. Two hundred and fifty thousand dollars."

"Jesus H. Christ." Sister couldn't help herself.

"Had it been Jesus, I think the bail would have been less," Marianne tweaked her.

"Yes." Sister laughed, always fond of Marianne's quick retorts.

"And Beryl says they can see Solange on her back porch with a telescope aimed right at them."

"Good heavens. Has that woman no sense?"

Betty could overhear Marianne, as Sister had the phone between them, and said, "Isn't she overdoing the wailing wife? In this case the spying wife?"

"She's certainly not suffering in silence. Maybe she really did love him. They seemed to get along."

"Let's assume she did. That doesn't mean Winston killed him. That has to be proven. And it was Andrew who threatened to kill Winston."

"Was. But here's the next part. The sheriff took in Georgia for more questioning. They wanted her at the station."

"Georgia was at the breakfast." Betty spoke.

"She was but she came in the back door late. Now, how Solange unearthed that, I don't know. My guess is someone trying to stir the pot, and there's always people who do, told Solange."

"Georgia wouldn't harm a fly." Sister used the worn-out phrase.

"Revenge. That's the bandied-about motive, at least from Solange."

"They tolerated each other." Sister filled that in.

"For Olivia's sake. That's what Solange is saying," Marianne replied. "And I expect there is a kernel of truth to it. Olivia was not going to give up her close relationship with Georgia. Solange was smart enough to know Andrew wouldn't challenge his mother."

"Marianne, I believe he wouldn't, but I also believe he feared she would change her will." Betty really had read a lot of mysteries.

"She changed it last year," Sister said. "At least that's what she told me. She wanted to give them enough time to adjust to it, and she wanted to manage it. She didn't indicate there was any trouble."

"Andrew was not stupid," Betty responded. "He wouldn't piss off his mother and Solange certainly wouldn't piss her off."

"She's now a rich woman in her own right." Sister stated the obvious.

"Does anyone know why Andrew threw off the beagles?" Betty asked.

"No, but as you know, Solange wants half the pack."

"She's nuts." Sister was vehement. "Those beagles belong to Winston. That woman doesn't know one end of a hound from the other."

"Now, Sister, that's not damnation. How many people really do know hounds?" Marianne sighed. "She declares she will hire a kennelman and learn everything."

"I expect that, too, will go to court?" Sister grabbed her teacup.

Betty rose to pour in more hot water.

"Who knows? It seems to me a murder charge takes precedent." Marianne thought out loud. "The real problem is, who else had a motive to kill him?"

"Apart from Georgia, whom they are trying to blemish?" Betty leaned closer to the phone.

"Right. It's awful, but who else wanted to kill him? I don't think either Winston or Georgia would do that, but who and why?"

"Do you think he was dealing drugs?" Sister asked.

"Oh, he took them when he was a teenager and in his early twenties, but he grew out of that. I never heard anything suggesting he would deal, and why would he? He didn't need the money," Marianne replied.

"The thrill of it?" Betty suggested.

"Maybe, but it's a far putt," Marianne again replied.

"A bad business deal?" Betty kept on.

"He wasn't exactly gifted in business. It's possible he blew up something or screwed someone, but would we know? If Andrew were in a business, he'd try to drag the rest of us into it or get us to buy whatever he was selling."

Listening intently, Sister agreed. "We would have known. I would never describe Andrew as discreet."

"Right." Marianne agreed. "There has to be a motive. Something we've never thought about or never known."

"Well, we'd better hope this is found before Winston goes on trial."

"And Georgia if they drag her into this. I don't know, as I wouldn't put anything beyond Solange. I can't decide if she's stupid or really smart." Marianne wondered. "Her grief is driving her misery, but in an odd way she's taking charge of things."

"Odd. It's all so odd. I never read her as stupid. More like just going along. Being agreeable." Sister then added, "Olivia never suggested she was sneaky or a backstabber. She never said she was fond of her but she didn't criticize her. She thought of it as Andrew's middle-aged crisis."

"A facelift would have been easier."

"Betty, men don't do facelifts for a pickup. They find a younger woman." Sister sipped her tea.

"Most likely. Or buy a Ferrari," Betty concurred.

"Here's the thing, Marianne. Whoever killed Andrew knows NTB, knows Farnley. Could be a member or could be someone who from time to time hunts with you. He knew enough to nail Andrew in the shed and dump him on the spider wheel tedder." Sister had an uneasy feeling.

A long silence followed this. "You're right."

They chatted a bit more, then the call ended.

Betty sat back in the chair. "So it's a beagler?"

"Well, it might not be a club member, but it has to be someone who knows that fixture so yes, I'd say it was a beagler."

"We can be glad it's not a foxhunter." Betty relaxed in the chair.

"Could be both. Foxhunters beagle and beaglers foxhunt."

"Motive, Sister."

"Betty, if we had the motive, we'd be halfway to the killer."

CHAPTER 18

November 1, 2024 Friday

"Why would I check my watch as I walked to the back door?" Georgia flounced onto Beryl's sofa while Beryl and Winston sat in opposite chairs.

"You know they are trying to establish time." Winston, who had endured way too much questioning himself, stated the obvious.

Georgia looked at him. "They wanted to know when I last saw you. And I don't remember a last moment seeing you, but I think it was when you and Russ and the whippers-in were putting the beagles in their separate temporary fenced yards. Andrew wasn't there. I wasn't paying attention to him. My focus was on the hounds."

"Do you think Sheriff Wolf or his assistant, Kate, understands how focused we are on the hounds?"

"Not for a minute," Winston replied.

Beryl, with a tight smile, replied, "Call Kate by her title."

"Why?" Georgia's voice rose.

"It will sound sexist to the keepers of our conscience that you call Dooly Wolf by his title but you just call Kate Kate," said Beryl.

A blank look crossed Georgia's pleasant face. "What is her title?"

"Deputy. Takes time to reach that high in law enforcement. So well, so there."

"I see." Georgia didn't really.

"I've been reading books. There's such drama over the impending election and lots of it over the so-called culture wars. Women should be called by their titles."

Winston laughed. "What culture?"

Beryl laughed with him. "That's another issue."

"Where was I?" asked Georgia.

"Keeping track of people," said Beryl.

"Right. Let me interject there that Dooly and Kate—no titles see, so I'm not placing him over her, but anyway—couldn't have been more pleasant. It wasn't like I was in a dark room with light shining in my eyes being grilled. But the questions surprised me. Things like, did you notice straw on anyone's clothing or dirt on their shoes?"

"All of our shoes were lined up outside the front door. Everyone had dirt on their shoes," Beryl replied. "So I assume yours were outside the back door."

"Of course they were. You know I would never go into Mrs. Abeles's house with my shoes on after a hunt. My socks were wet so I took them off, too. Rather thought of myself as the Barefoot Contessa." She paused. "I guess not very many people know that movie anymore."

"Only if they watch Turner Classic Movies," Winston informed her. "Ava Gardner didn't have to speak. All she had to do was walk in front of the camera. Whenever I'm ready to criticize North Carolina, I do remember they gave us Ava Gardner." He laughed. "But damn I hate it when UVA goes against them in basketball. Now, Georgia, back to your interrogation."

"Yes. I wandered off, but I do believe these side trails lead to interesting, even fascinating, information. For instance, how can you trust a woman named Solange? She's not French."

Beryl shrugged. "Well, she is from Watertown, New York, and there are lots of French Canadians in upstate New York, New England."

"I suppose. Well, then the sheriff asked me, did I get along with the girl from Watertown?" Georgia was a touch snide. "I said yes. I kept my distance, but we'd reached an accord because of Olivia. No one wanted to bring pain to Olivia. Of course I ask myself then why did Andrew ditch me for that?"

"Men think they are only as old as the woman they are sleeping with." Beryl's voice was calm, but she reached for her husband's hand to reassure him. Not that Winston indulged in affairs, but she didn't want to sound overly critical.

"He was an ass. A duped ass. Although she seems bright enough. But I never once saw her contradict him." Winston's eyebrows knitted together. "It kind of reminded me of when he was in college. Too much partying. Too many drugs. He didn't think. She was like a drug to him."

"Oh dear." Beryl grimaced.

"I think of our disagreements as moments to fully discuss issues." Winston meant that.

"You should have gone into the diplomatic corp." Georgia meant that, too.

"Okay, Georgia, what else?"

"Of course they asked did I like her, and I said no. How could I? Then they wanted to know did I love Andrew. Impertinent."

"No it isn't," Beryl interjected. "It could have a bearing on the case."

"Like I'm the murderer?" Georgia was deeply offended.

"Everyone is a suspect to some degree." Winston nodded. "It's a fair question. How did you answer it?"

"I said I loved him when we were young. He was spoiled but he never mistreated me. I felt his lack of ambition. But we traveled all over the world. We didn't have children even though I wanted them. He did not. We didn't argue about it, but I felt it. He wasn't perfect. Not that it's a reason to kill someone. Then Kate, I mean Deputy Kate—"

"Deputy Fortesque," Beryl gently said.

"Yes. She asked, when did I fall out of love with him? I thought about it and I said when I reached forty and realized he had no goals, only a social life. He wanted to look important, accomplish something on his own, but he was too lazy to work. Winston, did you think your brother had goals?"

"Not in the conventional sense, but he liked being at the top of the social order. He paid a lot of attention to the late Bunny Mellon." Winston mentioned Paul Mellon's widow. The Mellons had a multi-generational fortune. Paul's father was secretary of the Treasury. The son attended Yale. He was highly intelligent. Collected important art and gave generously.

"Andrew had to drop his name in every conversation at least once, even to those of us who knew him well." Beryl agreed with Winston. "But he did no harm. That's how I look at Andrew. Truthfully, I never took him seriously. I really don't think he was harmful."

"Not to you." Georgia's lips pursed. "He wasn't violent, but he drifted away as I aged a bit. I didn't think I looked that bad, and yet I was considering a facelift because of him. Fortunately no body parts had fallen when he dumped me. But it hurt."

"Did they ask for details?" Beryl pressed.

"Some. Like did I think he was having affairs when we were

married. And I didn't know. Then again, I wasn't looking for it. In retrospect, maybe he was. I missed it. It didn't occur to me. But I clearly stated that once I was over the shock of Solange I lived my life my way and I became happier than I was with him."

"And?" Beryl's eyebrows lifted.

"That's when I realized I was treading water with Andrew. We weren't going anywhere. We got along. At least I think we did but I clearly said if I was going to kill someone it wouldn't be Andrew. Why would I risk what I had found in life for a man I came to regard as superficial? Was I furious at being cast aside? Yes, for a time, but ultimately being rid of him was a blessing."

"Honest answer." Winston concurred.

"They asked other time things. Like when did I last see you? Did I think you hated your brother? I clearly stated I didn't think you hated Andrew but you were disgusted by him. Having to move the beagles set you off. Ridiculous."

Winston exhaled. "For a time I thought he was back on drugs. The divorce seemed so irrational," Winston said.

"You know, eventually almost everyone who was at that hunt will be questioned." Georgia sank farther into the sofa. "Time. All this will take so much time. If drugs were part of this, it will come out. I think I would have known about drugs quicker than about an affair."

"Would you like anything to drink?" Beryl asked, feeling a bit parched.

"No, but if I don't stand, you'll need a crane to get me out of this sofa." Georgia laughed for the first time since arriving.

Winston, ever the gentleman, rose, took his former sister-in-law's arms up to the elbows and lifted her up and out. "Come on. We'll retire to the kitchen and have a drink. It's early, but we could drink sherry and it wouldn't be out of place."

"Well," Georgia paused. "For medicinal purposes."

Beryl smiled. "I was about to toast the same thing."

They walked to the large country kitchen, a deck behind it. As it was unseasonably warm, crazy weather, the back door was open.

They each took a glass of sherry and walked to the deck to sit in the sunshine. Miss Priss, the retired beagle, padded after them.

"That sun feels fabulous." Georgia lifted her face to the rays.

"Tomorrow it will probably snow," Winston mumbled.

"Don't say that." Beryl crossed her fingers for luck.

They sat, drank. Beryl gave Miss Priss cookies.

Georgia shaded her eyes, looking toward her former home. "What the hell?"

Winston's gaze followed Georgia's, as did Beryl's.

"Solange is watching us through their big telescope!"

Georgia stood, looked right at the telescope and shot Solange the bird. Then she sat and knocked back her sherry.

Beryl, knowing her well, retreated to the kitchen, brought back the bottle and poured Georgia another glass.

"Maybe she's trying to find more evidence of my guilt," Winston grumbled.

"Nosy. Rude. And now rich in her own name. Damn, what a fool your brother was." Georgia then sighed. "And she's acting foolish. Maybe she's on drugs."

Beryl sipped her sherry. "The doctor has to have her on something."

"She can hide behind her doctor." Winston grimly gritted his teeth, realized it and stopped.

"Before I forget," Beryl changed the subject. "Did people notice you were barefoot at Mrs. Abeles's house? Did Damaris notice? She's her mother's daughter. Misses very little."

"Susan fetched me tea so I wouldn't stand next to Hetty as she poured. That way she wouldn't see my bare feet. Granted, we can't spoil her floors or rugs with muddy shoes, but I am not sure a lady in her nineties would appreciate seeing my feet, still wet, by the way."

They chatted and finally Georgia rose. "I want another sherry but I can't or I won't be able to drive home. Fortunately it isn't far."

"Do you think you'll be safe alone?" Beryl blurted out.

"Who would want me? As an ex-wife could I be a reasonable suspect? Yes. But would I or am I strong enough to lift his body and jam it on the spider wheel tedder? No."

"But people could think we acted in concert." Winston finished his glass.

"True." Georgia hadn't thought of that.

Winston, slower, said, "Whoever killed him really wanted him dead."

CHAPTER 19

November 2, 2024 Saturday

An hour of searching finally yielded a brisk run at Kingswood, a smaller fixture of soft, rolling hills. The more eastern fixtures, undulating, offered stiff gallops should a fox be found. In the distance one could see the Blue Ridge Mountains. So many homes in this area of the county did have views, just not close ones.

The jumps, great fun, were brush. The owners had seen Harvey Ladew's home in Maryland. They didn't have the skilled labor to create scenes of hunting with clipped boxwoods, but they did have brush fences, which took a bit of doing and watering during the hotter months. The Shelleys, not riders, enjoyed watching the hunt along with the social festivities. Today they followed behind Kathleen Sixt Dunbar and Aunt Daniella.

Sister, on Lafayette, kept a stiff pace but not so fast she'd run up on her hounds. The fox was moving, but the line wasn't that hot. He was probably a good half mile away, Sister surmised. But the day proved cool enough that although fading enough scent stuck and the hounds could make good on it.

Lafayette's long, fluid stride felt fabulous under her. One hunts for three hours—even four, depending—and a rough-gaited horse will wear you out. As a young woman, Sister figured out how to find the smooth-gaited horses and the sensible ones. If that animal has a Roman nose or some beauty blemish, fine. You can't put in what God left out, and the most beautiful horse in the world who is a nutcase or rough-gaited isn't worth the time or money. At least, to her.

On days like today, hounds need to focus intently, keep trying, because often the scent will fade, need to be found again. Then again, scent can heat up, making hounds' determination pay off. That was today.

A brush fence, maybe three feet tall, was up ahead and Sister remembered this was one with four strides and then another brush fence. This was a small challenge but a welcome one. People needed to see all manner of obstacles. If all one jumps is coops, that horse and rider develop a false confidence. What will happen the first time they see log jumps, logs lashed together? Or a bit more scary, an airy jump, one with a solid top line or board but airy underneath. For whatever reason, airy jumps caused more refusals than solid ones.

Sister could come up with many reasons for this, but mostly she wanted to get over, the devil with the reason. This was why when territory was opened or cleaned up during the summers, she bugged the fencing groups to create variety. Stone fences, logs, tiger traps, hog's backs, coops—some painted, some not. Then there were ditches. Not many, but enough. Don't look down.

The great thing about the brush jumps is horses could swish their hind legs through them if they so desired. Couldn't do that on a stone fence. One would be ass over tea kettle.

Lafayette didn't swish. He cleared the two brush fences with room to spare. Sister knew to sit tight on her gray Thoroughbred. He loved to jump and the bigger the better, she was fine jumping but her bigger the better days were over. Oh, she'd do it, but she wasn't looking forward to it.

Behind her, the Master heard swish, swish, swish and even a giggle. People were loving it.

Up ahead she caught sight of Kathleen sitting at a small county crossroads, the Shelleys behind in a brand-new huge Ford truck.

Hounds headed straight for the crossroads, paused, then shot left into a thick woods.

Suddenly the cry changed. Weevil, not far behind, kept up, as did his whippers-in. Sister, moving along, had drawn to within twenty yards of him. Close enough.

She saw her huntsman hold hard. The pack milled around something she couldn't see. Then the whippers-in came closer and they too stopped.

She saw Weevil gesture to Betty, who wheeled and headed straight for Sister.

"Turn back." Betty was brief. "As you pass Ben Sidell, send him up."

Ben Sidell, the sheriff, was happily out today.

Sister knew something was terribly amiss. Betty turned to rejoin Weevil. In the hunt field, one doesn't ask for details for the most part. It costs time.

She moved the field back a good fifty yards. They waited patiently as Ben Sidell rode into the woods. Tootie appeared out of the woods, as did Betty. Weevil then came ahead of his hounds, blowing them to him. He stopped and blew some more. They obeyed, but walked to him, didn't run.

Meanwhile, Kathleen and Aunt Daniella as well as the Shelleys waited.

Five minutes passed. Hounds kept heading back to the trailers. Ben rode out of the woods. He rode to the Shelleys at the crossroads.

Walter rode up to Sister and said, "Get Weevil to hold up. In case he's needed."

Sister watched as Peterson Shelley walked into the woods. Time passed. When he walked out he was visibly shaken.

Ben rode out again this time to Sister. "Get them back to the trailers. Everyone. Keep them there. I'll be there as soon as I can. I have to wait for my team."

"Yes." She nodded.

Once back at the trailers, the people knew something quite out of the ordinary had happened.

By the time everyone had eaten their second sandwich, Ben rode up, dismounted. He handed his horse to Walter, who took it so the sheriff could speak to the people while Walter took care of Nonni, a marvelous horse, a real packer.

Ben stood at the end of the table. "I'm sorry to interrupt the hunt and sorry to question you all at the table. Does anyone here know of any trappers?"

"Doesn't Garvey Stokes's brother trap?" Alida mentioned the man who owned Aluminum Manufacturing.

"He did. Had a heart attack last year," Sam filled her in.

Ben spoke. "If I need to ask any of you questions individually, I know where to find you. We've found—or more accurately, the hounds—found a trapper trapped by his own trap. He's dead. That's all that I can say right now."

"No one knows who he is?" Ronnie asked.

"No. Mr. Shelley didn't know. Had never seen him. I'm hoping someone can identify him."

"Foul play?" Ronnie knew something was up.

"We don't know that either. The medical examiner will have those answers. But I can tell you that his ankle was held by a powerful trap, powerful enough to hold a bear."

Once home, Sister and Betty cleaned their horses and Gray's horse, Cardinal Wolsey, too. Gray had left with Sam, as they intended to work on the Home Place, so Gray would spend the night. Nothing major. A drain pipe fell off the corner of the house. How was anyone's guess. The two of them could repair it a lot easier than one.

Once the horses were in their light blankets, as the night wasn't predicted to be that cold, the two women walked up to the house. Weevil and Tootie were counting hounds, checking for sore pads.

Sister put on a pot of tea. Betty had given her the details of the corpse.

"You'd think he could have pulled open his own trap," Sister wondered.

"It wouldn't be easy, but a strong man, one who could withstand the pain, might could do it." Betty used the bane of Southern grammar teachers, "might could."

"And you said you thought the ankle was crushed?"

"Sister, no doubt. He was in rigor, as I told you, so he hadn't been there long. His jaw was wide open, as were his eyes. Creepy that he stepped in his own damn trap."

"Or was pushed into it."

"Hey, I'm the one who watches mysteries. It would take more than one man to push another man into that trap."

"You're right. Thanks to Andrew's murder, my mind goes to strange places . . . You'd think he would have screamed. Someone would have heard him. The Shelleys' house is about a mile away, but they might have heard him."

"You'd think," Betty agreed.

"This is turning into a deadly fall." Sister shook her head. "Come help me feed my little babies while the water gets hot."

"How are they doing?" Betty asked.

"I've been feeding them every four hours. A little warmed milk with Esbilac and there's a small water bowl there. They're big enough to drink from it. But the milk is helping and I'll try some soft baby food maybe tomorrow." She sat and opened the crate, the three shooters filled and ready.

Betty watched as Sister gently put the needle-like plastic object in one cub's open mouth. The plastic was not too hard but not too soft either. "He's hungry."

"If I can keep these guys eating I think I can save them. They're so beautiful."

"They are," Betty agreed.

The teapot whistled, so Betty got up, made a proper tea in the old pottery teapot as Sister continued to feed the fox cubs. Golly watched from the counter. She could care less about the babies, but it might be possible for Betty to share a morsel. Even the corner of a cookie was something. The dogs were outside, so the cat could display herself to full advantage. She rubbed on Betty's arm. Purred mightily.

Sister fed the last little one as she rubbed his head with her forefinger. Finished, she placed him back in the crate, next to his sister and brother, already nestled in the blanket. It was cozy.

Standing, Sister placed the utensils in the sink. "What is it about feeling a heartbeat? With people dying around us a heartbeat is special. Hopeful."

"It is." Betty smiled as they sat at the table then changed the sensitive subject. "I didn't eat much at the breakfast."

"Me neither. I have some leftover lasagna from last night. I'll heat it up. Will take two minutes."

She did just that as she also gave an adoring Golly cat a Greenie, the best.

As the two women ate, they enjoyed warm food.

Betty broke the silence. "I am not fond of cadavers."

"Maybe only a pathologist is."

"How can anyone go into that line of work?" Betty was mortified.

"Answers. I figure they find the answers. Late, but still."

"I guess. I couldn't do it. I wish when Mother died we didn't have to have an open casket. She looked like herself. And my brother insisted on it. He wanted to sit with Mom. I gave in. Like I said, she looked good, but my last view of my mother was as a dead person."

"Every culture has its rituals. People are most conservative about marriage and death, ever notice?"

"Actually, I have. I mean, I've seen those funeral pyres by the Ganges. Or worse, the body is floating down the river. God, how can a nation allow something that unsanitary?"

"That's not what they're thinking. It's sacred to them, the river. When my mother died, she asked to be cremated, and this was before that became popular. What a fight. I finally blew my stack and told everyone that was her last wish and we had to honor it. They finally shut up probably because I so rarely lose my temper," Sister said.

"But you were right. It really matters. You know that's why I come back to Andrew's murder. Did he deserve it? Damned if I know. But he truly pissed off someone. People want to find the killer. Maybe they'll be next." Betty leaned back in her chair. "That was pretty good lasagna. And you're not even Italian." Betty smiled at her.

"Now, there's an ancient culture. Thousands of years. Beautiful buildings. Thousands and thousands of miles of roads and aquaducts and wars and, well, people to be buried."

Betty cleared the table. "While I'm up, would you like a drink?"

"No thanks, the tea was enough."

"I'm going to dip into your gin and make a martini. Seeing that man with his jaw wide open, his face contorted, held by a giant jaw, really, I could use a drink. Back to the thousands of years of war, the dead, and so on." Betty said.

"Yes?" Sister knew something was coming.

"We . . . well . . . those of us who are Christians . . . are supposed to rise from the dead."

"Yes. This is when we need Reverend Taliaferro and Father Mancusco."

"When we all rise from the dead after the millennia, where can anyone put us? Talk about overcrowding."

Sister burst out laughing. "God, Betty, where do you come up with this stuff?"

Betty laughed, too. "I don't know. Just pops into my head. But," she drew out the but, "what if the trapper was murdered? Anything can happen."

"Yes. Apparently, it is happening."

Betty threw that martini down her throat. "I feel better already."

CHAPTER 20

November 3, 2024 Sunday

Reverend Taliaferro gave a sermon on unsolicited advice. In short: Be careful.

Driving over to the Home Place, Bobby and Betty discussed it as Sister sat in the backseat and listened. "She's good. You know sometime we should go to Father Mancusco and hear one of his sermons. Bet he'd enjoy seeing his hunting buddies in a pew."

"He certainly hears us take the name of the Lord in vain out in the field." Betty gave thanks that she was far away from the field.

"You rarely give unsolicited advice," Bobby said to Sister as he glanced in the rearview mirror.

"Doesn't work, so why waste my time."

"There is that," Betty agreed. "But sometimes you can't help it."

"Well, Aunt Daniella will be in her chair next to the fireplace. The bourbon will flow and so will her advice."

"She's got a pass, being close to one hundred." Sister smiled. "Do you have any doubt that she was one of the most beautiful women of her generation? She could probably say anything." Sister put her hand to the heat source in the back. "Turn that up a tad, will you?"

Bobby reached with his right hand, pressing the dial then turning it up to 75. The backseat received heat as directly as the front ones.

At the Lorillard place, Betty stepped into the kitchen after hanging up her coat, while Sister first paid her compliments to Aunt Daniella in her favorite old club chair.

"Could I refresh your drink?"

"Oh no, honey. Let Gray do it. By the way, how was your sermon today?" She pointed to the wing chair and Sister sat in it.

"Aunt Dan, one minute. Betty, Yvonne, do you need me?"

Sam stuck his head out of the kitchen. "No, they don't. Are you being sexist, assuming the women should cook?"

"No. Were I going to be sexist, I'd think of something better than that."

He grinned, ducking back in but the two women all the way in the parlor could still hear the kitchen noise.

"Sam has been banging pots since he was tiny." Aunt Daniella reminisced.

"He has talent for cooking and horses." Sister wiggled backwards in the chair.

"And English. He never made less than an A in English, that's why Graziella and I," she named his departed mother, "thought he could go into law school or medicine. A good English student can usually do so much because they can read, really read."

"I never thought of that."

"True. Now, the sermon." Aunt Daniella folded her hands together.

"She discussed unsolicited advice. How it often does more harm than good. Her suggestion was if one is prompted to say something to warn someone, or help them in some fashion, don't frame it as advice. Frame it as an odd thought, or use an example, especially if you have been successful in the subject matter."

"Sensible. I fail on this subject. If I see something, I shoot my mouth off." Aunt Daniella held up one hand. "Don't be polite. I do, but I can't help myself. People are so blind. I've been blinded too by problems. Look how I avoided Sam's alcoholism, as did Graziella. By the third arrest for drunkenness in public, or drunk driving, we had to face it."

"Hard."

"Yes, it was. Our golden boys. Well, two golden boys, and one was ruining his life. Harder for him."

"Families often miss what's closest. Thank God for Gray. He finally prevailed."

"Having the money to put Sam in rehab certainly helped. And to give Sam credit he had to want to change. Never backslid. Not once." She smiled broadly. "Do you think you're born with the desire to drink or to take drugs?"

"I don't know, but when my son was killed, Big Ray went off his rails. Everyone saw it. There was nothing one could do. Best to just keep going, not focus on the pain."

Aunt Daniella nodded. "If you'd left him, I think he would have ended his life."

"I hope not. Miserable as he was, unfaithful as he was, I felt sorry for him. Whatever that inner fortitude is, he didn't have it."

"You did. But you had and have a strong faith, as I do. And that's why I listened so intently to today's sermon. Reverend Paige didn't just give a sermon, he thundered." She finished her drink with a flourish. "We are two days from the presidential election and his sermon was 'Render unto Caesar what is Caesar's. Rend unto God what is God's.' Some people would expect a Black preacher to stump for his candidate, but not Reverend Paige. He drew the line between temporary power and eternal power. And I will give him credit, he said that both parties were sullied with racism. What surprised me was he included sexism, too, and even climate change. Wasn't prepared for that. Then again, he's a young fellow in his mid-forties. Ordained. He did his homework. I was quite taken with the sermon." She paused. "If you think about it, maybe Reverend Taliaferro's sermon was also about not telling people how to vote. Unsolicited advice."

"Bet you're right." Sister blinked.

A little bell rang. Sister stood, gave Aunt Daniella her hand to rise, and the two ladies actually proceeded to the dining room, laughing as they did so.

The house, the first part what is now the mudroom, reached its final form in the 1800s. It really expanded when Monroe was president by the Lorillards, and the Laprades, who were keen business people and had been free Blacks since the 1600s. They never flaunted their success, which was wise. The dining room, fifteen by twenty feet, was ample, larger than many farmhouses had. The fireplace at the northern end of the room meant one wasn't eating in a forty-degree room. Bitter cold found its way through every crack in an old house.

After their prayer, Aunt Daniella, served first, asked Yvonne, "How was Father Mancusco's sermon? Sister and I were discussing Reverend Paige and Reverend Taliaferro. Was it political?"

"Not directly," Yvonne replied. "He drew our attention to the history of the Church, how persecution is part of being Roman Catholic. We are still persecuted today in parts of the world."

"Hard to believe, isn't it?" Gray carved the roast beef.

"When an institution has been in power as long as the Catholic Church, it is to be expected." Sister then added, "Religion invites persecution."

"Why do you say that?" Betty had never heard her friend mention anything like this.

"It's irrational. It pushes one to believe, to feel, not necessarily to think. Of course, that doesn't work. For centuries there are people who believe their logic can get you to believe their way. Fundamentally, it isn't logical."

"What about Martin Luther?" Yvonne was fascinated. "1517."

"That was about cleaning the Church, I think. Ending the abuses. He didn't think he was a bad Catholic."

"The world changed the day he nailed those theses to the door of the church at Wittenberg." Sam smiled. "And now everyone has their version of Christianity. It seems every large faith has factions."

"Waste of time," Sister bluntly replied. "If we spent time trying to help people whatever their faith, there's so much distress in the world, that I expect we would all be serving the Lord in one way or the other."

"Hear. Hear," Aunt Daniella agreed. "Now, what's this I hear that you all found a murdered man yesterday? Gray spoke of it as he drove me to church. Murdered?"

Betty allowed Sam to put mashed potatoes on her plate. "I can't prove he was murdered, but his foot was in a bear trap. So I expect something was wrong. Why would he step in his own bear trap?"

"True. Unless he tripped and fell into it," Yvonne added.

"Trappers fight over territory. Usually they are not invited to trap. Some landowners allow it, most do not. So the feeling is he veered onto another trapper's land. A trapper whom the Shelleys didn't know was using their land. They can be very clever at hiding traps." Sam finished serving the food and sat. "Think of how Crawford's land is or was used as you drive up the mountain. Trappers. Illegal liquor. You name it. The Buzzwells supported every generation since the 1830s with that stuff."

"Illegal activities often create harsh people. Interfere, you might die," Gray simply said.

"Well, maybe the dead man was warned. Maybe he had a bad reputation. For all we know, maybe he opened other men's traps and stole animals. Pelts bring money although this year the money isn't too good. Many of those men wouldn't have compassion for the dead man."

"But to kill him?" Yvonne sipped her wine. "Kill someone over a pelt."

"People kill for less." Aunt Daniella had seen a fair amount of bad behavior in her long time on earth.

Betty paused then said, "It's not yet Thanksgiving and we've faced two murders. One we have no idea about. We don't know the person, if he was indeed murdered. It doesn't really touch us, although we found him hunting at Kingswood. But Andrew, now, that's a different story."

"And that will drag on." Sister exhaled. "Both Winston and Solange can hire expensive, good lawyers. Those of us who were there will be dragged into it. Yet how else can the law work? Facts, times, relationships, all must be examined. It's not just the medical examiner. It's everything."

"You never realize how long justice takes until you're in the middle of a lawsuit." Sam savored the beef. "I don't like the way I left Harvard, but had I gotten my B.A. and gone to law school, I expect I would have learned a lot." He chewed a bit. "And not liked any of it."

They nodded in agreement.

"Had to be easier when the king or queen pronounced judgment." Aunt Daniella enjoyed the Sunday dinners and she enjoyed thinking.

"Even there best to delay it with Parliament or long investigations. I suppose if the king was furious it could be done with the wave of a hand, but no one in authority wants to look abrupt, unjust. Even the Spartans and the Athenians didn't want to look unjust."

Sam, who loved history, said, "Well, Xerxes and Darius didn't have to worry. Can you imagine being so rich that in the fifth century BC you could pay for over a million men under arms and have a huge navy? We have no concept of such wealth. Cleopatra. It's overwhelming."

"Don't you think they still had to keep the public happy?" Gray pressed.

"Secure. The definition of happiness is slippery in any century," Sam replied.

"Not for me." Aunt Daniella laughed.

They nattered on, happy in the twenty-first century. That didn't mean any one of them couldn't come up with some complaints, be they political or how their vacuum cleaner wasn't sucking up anymore, but in the main they were happy, surrounded by friends both four feet and two.

As the group ate a fabulous meal at the Home Place, Winston and Beryl finished a light dinner at Bradford Hall. Beryl concentrated on protein, some carbs. She was on another one of her health food kicks until it came to dessert. She was a good cook.

After dinner, Winston patted his stomach. "Honey, I need a brief after-dinner walk. How about it?"

"Of course. It's turned into a nice day. Mid-fifties. I'll grab my sweater."

They walked outside, followed by Miss Priss. Tidbit, the Yorkshire, fast asleep, missed the walk.

Their driveway was long and curving.

"When Andrew first started dating Solange I told him not to bring her home for at least two months."

"Why?" Beryl thought this odd.

"Because all rich people in the country have long, winding driveways."

She laughed. "You're right."

"Mother never denied being rich. When we were children, she used to say over and over again, 'To some, much is given and much expected.'" He smiled, remembering his mother. "Isn't that from the Bible?"

"I don't know. Could be Shakespeare. You know I'm not very literary."

"You read."

"Popular stuff. If you put a gun to my head I could read *Remembrance of Time Past.* Has another name now with a new translation. Doesn't matter to me." They reached halfway down the driveway. "What is that?"

Winston stared in the direction of her gaze. "Damned if I know. Come on."

Miss Priss ran ahead.

They reached the bottom of the drive in maybe four minutes. Miss Priss reached it before that. Tail wagging, she sniffed the base of a large sign.

Winston walked in front of it, as it was right by the turn to their driveway. In professionally painted, large letters were the words, "Murderer. Cain and Abel."

He seethed. "I'll kill that bitch. So help me."

Beryl, shocked, prudently put her hand on his shoulder. "It is tempting, but don't say anything like that. Truly. Anything you do, any emotion you show, will be used against you. And you don't know if she did this."

He kicked at the sign, then started to tear it with his hands. Seeing his fury, she helped. Miss Priss picked up a few pieces.

"It's on our property."

"Come on, let's get it out of here. We can leave the posts."

Took them ten minutes to demolish the offending sign. They then walked with great energy back up to their house, the dog leading.

"About the sign, say nothing. Don't even report it."

"It looked done by a sign painter. Professional."

"Certainly looks like it."

"She's out of her mind."

"She'll say it's grief. And again, you don't know if she's behind this."

"I think she is. Andrew was stupid. Stupid."

"She's trying to turn people against you. Your friends know you would never have killed your brother. Will a jury believe that? I don't know. You're middle-aged, rich, male, and white. Who is to say one or two of those jurors will believe guilt based on that? You can't do anything right with some people today. It, well, I don't know. I only know you would never kill him. A fistfight, sure. Show me two brothers or even sisters who haven't walloped on each other. But don't lose your temper. Especially ignore her."

The climb slowed them down. Out of breath they returned to their house, sat in the kitchen.

"She wants to put me away." Winston grabbed a scotch.

"I believe she's trying to turn people against you. But we can't prove that she put the sign up."

"Beryl, I'm beginning to wonder if we'll live through this. Maybe Solange, or someone, wants me dead."

"Don't say that."

"Unfortunately, Andrew and I argued more often. Mostly I ignored him but I criticized him more and more."

CHAPTER 21

November 4, 2024 Monday

Hound walk, early even in the winter, proved brisk this morning. Sister felt like everyone, including the hounds, walked faster, being eager to return to warmth. The temperature bounced around; warmish yesterday, cool today.

Once that was over, she drove to the big feed store in Charlottesville. Feed, delivered once every two weeks at the farm made life easy, but she had forgotten to order extra spring bulbs. Even though it was November, it wasn't too late for some daffodils, or even tulips.

Checking out, she returned to the car, rapidly wearing out, opened the door. "I got treats."

"Can we have one now?" Rooster could eat.

The pitiful face worked its magic. She rooted around in the big bag, found the box of treats, opened it, and popped a dog cookie in an eager mouth. "Raleigh."

"Thank you."

The dogs chewed their prizes while Sister negotiated the ever-increasing traffic in the university town.

"Didn't your mother tell you to shut your mouth when you chew?" she teased her dogs.

"No," came the unified reply.

One good thing about a truck or an SUV is the driver sits high. It's easier to see. Sister liked driving. She headed east, got on Route 20, and drove down to Brook Hill Farm and Stables.

Lynne Beegle-Gebhard, teaching in the higher ring, looked up, saw Sister and waved. Sister sat on a bench along with her dogs. She enjoyed watching Lynne teach, and the exuberant woman could teach anyone. Lessons were fun. They weren't designed to scare you half to death, but students left having done a bit more than when they'd arrived.

"So you think you could outrun a small Thoroughbred?" Rooster asked Raleigh.

"Of course. People think horses are faster than dogs but not me. I can be outrun by anyone," the Doberman bragged.

Rooster raised his eyebrows but kept his mouth shut.

Lynne put her four students through a course, watched each jump and the four young women, high school students, finished to praise. Deserved, too, as Lynne had raised the bar three inches. Doesn't sound like much but when someone is learning to jump they pay intense attention to height. The final goal was to get the kids to jump three feet six inches without fear, tensing up. In fact, to get them to look forward to it. Part of this meant teaching a rider to find their spot, which depended on their mount's stride.

The other key was getting a rider to relax. If you said, "Relax," they'd immediately tense up. Lynne stuck by that. Before they'd go over a course, she'd have them ride in a big circle, drop stirrups, pick up stirrups. Take one's hands off the reins and circle your arms. This loosened people. Then drop the reins, drop the stirrups. Finding that one could do this at, say, a brisk walk or trot sent confidence way up. So by the time the young women hit the middle of their lesson, there was no thought of fear. They concentrated on remembering the course. They paid attention to the footing and, of course, they were competitive with the other riders. No one said as much, but the competitive spirit was there.

One of the things Sister most admired about the daughter of her old friends was that Lynne didn't create mechanical riders. Sure, people could count strides, but Lynne wasn't emphasizing that. She emphasized feel. If a rider feels their horse, is in sync with the animal, it's so much easier. The pair are fluid, and even a rider with short legs looks a bit elegant. No one looks as elegant as a tall rider with long legs, male, female, or in-between, but to watch a matched pair, a pair that understood each other, was always a joy.

Sister couldn't help it. She sat there with a grin on her face.

Raleigh and Rooster, on the other hand, hoped they'd have a chance to show off.

As the four kids filed out of the ring, good footing, the two dogs took off, hurried into it.

"*Watch me.*" Raleigh soared over the three-log jump, a natural.

"*Ha.*" Rooster jumped it, too, then the two of them raced each other to the next jump. Sister laughed at her dogs while Lynne turned around.

"Next time I put on a show, how about you bring these two? We can have a dog challenge. Two dollars to enter the class." Lynne laughed as she climbed the hill to lean over and kiss Sister on the cheek.

"Good lesson. The redheaded girl started out stiff, or she was when I sat, and by the end of the lesson, she was much more comfortable. Eyes up, too."

"She has a strong leg. I'm working on her confidence."

"You're succeeding."

"Come up to the barn with me. Need to get the next group saddled and ready. They should be ready but a check never hurts."

As the two women walked up, Rooster and Raleigh also, Mark, Lynne's husband, slowed down. He was in a huge new tractor.

"Sister."

"Hello, handsome." She beamed at him.

"You say the nicest things." He flashed his big smile. He waved and continued up the hill. The farm, like any farm, took a lot of work, a lot of equipment.

"Lynne, that tractor looks brand new. Had to cost a damn fortune."

"Mark went to Kentucky to get it. It's maybe three years old. He can find things and then he can bargain. I can't."

"He found you." Sister smiled at her. "I dropped by on a whim but now that I'm here, I suppose you heard about the dead trapper at Kingswood?"

"I did. It was on the news, but Liz King called me and told me. She mentioned one of Farmington's masters, they've been having trouble with poachers. Keswick, too."

That was the other big club in the eastern part of the county, Farmington being in the western part.

"Any here?"

"I haven't seen them but Mark's found a couple of old traps up on the hill where it breaks over onto our neighbor's."

"I called around as did Gray and his brother. Between us we can cover a lot of territory so to speak. And the feedback we're getting is that money is tight. Pelt prices are down. Some trappers are even going after rabbits."

"That takes a lot of rabbits," Lynne mused. "If times get tough, trapping is the least of it. How about outright theft?"

As they reached the barn, Sister took a big breath. "Yes. I keep reading about all this shoplifting in stores. Stuff being locked up and people not buying because they don't want to find a store worker to unlock a cabinet. Crazy stuff."

"It is, but it's not as bad as the big department stores. Some of them have closed down," Lynne mentioned. "The tough part about trappers is finding them. The traps that Mark came upon were rusted. Left out. These guys have to move around."

"They do."

The two chatted while Lynne checked the tack on the horses for the next lesson. Each student has to clean and tack up their own horse. No servants here. You did it yourself and you learned.

Driving back home Sister enjoyed the scenery, passing old farms. The eastern part of the county being settled before the western, which was true up and down the East Coast.

Pulling into the drive, she let the dogs out, who immediately roared into the house to tell Golly what she missed.

Sister followed, dropped her shopping bag, went to the stove, and warmed some milk, time to feed the fox cubs.

That accomplished she put her purchases in the mudroom. She'd get to them soon enough.

Betty called. "Hey."

"Hey back at you."

"Wanted you to know that Ben reached me after hound walk. Still no identification of the trapper man but he did say once they got him on the slab they found he had been shot. Whoever did it opened his coat, shot him, closed the coat. They still aren't sure if he was in the trap first or put there after being killed. So it was murder."

"That will go round like wildfire." Sister sat. "What people are telling me is how those guys fight for territory."

She then filled in Betty on her brief stop at Brook Hill. They batted around ideas.

"Remember when you found the corpse at Bishop's Gate?" Sister recalled an event in the past. "Two bodies over the space of a year, in our territory. The one was solved. Then again trapping isn't something you'd think would lead to murder."

"Maybe it wasn't about trapping. Either way, I have no desire to find another body in the hunt field."

"You're tough about it," Sister complimented her.

"No, I'm really not. I simply know there's nothing I can do about it. Animals die. We die. Generally, we die in the hospital, in car wrecks, at hospice. We aren't often found out in the woods. If a body is lying about you know there's trouble."

"That's true."

As the two friends talked, Beryl Bradford stood at the entrance to her farm. Solange Bradford pulled up, cut the motor, and got out.

"Did you put that sign up?" Beryl said in lieu of greeting.

"No. Why would I do that?" Solange's face reddened. "No hello or anything."

"Accusing my husband of murder won't help anything either. Winston didn't do it."

"The trial will establish that." Solange's jaw jutted out.

"How many other people wanted Andrew dead? And why? Could be anything." Beryl wasn't backing down. "Maybe your handsome gardener had a fight with him. He was jealous, took it out on Scott."

"That's absurd. Winston had a motive and for that matter so does Georgia. But that's not why I'm meeting you here."

"Right." She held out her arm as Solange pulled a luxurious sable out of the backseat, draping it over Beryl's arm.

"All yours."

"Why didn't you sell it?" Beryl questioned, taken aback.

"Then I'd look poor, which I am not. But also, I couldn't do that to such a wonderful gift from Olivia. I never showed interest in furs but she left this to me in her will. And she had a note in the pocket saying it would match my hair."

"Well, it would if you let your hair go natural." Beryl couldn't resist.

Another flush of red crossed Solange's perfect features. "A touch up here and there. Anyway, Olivia was generous. She loved Andrew. She liked me. I don't know as she loved me but this was a magnificent gift. Andrew was ecstatic."

"It's beautiful. Nothing like sable."

"Maybe she hoped I'd have a daughter and the coat would be passed down, but I can't wear it. I just can't. I am so against animals being killed for fur. So this way it stays in the family and I don't feel guilty. And I don't feel ungrateful to Olivia. If I wasn't going to wear it, she would have wanted you to wear it."

"Perhaps." Beryl's voice softened, for she did adore her late mother-in-law.

"Well, I'll go back home." She stopped, turned again to her sister-in-law. "I don't have the best judgment right now, but I think this is good judgment. I feel okay, then I crash. The worst part is waking up in the morning, reaching for him and he's not there."

"Taking Winston down the tubes isn't going to bring Andrew back."

"No." Solange's eyes glittered defiantly. "No, but if Winston killed him—over and done with. If he didn't, maybe what is to come will lead us to the killer."

"Maybe you don't want to know. Maybe Andrew's murder is worse than either of us can imagine."

CHAPTER 22

November 5, 2024 Tuesday

Thinking few people would be out as it was Election Day, Jefferson Hunt put Old Paradise on a fixture card. Sister looked forward to a no-pressure hunt at the huge estate that sat across the road from Tattenhall Station, another vast estate. She knew how lucky she was to have so much territory in one place. She wanted to poke around if the day proved slow.

While not a barn-burner day it wasn't slow, given that Tuesdays were usually small in number, election or not. Today the group comprised of fifteen people.

As hounds drew from the main old stable, stone, Earl, who moved from there to the carriage house, watched. As the restoration progress continued there were too many people in and out of the main stables, so Earl had moved to quieter quarters. Proved better than he'd hoped. The old carriages, immaculately kept, lined the sides of the large structure. The middle of the buildings was an aisle. Both ends of the building had double doors, which made it easier to get out a carriage. A four-in-hand carriage, big, needed space. No point scraping one of those shiny sides because the entrance and exit were too tight. There were even a pair of double doors in the middle of the barn, facing the mountainside. Rarely used, a handsome carriage sat there, built for two. If Earl felt like it he could sit in the driver's seat to see everything around him and even what was going on up in the cemeteries.

Each carriage had a few blankets folded on a seat. This kept people warm for the half of the year when trotting along in a carriage could be cold. If nothing else, a touch of speed meant that breeze would hit you in the face.

The day, low forties, nice enough for a fox with his double winter coat, saw the fellow sitting on a blanket. He watched as the hounds trotted by. A few stopped to sniff, but his scent wasn't fresh. He'd been in the carriage house for a full day, having stashed a healthy amount of food in there. Earl wasn't lazy, but why work harder than necessary?

Pookah stopped, nose down. *"Red."*

Zandy, older, advised, *"Earl. We won't get a chase. Come on. Don't tarry."*

Earl watched them pass another outbuilding, the stable for the workhorses. Sarge, young, made a den in there. The old but tidy barn also had blankets. Every stable, there were three plus the carriage house, was fully equipped even if rarely used.

Hounds moved past the workhorse stable. Earl observed the slow pace. It should have been a good day for scent. He figured they'd pick up something somewhere. He often knew what other animals transversed the big estate including humans. Old Paradise, five thousand acres, once twenty-some thousand, offered places to hide if a human was so inclined. The bootleggers often came down from the mountains, coming over from the western county, which adjoined Albemarle County at the top of the Blue Ridge. He hadn't heard them yet this year. The place was quiet except for the deer hunters up on the mountains. They poached, but being high, their presence didn't disturb domesticated or wild animals below. Infuriated Crawford, but he would need a platoon of men to patrol those higher acres. His own, rough acres, still had the remnants of a still on them. He never went up there. No reason to go.

A low bellow, had to be Ace's, Earl thought. He knew every hound by voice as well as by sight. The A line of Jefferson Hunt had deep sonorous voices.

Ace picked up a coyote line. Not burning, but still easy to follow. The pack moved at a fast trot. Not all hounds opened, but all were on the line.

Sister on Midshipman, five, young but steady, gave a light squeeze. She had picked up Matchplay and Midshipman as yearlings a few years ago when a Thoroughbred breeder went out of business. As was her method, she took them slow. Same with the hounds.

By five the young horses had been exposed to everything but ostriches and alpaca, which one could run into without knowing they were there. Some of the new people in the county thought they would make money on exotic animals and their farms abutted fixtures.

Midshipman's ears swiveled. A loud crack diverted her attention. A mid-sized black bear bolted out of the ditch, trees on both sides. Midshipman jumped sideways. The bear, surprisingly fast, hurried in the opposite direction.

Sister heard the "oof", "oof" of people coming off behind her. Many horses feared bears. But she tried to introduce her youngsters to everything. As there were bear at Roughneck Farm and After All, she accustomed her horses as well as the hounds to the scent. Rarely will a black bear create a problem unless a mother with cubs. This was not the case. He wanted to get away from the Jefferson Hunt as much as the horses in the field wished him to do so.

Walter, bringing up the rear for First Flight, had his hands full. Bobby waited.

Walter stopped as the bear suddenly was running toward them, a pack of hounds on it.

The tall man stood by the most nervous horse and rider, Lorraine Shoemaker, Cindy Chandler's new neighbor.

Hearing another pack of hounds, the Jefferson Hunt pack stopped.

"Lieu in," Weevil yelled, telling them to go back in, look for scent in the woods.

They did, but the commotion behind them scattered their attention.

As the pack of bear hounds, Plott hounds, blew by, the bear, safely ahead, reached a massive oak in the middle of the cleared field. Woods would have been safer, but the pack was too close.

He reached up, climbing up.

"Goddamn," Bobby whispered under his breath.

No Jefferson Hunt hounds followed this pack.

Walter patiently waited for everyone to settle and knew whoever was hunting that bear was poaching on Crawford's land.

One of Crawford's workers, back at the main house, observed this in the distance. He gathered up another man and they each took a hound truck, aluminum housing on the back, these trucks were used to follow hounds apart from the mounted people. The large hound trailer sat wherever a fixture started. These trucks picked up stragglers, confused or injured hounds.

Sister, ahead, did not see the two employees, men who knew all manner of hunting, arrive at the tree. They picked up the bear hounds, putting them in the two trucks.

Finally, Walter, now on the ground, gave Lorraine a leg up as she had come off. He mounted. Pete Jensen, horse also a bit frazzled, calmed his expensive animal, and the back of First Flight slowly walked forward. This was not the time to catch up.

The bear, observing all this from the tree, wanted to be rid of everyone.

The two men drove back to the main house. After discussion with Crawford, on the road, they put the well-kept hounds in a kennel near the kennel for his Dumfriesshire hounds.

Crawford had everything. And he had lived long enough in the area to assume whoever poached would not come to pick up their hounds. He now had a pack of Plott hounds.

Sister, unaware, crept into the woods at the base of the mountains. The coyote utilized the delay to his advantage.

Hounds worked, but nothing. Weevil, furious, rode back onto the pasture and headed south, in the direction of Bishop's Gate, which was four miles down the road.

Nothing.

Odd. One would think something would be picked up, but animals get spooked, including wildlife. It proved a shot day.

As they rode back to the trailers at the main barn, Sister and everyone heard one shot. Then another, from the opposite direction. Then a fusillade.

"Jesus Christ," she whispered to herself.

Once everyone was dismounted, their first concern was the volley of shots.

Sitting in the main barn, the tack room warm, they talked while eating the potluck food. As there weren't many people there was enough but not overload like most Jefferson Hunt breakfasts.

"Wonder where the bear is?" Lorraine nibbled a croissant.

"Back at his or her den," Walter answered. "Bears are territorial as most animals are. Their territory is big. Can be fifty miles or more depending on where it is but he'll be back. They're smart."

"If anyone comes to pick up his hounds Crawford will call Animal Control. And he'll sue. He'll make an example out of whoever. You come out swinging, hurt people, cost them money in court, they tend to back off. Leave you alone."

Sam shrugged. "Except for those that would set your barn on fire."

"My Lord, do you have those?" Lorraine was aghast.

"No, not recently but in the old days that's how poor people would get even with rich people," Gray answered. He had ridden up front that day. "This territory, for years, had the Buzzwells making liquor at a hidden still. You left them alone."

"The lowlifes have their ways." Bobby didn't pretend to be liberal. "They'll key your car's paint job. Kill the shrubs around your home by putting poison at the base. It might take years but eventually we find out who those people are. Now, I'm talking about in the sixties and seventies, when I was young. But eventually those guys do something worse or get sloppy. And they get put away. So whatever business they might have goes to hell. The wife is stuck trying to feed the kids."

"There are always people who think they can outsmart others." Walter sat, glad to stretch out his long legs. "Crime is based on it."

"We'll never know who did get away with wrongdoing." Sister stretched out her legs, too.

Ben Sidell, in Second Flight that day, spoke. "We know what crimes are unsolved. It frustrates me as a law enforcement officer, but if you consider how big our country is, we don't have that many unsolved crimes."

"But some of them are sensationalized." Yvonne wondered if

that bear would show up to her door since she lived across the street, down two miles.

"They are," Ben agreed. "As technology advances, some of them are now being solved. Still, it grates on my nerves."

"What? An unsolved crime?" Sam fetched Yvonne another drink, hot.

"Crime in general irritates me. Most of it is unnecessary. Anger. Ego. Family drama. Now, crime leading to profit, that's another issue. And that often takes longer."

"White collar crime?" Lorraine asked.

"Yes," Ben answered.

"What about political crime, since this is Election Day." Gray smiled slightly.

"Doesn't count." Yvonne grinned. "We expect them to lie, to be corrupt."

"Yvonne." Betty then added, "Maybe that is how many people feel today. Those that actually believe in a candidate will be sorely disappointed down the road. Well, I amend that. One group will be disappointed tomorrow."

"Aren't you glad you aren't in politics?" Walter asked the group.

Most agreed, except for Ben. "I'm not exactly in it but not exactly out either."

They talked on, the group breaking up after an hour of breakfast time and talk.

Earl watched the trailers go out. Then he curled up on a blanket in the tack room. Electric heat set at a low temperature kept the room reasonably pleasant. The electric heat in the washroom ensured the pipes wouldn't freeze. Sixty degrees kept all safe.

Sister and Betty wiped down the horses, put on blankets, and cleaned tack. Sister usually cleaned Gray's tack, as he did house chores. By the time she entered the kitchen she could hear the election news on the small TV in the corner.

"Too soon to tell," he informed her.

The phone rang. Sister picked it up. It was Crawford. "Sister, Crawford here."

"I'd know that voice anywhere."

"I'm not going to talk about the election."

"Me neither. Too soon to tell."

"The gunfire you heard today, my boys told me about it, turns out to have been the bear hunters versus the deer hunters. Both groups poaching. As you know, I have the bear hunters' hounds."

"Nice-looking hounds."

"I'm buying three drones. I'm hoping that will keep my ridge clear. If you have any trouble at any other fixtures, you might suggest it."

"Crawford, that's an excellent idea."

They spoke a bit longer, then Sister hung up her wall phone, told Gray.

"Sounds like a good idea."

"If the two groups of hunters became that angry with each other, doesn't presage good things."

"No, but I doubt they'll kill one another."

"With what's been going on around us, I wonder."

The phone rang again. Ronnie Haslip.

"Heard you had a small battle today." He started the conversation.

"It will pass. I hope."

"I have good news for a change. A small group from Bull Run and Deep Run, old friends, have rented Wolverhampton for the weekend after Thanksgiving. I'll hire someone to spruce up the stables. And I'll get the heat turned higher two days before the week-end. Take the chill off."

"Ronnie, that is good news."

"Thought you'd like to hear it."

"We'll be across the street from Wolverhampton. Fixture is Close Shave. Oh, Ronnie, I hope this means things are looking up."

CHAPTER 23

November 6, 2024 Wednesday

On his hands and knees Ronnie crumpled paper, putting it in the woodburning stove in the Wolverhampton tack room. After filling up a goodly amount he put in dried, split wood. A match, and whoosh.

The stove sat on a heavy slate base, the pipe going out of the roof.

Given the fourteen-by-fourteen size of the tack room, ample yet easy to heat, he sat for a moment in the old chair, watching the flames through the glass front.

The last time Wolverhampton was remodeled was the 1980s. Baseboard heat ran around the bottom of the washroom. In case the weather turned brutally cold, light fixtures in each stall as well as the wash stall could hold a heat lamp.

Today the temperature stuck in the mid-forties. One needed a coat, a sweater underneath, and gloves if one's hands grew stiff with the cold easily. His did not but he always had gloves in his work jackets. He had his Carhartt for today and a heavy lambskin jacket for bitter cold.

Sitting there enjoying the heat, he double-checked his list. He'd bought eight water buckets, eight feed buckets. He'd also bought a dozen buckets for odds and ends. You can always use a bucket. Every stall had an iron thin rod across the midpoint of the door. This was for the blankets or saddle pads. Next to the door a strong hook, high, could hold a bridle and even a blanket if you hooked it at the neckline. The stable, originally built in the mid-eighteenth century, solid and tight, was easy to work in. In the summer, just throw open the doors at each end, open the top door of the Dutch doors, and a breeze from the mountain not two miles away to the west refreshed man and beast.

He looked up at the thick rafters, hand hewn. Stables now used I-beams, depending on the stable or four-by-four posts. He much preferred the hand hewn. Those with highly skilled labor and deep pockets could afford to have their stables with space over the center aisle, like the center aisle of a church, beautiful curving wood, high.

It made him think of Notre Dame, rebuilt. He had visited the extraordinary structure his junior year in college. His parents gave him enough money to get to Europe and then wisely left him alone. Like most everyone who had set foot in the cathedral since 1163, he'd felt awe, a connection to the past and also that this church represented France.

Sitting there, he tried to think what represented America. Was it the White House? Congressional building? Maybe it was the Grand Canyon, the Blue Ridge Mountains, or the Rockies? A Maine lighthouse? Now that he'd gotten himself on this kick, he pulled himself back. Work to do.

"Hello," a man's voice called from the end of the stable.

Ronnie, jacket back on, stepped outside. "Can I help you?"

"Are you going to allow deer hunting? I'm part of a hunt club and we will pay."

Ronnie recognized this man as the fellow who'd challenged Sister with a bow.

The man didn't recognize Ronnie, who had been with First Flight that day, not up with Sister. Also he had worn a hunt kit, and people often look different without it.

Ronnie reached out his hand. "Ronnie Haslip."

"Ames Dewey." He removed his glove to shake hands, so Ronnie knew Ames possessed some manners even if he'd been foolish enough to challenge Sister.

"Cold. Would you like to come into the tack room? It's warmer in there."

Ames followed Ronnie inside the room, which quickly warmed up. He sat in one old chair, Ronnie in another.

"Do you own Wolverhampton?" Ames asked.

"Yes. I'm part of a syndicate that does. Three of us live on Chapel Cross Road. I live closer to town. It's a big house. Well built, as is this barn."

Ames glanced up at the lowered roof of the tack room. "Different times. Different people."

"True."

"Deer season, bow season, started October fifth. We're almost at the beginning of rifle season, another ten days. We would pay seven thousand dollars."

"That's a starting offer." Ronnie smiled, he loved to bargain but not this time. "I respectfully decline. I am not opposed to deer hunting, but Wolverhampton will be rented on weekends, perhaps even for months, by foxhunters. If you're hunting deer, even if you aren't out there when people are riding, our game sits tight. Obviously, if people rent this place, we want to show them good sport."

"Right."

"Have you run into trappers? Had trouble?"

Ames weighed his words. "We aren't on the same land."

"I would think not, but surely they must poach your hunt territories. They're poaching everyone else's."

"They can be a problem. I guess you know there was, oh, some gunfire the other day. Stupid really."

"Never a good idea to point a gun at someone. Tempers flare. People lose their reason."

"They do. I'm glad to have met you. If you or the other people change your mind, you can find me at Parker Auto Repair. And should you all ever change your mind, I would give you a discount for any car repair." He rose, as did Ronnie.

Ronnie walked him out. "That's quite an offer."

As Ronnie watched Ames drive away in a big old Ram truck, he figured Ames and his hunt club had hunted Wolverhampton as it sat empty for years. Although so close to the Blue Ridge, it was on the east side of Chapel Hill North Road, having more good pasture land, a few flattish fields.

He returned to his barn chores and kept feeding that stove. Every now and then he needed to warm up just a little.

Bradford Beagles were showing good sport at Whippoorwill Hollow in the southern part of the county. Winston, hunting the hounds, Georgia whipping in to him as well as his wife, hit it just right. The scent lifted off the ground. The temperatures, in the mid-forties, felt warm when one was running flat out.

Hounds pushed out four rabbits. Lots of "Tally-hos." The field, small on a Wednesday, would be bragging to everyone who missed the hunt. It was that good.

Picked up Winston's spirits. Being accused of murder had devastated then infuriated him. Hunting his hounds gave him some stability and today he actually felt happy.

After the hunt, the small group ate sandwiches, drank tea and coffee. The beagles had some kind of small breakfast. The big breakfast was on Sundays for the people. Weekdays, whatever was back at the trailers was welcome. The beagles ate a bigger breakfast once back at the kennels.

The small group sat, as everyone had brought folding chairs. The election focused everyone's attention, until Solange drove by, slowly, her handsome gardener driving.

Beryl smiled at her husband, the message being, "Don't bite."

To his credit, he didn't.

Georgia dryly commented as the big truck rolled by, "Perhaps she can get an appointment in Trump's new cabinet."

Not everyone there had voted for Harris, but everyone there did have a sense of the absurd. They laughed.

Later, Winston, feet in a small tub of Epsom salts, remarked to his wife, "I'm thinking about counter-suing."

"Winston."

Miss Priss, hearing the tone of her mom's voice, came over to sit at Beryl's feet. Tidbit, the Yorkshire terrier, sat there, too.

"I am being falsely accused of murder. What if I falsely accuse her of something?" Winston's voice had sharpened.

"More time. More money. You did not kill Andrew and the truth will come out," she replied.

"Honey, I now think the truth has nothing to do with the law, with politics, with . . . well, you name it. I can sue her for anything."

"Like what?"

"Drugs. That would bring her low."

"Winston." Beryl's voice was firm. "Do not do that. No matter what she does, don't lower yourself."

"And if I'm acquitted, what happens then? She walks off?"

"She walks off with huge legal bills, and she will be maneuvered into paying yours. You have good lawyers. You know that will be part of the demand because once you are in the clear, you can retaliate, legally. No making up horrible deeds."

"What if she loses her case? And she continues to live next door?"

"Darlin', let's cross that bridge when we come to it."

CHAPTER 24

November 8, 2024 Friday

"We got more rain than you did," Sister commented, walking with Marianne and Susan at Farnley.

"Sprinkle." Susan turned to look back toward the house.

"Be dry by Sunday." Marianne looked back as well. "It doesn't seem that far to get back to the house and the barns, but after an hour of running and trotting when hunting, I need a breath."

"A half mile?" Sister suggested.

"A little more." Marianne put her hands in her pockets as a chill wind came up. "My weather channel did not predict a falling mercury."

"It's supposed to be thirty-seven degrees on Sunday," Susan helpfully told her. "I'm wearing two pair of socks."

"Me too. It's my hands that get cold. If you wear a warm pair with fur lining the glove is too thick to open gates, fix chains. If you wear a pair thin enough so you don't have to take off your gloves, then your hands get so darn cold you can barely move your fingers."

"I am a sucker for any ad in a catalog where the item is on

someone's hands and the person is hiking in snow. I can't help it. I order a pair and it's one or the other, flexible but you get cold or clumsy." Sister half smiled at her predicament.

"But aren't there heated gloves now?" Susan asked. "Swear I've seen them advertised. Bet they have wires in them."

"Well, if I see a pair, I'll buy them," Sister promised.

"Ready to head back?" Marianne asked—but really, she ordered.

The three, collars flipped up, walked on the farm road back toward the house and some buildings.

They stopped by the large hay bale piles, big round bales.

"A fewer number than when we last hunted here," Susan remarked. "There are still some out in the field. It's amazing how much hay ponies, horses, and cattle can go through just in one week."

"We didn't have a good hay year." Marianne counted the bales. "But these are serviceable. I count thirty-nine."

"You count fast," Sister remarked.

"I do. But there is enough here to get through the winter, unless it's a late spring."

"This line has been left intact." Susan pointed to the row of bales next to the big shed.

"The sheriff's department didn't want this disturbed so the farm manager has pulled hay from the other end."

"So far nothing has showed up," Susan noted.

"They're thinking someone hid between the bales?" Sister thought that could be possible.

There was enough room for a thin human if kneeling down no one could see him.

"Could be. They've slowly wedged though the margins with metal detectors. Nothing." Marianne then added, "I never realized how much there was to do at a crime scene. For instance, what if someone lost a cheap lighter? Or a chain? Little things. They may not belong to the killer and then again they might. Let's go in the shed."

The three walked through an aisle where hay had been moved to feed, then walked in front of the lined-up bales.

Now standing in front of the shed, Sister paused. "No spider wheel tedder."

"They took it down to a big shed at the department. One of those long Morton structure things. Sheriff Wolf said this might prevent the killer from coming back if he had forgotten anything like pulled a glove off and touched a spider wheel tedder. And as the season is over for turning hay, this doesn't inconvenience the farm manager." She paused. "They allowed him to park the really old tractor on the other side."

"Right," Susan agreed. "Have they determined how much Andrew weighed? I would guess he weighed about one sixty."

"Why?"

"He was, as you remember, dropped or placed on a lower wheel. So someone had to be able to lift him."

"He weighed one hundred seventy pounds," Marianne informed them. "I asked Sheriff Wolf. So we figured the person who shoved the body on the wheel had to be strong."

"There was someone probably waiting for him," Susan said. "And most of us are fit from hunting. With difficulty someone could have lifted him up."

"I think this murderer hunted with us." Marianne sneezed from the dust in the shed. "If someone had parked a car down on the state road and walked up, someone had to have seen the car. I can't think of who this could be, well none of us can but whoever killed him was already here. And, of course, Winston wasn't immediately at the breakfast, nor was Georgia. Susan and I made a list of who we could remember at the breakfast, the coming and goings, we got some of it but there were people who used the bathroom off the center hall then left by the front door. Nothing or no one jumps out. We don't have it all plus we were engaged by the breakfast."

"Let's try something." Sister walked to the side of the shed where a rope was hanging on the wall. She took it down, walking to the site where the spider wheel tedder had been parked.

"Catch the other end." She tossed the rope up over a heavy rafter.

The two women caught the end.

"Got it." Susan held it and Marianne stood back.

"Marianne, put your hands above hers," Sister ordered.

"What are you up to?" Susan asked.

"Okay, I am going to hold on to this end. See if you can lift me. Say up about four feet. I've got it tight."

The two women, fit, gave a yank, kept pulling and indeed they pulled up Sister four feet then gently let her down.

"I get it." Marianne frowned.

"Two people." Susan threw the rope back over while Sister rolled it up.

"Two people maybe, or one person who could easily heave a corpse or haul one. For two people it would be easy and fast. But a beagler could probably lift him up if need be. It's a horrific end."

"Never thought of two people." Susan looked up at the beam again.

"This doesn't prove there were only that there are possibilities we didn't consider. Marianne, did the farm manager mention when he put the old tractor in here? With the weather coming in best to get equipment out of it."

"After the sheriff moved the spider wheel tedder, there really was no need to keep the shed empty," Marianne answered.

They stood there a few minutes more then walked to their respective cars.

"Thanks for coming up to help with cleaning up some of the territory. We covered a lot of ground today." Marianne thanked Sister.

"I'm glad we ended back here right about the same time we hunted here. It's overcast but enough light. That's another thing we didn't consider, but perhaps Sheriff Wolf did. Shadows. We hunted on a sunny day. A person can hide in shadows depending on where they are. Even behind a tree."

"True." Susan noticed a short shadow at the edge of the shed, a bit of sun beginning to pass that way west.

Driving home, Sister couldn't prove it, but she felt the killer was already in the shed, which meant Andrew was in the shed, too. There had been no signs of a body being dragged. Granted he could have been made to walk to the shed at gunpoint but no one noticed him going anywhere. The more she thought about it the more she thought this wasn't an act of fury, a lapse in judgment. This murder was planned. The murder weapon was with the killer and he walked away with it. The medical examiner declared he was stabbed. Would Andrew have seen a knife? Her mind was spinning. It's possible that this wasn't fury. Maybe Andrew had something on his killer. Something that could put that person away or ruin their life, cast them down. And maybe the killer was at the breakfast with the murder weapon in his inside pocket. This was an unnerving thought.

The longer she drove, the more convinced she was that she had found a few important points. What could Andrew have had over someone?

CHAPTER 25

November 9, 2024 Saturday

A fine snow fell steadily. The weather channels had not predicted snow. It started about a half hour after the first cast at a new fixture, Nickle and Dime. Bracing against the wind that came with it, seven to eight miles an hour, the field members hunted this fixture for the first time.

No houses yet stood on the newly tended pastures. The three-hundred-acre land abutted Prior's Woods down Chapel Cross Road. New paths snaked through the woods, the pastures now frozen and bare would eventually be lush. That might take three years, but it would happen, as the owners, the Powers, intended to create a modest, practical farm.

Tiny flakes of snow stuck in Sister's lashes as she trotted toward the edge of the land, so named because the Powers declared they wearied of being nickel and dimed where they lived outside of Pittsburgh.

Not having lived in Pittsburgh Sister thought any place near a big city was bound to become more and more expensive and more and more difficult. Rules, regulations, homeowners associations would make any change drag on and on.

It wasn't that there weren't county ordinances in Virginia and some counties proved more burdensome than others, but compared to states above the Mason-Dixon Line, even Mid-Atlantic states, the Virginia counties seemed to be less restrictive.

Sister was grateful that everything at Roughneck Farm, except for modern electricity and pumps, had been dug or built starting in the early 1800s. Being historic, many things withstood time's fury. And also what withstood time's fury was regular rereading of whatever new county ordinance passed through the commission. Not that she wanted to build or change anything, but should the need arise she wanted a hint at how difficult it would become, how many engineers would one hire and what law firm to use.

The Powers would be encountering all that.

The club built jumps into Prior's Woods. As they headed the opposite direction encountering a distant fence for Beveridge Hundred, Jefferson Hunt refurbished many of those jumps. A simple tiger trap, painted black, was right ahead. The freshly painted black fence appeared more formidable than it was. But Aztec took it without a blink.

Once over, they landed in a thick wood. The hounds had picked up a line, following it diligently. It wasn't a roaring go, but they were speaking, noses down. Good.

Betty moved along fifty yards to the right, that trail was narrower but possible, while Tootie followed out on the road just in case the fox crossed. She felt they were on a fox at a decent pace.

Beveridge Hundred, not as vast as Tattenhall Station, at two thousand acres, or Old Paradise, at five thousand acres, added to the distinctiveness of the fixtures in Chapel Cross.

Hounds veered to the left, now faster, blasting through thick woods. Sister spurred Aztec along as she knew a cleared path that intersected the one she was on was up ahead. They would make better time taking that than following immediately behind the hounds in thick woods.

"Tally-ho," Tootie called out as the fox, then the pack five minutes later, crossed the road. She followed, realizing the fox was far enough ahead to give the hounds the slip.

The other side of the road had not been groomed. She galloped toward the north, found a deer path, plunged into the heavy woods.

Hounds stopped speaking. He'd dumped them. Tootie rode up to a large rock outcropping that she knew from hunting here over the years, starting with her student days at Curtis Hall. She stopped because the hounds had stopped. Some on the rocks, taller than she was even on horseback.

Weevil caught up. He reined in Hojo.

"Get 'em up. Get 'em up."

Arnie nosed around the bottom of the rocks. *"He had to be here."*

Trinity, older a bit, looked up. *"Arnie, he could jump up on the lower rocks. No scent down there. He may have a den in there that he can get to, being smaller. We can't."*

"Not fair." Arnie puffed, which made the slightly older hound smile.

Weevil waited. The field stood out on a road, but at the edge. Not much traffic on this part of the road. Sister wasn't worried. They waited. Weevil rode out hounds walking obediently.

He cast toward the crossroads. Hounds moved back into the woods, found a trail, but no success. The snow thickened.

Sister rode up to Weevil. "Lift. This is coming down faster. Will make driving difficult if we wait too long."

They got back to Beveridge Hundred in twenty minutes.

As Yvonne had a breakfast, people stayed long enough to eat, thank their hostess.

Weevil, Tootie had headed back. Betty waited for Sister. They drove back home a half hour later.

"It's coming down now." Betty was glad to be in the warm cab of the truck.

"Tough day. I thought we'd do a little better."

"You never know." Betty shifted in the seat. "At least we weren't surrounded by deer hunters."

"Right. Our fixtures out here don't allow it, but places like Prior's Woods, or across the road where we waited, you never know."

"Found this." Betty reached into her pocket, plucking out a plastic lighter. "The little glitter at the top caught my eye. Waiting around, I picked it up. So someone is back there." She dropped it into Sister's outstretched right hand.

"Someone's been back there. Not a surprise really. No one polices those woods."

"Well, no one was there today. Or if they were they were well hidden."

CHAPTER 26

November 10, 2024 Sunday

"Dammit!" Gray yelled.

Sister, upstairs at a small desk in the enclave, looked up from her papers and smiled.

Raleigh and Rooster, at her feet, snuggled on a plush bed she kept there. Those expensive beds were all over the house. The fox cubs, too little for such a bed, had a thick, small blanket in their tiny kennel, which Gray had built for them. Sister didn't like keeping them in a big carrying box. They were growing, still using the bottle, but she felt in a day or two some wet food might be offered.

Right now she sat there, the desk lamp providing warm light. Her husband loved his Sunday football games. After dinner at the Home Place, everyone had watched the noon game. Now, home, he was roaring about the afternoon game. Clearly his team was making mistakes. She flipped open her Calendar again, a large *New Yorker* one.

Raleigh lifted his head. *"This bed is perfect."*

"The hall is cold. That's why that insufferable cat stays down in the li-

brary. She has the couch all to herself while he's carrying on about football. I've watched football. Doesn't seem so exciting to me. The humans are so slow."

"Since it's human versus human, that doesn't matter." Raleigh laid his head on the high side of the bed.

"Never thought of that." Rooster put his head on his paws.

Sister had a wool throw over her legs, a cashmere sweater on. Wasn't as toasty as being downstairs with the fire roaring in the library but the throw and sweater made it warm. She would have worked in the kitchen with that large fireplace, but she didn't want the light to keep the fox cubs awake. Eventually they would have nestled together, but if she made phone calls that would be disturbing. She was growing to love the three gorgeous creatures, who would squeak when she opened the screened door to their housing. They'd wobble to her, she'd pick them up, put them in her lap while Golly watched. The dogs evidenced little interest in the orphans. Golly showed more curiosity.

Her cellphone on the desk, she peered at the large square on the calendar, she'd turned to the month-at-a-look page. She also had in front of her her Calendar from the Audubon Society, which featured big squares, whereas the *New Yorker* calendar started with the entire month then each page was a day in that month.

She picked up the scribbled fixture cards. Not yet set.

"Scheduling."

"I thought she already did that," Raleigh remarked.

"She did, but remember she had some days where she couldn't pin down a fixture. Couldn't get the landowners. It's a lot of work." Rooster usually only concerned himself with his feeding schedule.

"People worry about time." The sleek Doberman thought it silly.

Sister picked up her cell, dialed Betty. "Hey."

"You aren't watching the game?"

"No. I'm fiddling with the to-be-announced days. Good old TBA. If you're watching, I'll call tomorrow."

"Don't care about either of the teams. I still like the 49ers."

"You are loyal," Sister joked. "Thanksgiving is at Mill Ruins. November 30th will be at Tattenhall Station. December 1st will be at Old Paradise. Thanksgiving is always a big day. So often the weather conditions are perfect. Lots of people out."

"Close Shave is for November 17th. We'll be across from Wolverhampton and if we wind up there maybe we'll get better ideas for paddocks and then jumps. There's still a lot to do."

"You have a point. Okay. I'll call owners and double-check. They've cleaned up those old outbuildings. New roofs. Some have insulation even under the roof. It does help stabilize temperatures."

"Does. It will probably be cold." Betty considered her clothing, as it seemed she needed shirts and vests a bit warmer for each hunt.

"It will. I pray it doesn't rain. Snow is easier than rain," the Master said.

"I'll ask their whippers-in to ride with me and Tootie."

"Wonderful."

Sister smiled. "Okay. Let me call the foxhunting masters as well as the beagle masters. Just to make sure they don't need something we haven't considered."

Betty then added, "Too bad our flasks don't keep liquid warm."

Sister agreed, then clicked off and called Beryl.

"Sister, did you get snow yesterday?" Beryl asked.

"Thin little flakes but it came down. Maybe an inch out there now. Should melt off tomorrow. Supposed to get into the forties."

"We've got a warm small barn at Tattenhall Station. It's easy for you all and NTB to put your hounds in there yet keep them apart. The stalls will be filled with deep straw plus an old horse blanket in each one."

"Sounds fabulous."

"Before you call Marianne let me tell you the latest. Solange is now remodeling the kennels to be a greenhouse. So she's given up on trying to get her half of the hounds."

"She sounds oh, what expression, all over the map."

"*Unbalanced* is how I'd put it. Georgia and I were parked on our side of the road to watch and Solange came out to cuss us. Ann and Scott hurried after her. If she didn't have them, I think she would wind up in some kind of halfway house for loonies. I mean, standing there screaming at us. The Howletts take it all in stride."

"Maybe she needs better drugs," Sister wryly commented.

"There's a thought. Georgia laughed at her, which made it worse. Can't blame her. Ann put her arm around Solange's waist to walk her back into the kennels/greenhouse. She's not seeming to get better. That greenhouse won't be a cheap transformation. Lots of glass, humidifiers, lights. What's she going to grow in there?"

"Poinsettias," Sister quickly answered. "She'll have a Christmas business, or how about Easter lilies?"

"You're going for the holidays," Beryl teased her.

"I am. They are rushing upon us. Not Easter, but we've got Thanksgiving then Christmas then New Year's. I'm never sure how I'll get through it."

"You do a beautiful job. As I recall, your Christmas tree is so nineteenth century. Beautiful."

"Thank you. The best is my cat, Golly, is usually up in it. So instead of electric lights, a pair of bright green eyes are looking at you." Sister laughed. "Okay, let me call Marianne."

"I called her about Solange," Beryl confessed. "It was too good not to pass on."

Sister then called Marianne. The barn worked for her.

"Good. Then Alida can send out an email. She's turning into a wonderful hunt secretary."

"That's a job I wouldn't wish on anyone." Marianne thought the detail way too much.

"Being a master isn't so easy, but we get to focus on hounds and landowners. Hunt secretaries have to check and double-check and then send out stuff. People don't realize how much there is to do with hunting. It's a small business really except you don't make money, you spend it."

"If we break even, I think it's a great year." Marianne spoke the truth.

"A few hunts have funds in the stock market. But then it becomes 'Don't touch the principal,'" Sister acknowledged. "Ray left what was a decent sum for our hounds at the time and, Marianne, we now need fundraisers to pay all the bills. Every time I turn around, a price has shot up. Whether it's food, meds, nothing goes down."

"I know," Marianne agreed. "Russ and Peter and I talk about this. We're okay, but something like a new virus can shoot those vet bills skyward. Russ and I check and double-check. Using that Musher's foot pad stuff has been a big help. Sore feet slows a pack."

Sister said, "To switch, you heard about the greenhouse at Bradford?"

"I did. You know, I used to wonder why Andrew allowed Solange to keep her friends with her. I thought Andrew would be jealous of Scott. They are especially good-looking. They were so close. He gave them good jobs, and truthfully, they are good gardeners. Well, now I know. They keep Solange level, or did until Andrew's murder. I had no idea she was so, uh, so dramatic."

"That's a thought."

"Andrew was a jealous person in his way but he tolerated the Howletts. They no doubt did him a favor. It's odd what you figure out or think about. We can usually figure out who is drinking too much. Shows over time. Drugs, well, depends on the drugs. Harder." Sister tapped her fingers on the desk, which made Raleigh bark. "It's me."

"*Sorry,*" he replied.

"How long before this goes to trial?" Sister asked.

Marianne said, "I don't know. If it can be delayed I don't know if that might work in Winston's favor. I expect both lawyers are working overtime. There's not much in the way of hard fact regarding Winston and Georgia. They weren't at the breakfast until after the rest of us were there. That's all that can be proven so far. No weapons found. No footprints." Marianne paused. "Whoever killed Andrew was smart enough to rake the shed. No footprints. Probably medical gloves. Your experiment with the rope makes this even more confusing. It makes sense that maybe there were two killers, or a killer and an accomplice. What I do know is this isn't helping the community. Most people think Winston is not a killer, but there are those who do. It tears apart a community. I just want it over."

"Yes," Sister simply replied. "And even when it's over, no good can come from this."

"Not that I can see."

"Well, there is one thing. You might get new members."

"What?" Marianne was surprised.

"People are drawn to murder. It's like people slowing to see the remains of a car wreck."

"Ugh."

"With that happy thought, I leave you."

"Sister, I'll get you for that," Marianne promised.

"I know you will. You'll probably run me to ground when we're hunting."

After that call Sister went downstairs, warmer already. Rooster and Raleigh followed. Gray was sitting on the couch, the TV remote in his hand. Golly was asleep in his lap.

"*Stay off the couch,*" the cat lifted her head and ordered the dogs.

"*There's room for us,*" Rooster grumbled.

"*I was here first. I'm calming Gray. His team is losing. He needs me close. You'll get in the way.*"

"Bother." Raleigh sat at Gray's feet.

Sister briefly gave Gray the plan for December 1st. Noticing his empty drink, she picked up the glass.

"Can I get you anything?"

"A new quarterback. Three interceptions in the first half. Three. They paid sixteen million for this guy for two years. Don't get me going about the two years but he's a disaster. I wouldn't give you fifty cents!"

"That is damnation." She nodded.

"Oh, yes, I would like a refill. This way I don't have to disturb Golly."

"He needs me," Golly informed Sister.

She refreshed his drink, kissed him on the cheek, and climbed the stairs back to her little desk. She had a bigger one down in the library but this little one was useful, out of the way, and if something occurred to her upstairs, she could sit down and scribble it out.

She called Yvonne.

"I was just going to call you. That dressing you made for the chicken today was wonderful. Having Sunday dinner with the boys, you, and Aunt Daniella is the best. It's fun when Betty and Bobby come along, too. Anyway, here is why I was going to call you."

"Sounds exciting."

The two dogs came upstairs and snuggled back in their bed.

"Remember me saying today that I wanted to talk to Ben Sidell about parts of Chapel Cross Road South being unprotected?" Yvonne mentioned.

"I do. He hunted with us yesterday, so he certainly knew what you were talking about. That far end of the road is left alone except for Bishop's Gate, thanks to you. But across from you it's rough. I wish those people would sell. Why, what's up?"

"Our good sheriff came today and went across the road. There's no way to drive in there so he left the county SUV here and he and Jude walked in." Jude was his young officer. "They went back to the rock formation. He did say there was fox scent. Anyway, there are some places where there's room to stash things. Not dens. Too easy to get into since he said these were at the edges of the rocks. They found a stash of rifles and guns."

"What?"

"Rifles and guns. Serial numbers filed off. I asked what did that mean and he said it could mean a couple of things. One is, these are stolen and will be sold."

"Why wouldn't the guns be kept in a building? Even an old garage?" Sister murmured.

"I asked that, too. He said the problem there is if anyone had a camera, they might become suspicious. Out here, that's not going to happen. There's a big profit in guns that can't be traced."

"Yes, I suppose there is."

"He also said this could be planning for some kind of attack. After all, there was gunfire out here between deer hunters and such."

"A war between hunters or between hunters and trappers. That would be supremely stupid." Sister pulled the wool over her legs, as she was getting colder.

"Seems so to me, too. A little like a war in a big city between gangs." Yvonne had lived through this stuff in Chicago. She lived in a wealthy section but there were shootings every day in parts of the city. One had to be careful what colors you wore going into those sections. Mostly no one wanted to go in there.

"I don't think anyone is coming for me or my neighbors, but it is unnerving."

"It is. What if there is not a gang but, say, people here who need those guns? People selling other kinds of contraband? I don't know if our county is more criminal or safer but I know times are crazy. If you're going to be shooting at people, best the guns can't be traced."

"Makes me crazy." Yvonne rubbed the ear of her adorable Norfolk terrier, Ribbon.

"Reading history as I do, there has never been a time that didn't have killings, diseases, fights over borders. But now we hear about stuff twenty-four hours a day. Then you had to wait for the town crier." Sister mentioned how news was transmitted.

"In Rome, there wasn't a town crier but an announcer at the Forum. People got the news, it just took longer," Yvonne responded.

"Before I forget why I called, would you consider helping Kasmir and Alida with the breakfast? We prevail upon them far too much."

"Of course," Yvonne readily agreed. "I'll woo Sam into it, too."

"Two minutes." Sister laughed.

"I haven't noticed you struggling with his brother," Yvonne teased her back.

"They are good men." Sister then told her about Solange's greenhouse project.

Building a greenhouse wasn't strange, but Solange certainly had been acting strange. First Solange wanted half the hounds back, realizing she'd never get all of them. Then she decided to turn the kennel into a greenhouse, as once Winston said he'd got to the National Beagle Association Solange thought she didn't need bad publicity. There was still quite a bit of sympathy for her loss.

"Maybe she really loved Andrew," Yvonne posited. "I only ever saw them together beagling, and only once at that. But maybe it was a love match."

"It only crossed my mind because of my long friendship with Olivia. She never spoke of it, good or bad, but if she thought Solange wasn't good to her son she might have said something. She kept him happy."

A long pause followed this. "I doubt that was difficult."

"Right," Sister replied and they both laughed.

CHAPTER 27

November 11, 2024 Monday

A light flurry swirled around. Sister, standing outside the Wolverhampton barn, noticed a brilliant cardinal walking across the white ground, lifting off only to land on a fancy bird feeder. Another bird feeder stood outside the back door of the house.

Ronnie, singing inside the barn, had no idea his theatrical improvisations were being heard. He made Sister laugh. Then the singing stopped.

"Hello, boys," Ronnie greeted Raleigh and Rooster, who barreled into the barn shortly followed by Sister.

"You've gotten so much done." She didn't inform him she'd heard his Broadway tune.

"Always takes longer than you think." He patted Rooster on the head. "Come into the tack room. Tell me what you think. Also it's warmer."

"It is getting colder, and the snow never showed up on my weather apps."

"Oh, we're by the mountains. We have our own weather system."

"True." She stepped over the threshold into the inviting tack room, very plaid.

"The baseboard heat is old but I did have the electric company come check everything. House, too. It's the potbellied stove that does the job."

"I can feel it." She removed her gloves.

"The split wood pile is over here. Well, you can see it. I've got it in a firewood holder. Tractor Supply." He named the store where he bought it. "Over here in a more contained box is the fatback. Don't want anything near the fire. But look at where I put the bridle holders. Did I put them too high?"

She walked over. "Not for me, but for someone short, like Beryl Bradford, yes. So put up a few lower ones in between the high ones. There's room."

"All right. Speaking of Beryl, they are all coming for the fox-hunt on the thirtieth as well as the beagle hunt. Beryl called, Marianne called, folks from Old Dominion called, as well as a few from Blue Ridge Hunt. This place will be packed but they all know one another. Beryl organized it. Bull Run has the rooms in the back on the first floor. Everyone else is on the second floor."

Sister smiled. "Anyone in the servants' quarters?"

"Four grooms. If there's a need I can put a cot in here but the third floor of the house will do for now. I've tested the baseboard heat up there. With the fireplaces, it will be warm. No double window panels. Don't touch the glass." He smiled.

"Good." Sister took steps to the saddle racks. "Weren't these left here? I remember a pile in the corner."

"Old, but perfectly serviceable. I lined them up and you'll notice I have a sturdy stepping stool. Even if you're tall a saddle is a bit unwieldy. Stand on this and slip it on a rack."

"You painted the racks."

"I did. Hunter green. Well, Charleston green but who will notice?"

"I did." She grinned at him. "Okay, show me the stalls and then let's come back here, sit in the warmth, and plan the hunting and beagling. Going to be a big weekend."

"It is a plus we have Thanksgiving hunt on Thursday. The great thing about that is, no breakfast. Everyone rushes home, but we'll have two breakfasts that weekend. One after the foxhunt and one after beagling. So Tattenhall Station, and then where?"

"Old Paradise; Crawford and Marty volunteered. Bless them."

They walked to the stall right outside the tack room.

Ronnie pointed to the light overhead. "I put in heat bulbs. If it's nasty cold this will help. The lights in the center aisle are regular. I'm trying to balance cost with warmth. The temperature has been bouncing back and forth."

"This looks nice. You've already got straw in the stalls."

"One less worry. The little outbuilding behind the stable, full of straw on the left side, hay on the right. People are to bring their own feed, but it's best we supply the hay. You know they'll all give something to the hounds for all this."

"Right. But you have thought of everything."

"Thank you." He was happy she'd noticed everything. "Over here in this trunk are extra blankets. That one, too. Called around to some of our members. Most everyone had an old blanket or two. If anyone forgets a blanket, they'll be okay. The other thing is, I bought sponges, leather cleaner, small buckets. Also boot pulls and a big boot pull that I've chained to the wall here in the corner. They're almost four hundred dollars now. Old towels." He pointed to another tack trunk.

"You've thought of everything. Stacking split wood is smart. Who cut it?"

"I did. Could use the exercise. Oh, lead shanks. Over here. We know someone will have that on their horse's halter, walk off with it, and not figure it out until they get home and lead their horses off the trailer. I'll factor in that cost."

"Ronnie, you're amazing."

He beamed at her praise. "My goal is that Wolverhampton will begin to pay for itself after one year. This is if we don't sell it."

"I hope you're right. You, Gray, and Alida can look into the future with dollar signs. I can't. Before I married Ray I rented an apartment in Staunton, paid bills, put some money in a savings account. I thought I was doing pretty good."

"You were."

"Small beer, but I had no idea about investments. Ray certainly did. He had a feel for the market. I was still fairly young when he died. Thirty-one. Admired him. Thanks to him, I focused on arithmetic. Knew better than to be a stockbroker. Don't have it. But I've done okay. Come on, let's go back to the tack room and go over the schedule."

They sat opposite each other in front of the stove, which Ronnie had fed.

Sister removed her work coat; one feels freer without a heavy coat. Ronnie shed his, too. They pored over the hunting schedule, worked out where to put up the beagles so they would be both safe and warm. Wolverhampton would have horses in the stable. Ronnie mentioned that Kasmir's small, unused stable, which did have heat, could be used if needed. The Bradford and Nantucket-Treweryn beaglers would bring everything they needed. Having a bit of heat in that small stable would be a godsend, plus the beagles could be separated by hunt.

"I'll check with Kasmir," Sister volunteered. "We can both go over the stable. They'll bring a lot of stuff, but we should have water buckets, and hoses for inside, and let's take a few of the blankets you have here. Between deep straw the blankets could help if there are one or two older hounds or someone a little light."

"That's the thing about hunting hounds. If they lose weight during the season it's hell to get it back on." Ronnie knew hounds.

"Weevil and Tootie do a great job."

"They do. Has she heard from vet school yet?"

Sister replied, "I don't think she'll know until after the new year. I figure she'll get into every school to which she's applied. It will throw us into a tailspin. What if Weevil decides to go with her? They'll be far apart and that will be for, I don't know, how many years is vet school?"

"Four years. Lots of math." Ronnie stretched his feet toward the stove.

"She'll be an equine vet. And she'll have to work for someone else, like being an intern, before she goes out on her own. Rigorous, but she's been clear about her dream."

Ronnie thought a moment. "Her mother will pay for everything."

"I'm sure she will. Tootie hasn't wanted to take money from her mother, but this time I think she will. I don't see how anyone can work while studying at vet or med school. Too intense. At some point you do have to sleep." Sister added, "Even when I was young, I needed sleep. Need more now. By the way, Betty called you about the guns hidden at the rock outcropping?"

"She did, and I was tempted to go over there today, walk back to it. I bet where the stuff was hidden would be easy to find for us anyway. We know that territory. Then I remembered that Betty said the department put up cameras in the trees. I don't need to show up on the sheriff's department cameras."

"You'd look fetching." She touched his toe with hers.

"Well." He had known her all his life and loved her. "Here's what I think. Whoever is involved in this will go back there and shoot out the cameras. They have to be smart enough to know they are there."

"True, Ronnie, but do they yet know the rifles and guns are gone?"

"Good question. I sure don't want to get involved in it. There has to be profit in this or why take the chance? Profit and no taxes."

"Oh, that's the Devil's song." Sister smiled.

They talked about horses, more scheduling, who was doing what and then finally Sister got up to go.

"Ronnie, if you need more help, you know I can push people."

"I'm fine. Sam and I have worked together on some of this, and Kasmir, Yvonne, Freddie, and Alida have transformed the house. Once the basic work was done those four created a home. Kathleen and Aunt Daniella came up with furniture. It's been a group effort. Brings us all closer together. All right, I'm off, too." Sister kissed him on the cheek, he helped her on with her jacket, the dogs followed her out, and off they went.

She reached Chapel Cross Road, Crawford's estate, to the right, the church to the left on the corner. She turned left to head home, remembering the fun they had years back when the Gulf station, the little restaurant, was open. People would stop in, including the family making moonshine to the west of the crossroads up the mountain. No one discussed it, but if you did want some of their outstanding product, you talked about the weather and pro football, rooting for the Redskins meant a fifth of those special spirits would be left at the restaurant the next day. It was all very civilized. She missed it.

CHAPTER 28

November 12, 2024 Tuesday

Devil's Chair, a new fixture behind After All toward the east, was aptly named. Jefferson Hunt built jumps there over the summer and during cubbing. They were lucky to get the place to hunt and owed that favor to the Bancrofts, who helped their new neighbors, a lovely couple from Nebraska, where he had been a professor of geology. Yes, Sister and Walter produced the obligatory paperwork holding the landowner harmless. Everything these days was legal, liability, insurance.

As Sister slid down a steep incline into what gave the place its name she appreciated why any newcomer or non-hunting person would harbor fears. The land, three miles from After All's border, enjoyed rich rolling acres. However, those rolling acres from each direction sloped down into what was the seat of a large chair. The surface, depending on your direction, proved uniform, but bits of earth gave way.

Matador, tried and true, literally squatted down, his forelegs out in front of him and straight, and down they slid.

"Tally-ho," came the cry from Betty. First Flight saw a saucy red blazing away.

"That was worth a twenty-minute run," Sister said to herself, feeling any viewing made the day that much better. She knew the fixture abounded in foxes. First off, they traveled through to get the garbage at After All. And then the owners, the Astridies, put out deer food. No deer hunting. Jefferson Hunt put out dog kibble in the four corners of the farm and one big barrel with holes and a place to hide, in the center of the farm. Foxes loved that dog kibble. Good food. Little work. What a deal.

Small flurries continued. Much like yesterday's weather, the snow was swirly and light. The mercury hung at thirty-two degrees. Cold, yet in sunny spots the earth was slick and soft.

As Sister and Matador slid down the steep incline she heard no shouts behind her. People hung on.

The field today, larger than she'd anticipated, numbered sixteen, actually a perfect number for a dicey day at a new fixture. Everyone could ride, and Rev. Sally Taliaferro with Father Mancusco offered prayers to those a bit loose in the tack.

Once at the bottom, Sister beheld the pack beautifully together, racing across the wide bottom. Weevil, behind, blew "Gone Away."

That was a sound to lift hearts hound, horse, or human. And gone away they were.

The fox knew the territory better than the staff or field. They'd cleared trails, built jumps, which helped. Still, not the same as memorizing land, which imprints itself on the brain as one hunts it.

Weevil, well mounted on Kilowatt, kept up, but as he approached the other side of the large bowl, a climb loomed. The ground was slick, it was the sunny side of the bowl. Hounds made it, no problem. Kilowatt stretched, made it with a little backsliding. Betty, to her great relief, was charging up the west side of the chair, so to speak, the sun had not hit that yet. The footing proved tight. Same for Tootie on the other side.

Sister leaned far forward, grabbed the jump strap she swore she would never use, and made it. Betty had convinced her to use a jump strap. After far too much bitching and moaning, Sister did. She reminded herself to give Betty a present for banging on her about making riding easier.

Once on top, the land evened out. Hounds gained ground, but the fox simply turned hard right toward Betty, literally ran right by her then down into the chair's seat again.

Well, at least this time riders were ready. Betty kept going straight. Weevil galloped down the side. Sister chose to slowly go down. Going down truly is harder than going up. Her leg, strong, would hold her, but if she flew down people behind her would part company with their mounts. No need to show off while others endured involuntary dismounts. Coming off going down did mean usually one was thrown farther from one's horse, which is safer— not that coming off is safe.

Down in the bowl again, Sister saw the fox go right back up, reverse direction.

Devil's Chair had a devil fox. Much more of this and the horses would be exhausted. Having hunted with Red Rock in Reno, Nevada, Sister appreciated a hard high climb, not that this was as arduous as Red Rock, but it was arduous enough. Then again, the footing couldn't have been more different.

Up again, Sister, breathing hard, watched her huntsman, early thirties, in peak condition, fade away with speed. She trotted once at the top. She'd find him sooner or later, thanks to horn calls. Leading the field brings many decisions; she'd move out a bit.

She could no longer see Weevil, nor Betty or Tootie. Where in the hell did they go so fast?

Then she heard the three long calls on the horn.

She slowed considerably. Three more long calls. He was calling hounds back, which meant they'd lost the scent or the fox had pulled a maneuver that no one could follow, such as going into forbidden land. However, at this juncture there was no forbidden land.

Finally reaching Weevil, hounds around him, she waited at twenty yards. He was praising the hounds. All eyes looked up at their huntsman. They were foxhounds that hunt out of love, not ones that hunt out of fear. She hated to think of those few hunts where, by her standards, hounds were mistreated or trained too harshly. Fortunately, there were very few, and like any other Master she knew she could never tell the Master of such a hunt. A few knew. Others did not, as their huntsmen were successful liars.

How many professions indulge liars? They have to be good at it to succeed.

Finally looking up from his charges, Weevil's eyebrows shot up. Sister then walked toward him as Betty and Tootie stayed in place.

"I have no idea how we lost that line," he confessed. "Red hot."

"Someone or something fouled it," Sister acknowledged. "And we don't know if there are deer hunters back here illegally. If they killed and dragged the deer off, the blood would ruin the line. That fox is smart enough to simply walk on the blood then skedaddle."

Weevil cocked his head. "I never cease to be amazed by our quarry."

"Huntsman, I am a good forty years older than you and I never fail to be amazed by our quarry. People who don't live close to wildlife think we make this stuff up."

He grinned. "I'm not imaginative enough to make it up."

"Snow is falling a little heavier. The ground in some places is, well, fools you. We've had a blasting run on a new fixture. Let's walk back. I think everyone will be grateful if nothing else that they are still upright."

He tapped his cap with his crop. "Yes, Madam." Then he looked down at a pack he loved. "Come along, children."

Weevil knew huntsmen usually didn't call their packs children, but he couldn't help it.

Walking back, Sister dropped her feet out of her stirrups for an instant to wiggle her toes. Toes grew cold first. The little wiggle created a little pain, but that was okay. She looked behind her, motioning for Freddie to ride up with her.

"How did everyone do?" Sister asked. "You started in the rear and moved up."

"Well, Pete Jensen and Lorraine stayed in the rear. Sally and Father stayed with them, so I felt I could move up. Everyone did amazingly well, considering the footing. The real problem is, you can't tell by looking. The ground is frozen underneath. That usually scares me even more than a green rider on a green horse."

They both laughed, then Sister quietly said, "Thank you for keeping your eye on our newer people. They are coming along. I would hate for anything to dampen their enthusiasm."

"I enjoy new people. The Saturday fields are more difficult."

"The most people I remember in my years of hunting was two hundred and forty. A huge hunt at Mill Ruins. Big Ray was alive. I couldn't tell you why there were so many people. It was a joint meet with Blue Ridge, they traveled a long way. Great hunt. I think lots of other people came, camped, as this was when joint meets still meant you put your packs together."

"Still happens, but not much," Freddie acknowledged. "It was the leishmaniasis scare that did that wonderful tradition in. Oh dear, bad grammar."

Sister laughed. "I try to obey good grammar, but sometimes

everyday usage wins out. Here we are. I readily admit, I am glad."
Sister dismounted and when her feet hit the ground she winced.

Everyone tended to their horses, some tying them to the side
of the trailers. Others put them inside because of the snow. Everyone threw a blanket over.

Hounds eagerly rushed into the party wagon, which was essentially a two-horse trailer, the inside altered for hounds, with half a
second story.

"Madam, I want to get them back."

"Of course, Weevil."

She found her husband and his brother, along with Yvonne.

"Everyone ready?"

"Hot coffee." Yvonne was colder than she realized.

Kasmir, Alida, Reverend Taliaferro, Father Mancusco, Lorraine, all the regulars were there, along with Kathleen Sixt Dunbar
and Aunt Daniella.

The inside at the Federalist home, warm, pleased everyone.
The Aristides decorated keeping to the period in mind, but Helene
could mix periods and make it work. The table filled with dishes appropriate for a hunting breakfast including scrambled eggs, deviled
eggs, small cooked hams, surprised people. The host and hostess
had outdone themselves. Their Shenandoah coffee was especially
outstanding. People needed a hot drink.

Alida, plate in hand, sat at one of the small card tables set up
so people did not have to eat with a plate on their lap. Helene came
to greet Sister, as she had met the Barbhaiyas at the Bancrofts'.

"Helene, where did you get these recipes?"

"From the hunt books. I drove up to Horse Country and
bought every food book that was there. Some of the recipes are
fabulous. I can't take credit."

"Of course you can. Who can cook like this?"

"My husband helped," the attractive middle-aged woman replied.

"A man who can cook. That's a keeper."

Everyone gabbed, enjoyed the warmth, the food, and the company. Oftentimes mid-week hunts draw people closer together, maybe because they have a smaller number.

Betty regaled Father Mancuso with her reading habits.

"You don't fall asleep?"

"Sometimes, but I have this little booklight that hooks over the top of the book. That way I can read without disturbing Bobby. I love to read in bed."

The host sat with Sister, Gray, and Kathleen. Aunt Daniella was holding court along with the Bancrofts, at an adjoining table.

"Thank you again for allowing us to hunt your farm." Sister thought the scrambled eggs perfect.

"It's something to see. The coats, the fancy horses. And I never realized how hounds sound. Gets one's blood right up," Timon enthused.

"I've never had the chance to tell you that I got my Ph.D. in geology and taught at Mary Baldwin as a young woman."

He brightened. "Not a lot of us. I don't understand why. Geology is fascinating."

"Feel the same way. I had Latin in high school, kept it up in college. Devoured Pliny the Elder. Can't read Greek but I did read Xenophon, in translation. Aristotle of course. A lot of geology, although that word was not in use."

"As my family is Greek, Mom and Dad made me take Ancient Greek at USC. I wasn't meant for California so I transferred to Virginia Tech, kept up the Greek and jumped into geology."

"So that's how you found out about Virginia?"

"The land is so beautiful. When I retired, I swore I'd come back here, and fortunately Helene agreed."

"Were you always fascinated by geology?"

"I was. I grew up by the Santo de Christo Mountains. I learned a lot by living there but didn't know I was learning. You know, we don't often know what we are standing on."

She smiled. "I know. What I remember apart from learning the ages of rocks and fossils, what was covered by a sea, what was not, was the continents breaking apart. Fascinating stuff. And I remember the darndest things, like Aristotle writing, 'Nothing is what rocks dream about.'" She laughed.

"You know his mother was rich. Very rich. I suspect Aristotle was a momma's boy." He rested his chin on his hand.

"Lucky fellow. She sent him to Athens, where he wanted to continue his education."

"You really did study." His gray eyebrows raised up.

"I did. Keep most of it to myself. So it's refreshing to talk to you." She then added, "And my husband, who dutifully listens."

"It's not dutiful." Gray intruded into the chat.

"He's good to me." She looked at her husband.

"Well, didn't mean to dominate the conversation. Mrs. Dunbar—" Timon looked at Kathleen.

"Please call me Kathleen. Your house is the most delightful mix of art, furniture, colors. You probably pass my store, the 1780 House."

"I do. My wife says it's got everything she wants."

Kathleen smiled. "What a hopeful thing to say."

They all laughed.

Gray and Sam left together. Gray would be home late. Sister and Betty stayed an appropriate amount of time, then left to drive the horses back.

On the way, slowly, the snow continued, again fine flakes but fine flakes do accumulate, Sister relayed how wonderful it felt to be talking to a geology professor.

"You rarely talk about it." Betty unzipped her coat, as the truck heater was doing a good job. "You know I'll always listen."

"I know that, but geology is a specialized interest. If kids want to know about it they always want to know where are the dinosaur bones and the fossils?"

"The fossils are in Congress."

They both laughed. "I don't know. Maybe we'd do better if there were more of them. Less bombast." Sister shrugged.

"Speaking of rocks," Betty watched as the headlights shone against the snow, the dark came early thanks to the low clouds, "ask Ben if you can go back and study the rock outcroppings."

"Why?"

"Maybe there's something there that attracted whoever put the guns there. Can't hurt. You'll look at it differently than we will."

"Never thought of it."

"Betty, have you ever suffered so much pain you couldn't think?"

The immediate reply. "Giving birth. And I was so dumb I did it twice."

"Once was enough for me." Sister slowed, turning onto the farm road. "Would you do it again?"

Betty thought. "If I were young, yes. What about you?"

"Yes. It was painful, but maybe there are things that are worse. Like a heart attack. People say kidney stones are awful."

"Kidney stones. Ugh."

"I can't imagine it."

"Tired. That hunt wore me out. Thinking about stuff. Bet those guns in the rocks were for criminal purposes."

"Betty, you have got to stop watching murder mysteries and reading them," Sister admonished her.

"Some of them are really good."

They pulled in, unloaded the horses, took a good half hour to make sure the horses were wiped down, covered with fresh blankets, put in a stall with water and good hay.

Then they dragged themselves into the tack room to clean tack. Best to get it done.

"Thank God you spent the money to heat this room." Betty sighed.

"Building anything always costs double or triple what you think it will cost. I bet that greenhouse Solange Bradford is building will cost buckets of cash."

"She has it."

"Andrew's death was useful in that respect. She doesn't have to ask for money. Beryl said Solange and the Howletts are foxhunting everywhere. God, I hope they don't come down here for the joint meet." Sister squeezed her sponge.

"Oh, I'm willing to bet you fifty dollars they'll be here. Solange likes to be the center of attention."

"You'd think she'd hang back. Given her beauty, she's always been the center of attention," Sister replied. "Does she need attention that much?"

"Tears flow like water." Betty paused. "That doesn't mean she didn't love him. She's reveling in the sympathy as near as I can tell. And I expect there are men planning to take Andrew's place."

"I expect that was going on while he was alive. Not that she encouraged anyone," Sister hastened to add. "What if the will states she can't remarry and keep the money?"

"We'd know by now, wouldn't we?" Betty replied.

"Maybe." Sister hung up the bridle. "I don't know what to think."

"If she comes here, maybe she'll wind up dead in her truck."

"Betty, how can you think that?"

"Well, I don't actually, but all we know is whoever killed Andrew is part of Bradford Beagles or even NTB. Has to be someone who knows the lay of the land."

"I get that. I don't get what the reward is for killing Andrew?"

Sister drew out her sentence. "Covering a debt owed to Andrew? Someone crazy for Solange? Far-fetched, but not impossible. People do the damndest things."

"I'm more worried about the guns hidden behind or under the rocks. That's a criminal activity. Big bucks. That makes sense to me. Killing Andrew doesn't."

Sister shrugged. "What I know is, I don't want to be dragged into anything. We'll all wind up at Winston's trial because we'll be questioned on the witness stand. That's a given. Thinking about contraband, that's not reassuring."

"Well, I wouldn't hunt back there until Ben knows more."

They put on their jackets, cut the lights, and stepped outside.

Sister walked Betty to her car, which was right in front of the stable. "I have thought about switching around a few fixtures until we know more."

"We can't really upset gun dealers." Betty closed the door to her old Bronco, blew Sister a kiss, and got ready to back out. "Be like the old days. You didn't upset the Buzzwells. In fact, you bought their liquor. However, we don't know who is selling guns."

Sister walked to the house, where she was rapturously greeted by Raleigh, Rooster, Golly, and J. Edgar Hoover. She went to the stove, turned on the heat and warmed a bit of milk for the fox cubs, who were now awake. Stirring the milk, she thought of what Betty had said. There probably was a lot of money at stake. She rather hoped they didn't find out.

As she sat with the cubs in her lap, feeding each one she thought about how beautiful they were, how true to their natures. Whatever was true human nature it seemed to be a mess.

CHAPTER 29

November 13, 2024 Wednesday

"They shot out the cameras." Ben Sidell pointed out an overhead camera in a white pine. "I thought the needles might help obscure it."

Sister stared upward. "Country boys are smart about such things. That's how they get away with poaching."

The two walked around the large rock formation to the back. Sister closely looked at the huge rocks.

"You can see here where the box, long, was found and over here the two smaller ones, handguns."

Kneeling down, she inhaled. "Fox. Not that he needs contraband."

"Do you have any idea why someone would use this location? I think it would be easier to dig a hole somewhere. Or even use a storage unit. People see one drive in and out, but carrying a carton or two, a long box, would not be out of the ordinary. I'm trying to think more broadly than I might but then again I am not a country boy."

She looked up at him. "For one thing, if the boxes are found on someone else's land, it doesn't lead to you. The owners of this rough patch are in New York. They don't visit it. An inheritance, I think, and that was years ago. So there's not a lot of interest. I do know real estate people have called because they call me." She stood back up. "I expect one day they will decide what to do with it."

"Someone put up the No Trespassing signs." Ben rubbed his chin.

"Yvonne."

"What?"

"She and Sam put them up hoping to keep hunters away, as this is catty-cornered across the road from Beveridge Hundred. If you think about it we trespass. The hounds go through if they're on a line. We don't come through here often, but we widen, the smallest bit, deer trails. No point inviting a truck back here."

"Whoever brought the guns here was strong, or there were two of them. Guns are heavy."

"Do you have an idea of what the haul would bring on the black market?"

"Smith and Wesson, Colt, Remington, older models. Well maintained. No Italian guns. No English either. Basic USA, but again older and well maintained. Couple hundred thousand at best."

"Collectors' items?"

"Collectors' items that could be used. They are good guns. My thought is, they are especially useful in crimes. People, well, law enforcement, expect a Glock. Stuff like that. Beretta. Bernelli. Well-made firearms but there is a romance attached to the older guns."

"And even though the serial numbers are filed off I expect it would be harder to determine what was fired."

"The cartridges help, but that doesn't identify a specific model."

"Useful for crimes?"

"Yes. Any gun that can't be traced is worth more than one that can." He looked around. "Is there anything there that would draw someone here? You know, a feature of landscape?"

She touched the huge rock outcropping. "The Blue Ridge Mountains, so old, have ravines, peaks, forests, meadows, lakes. The trick is to find where most people don't go, if you want to hide things."

"Gold?"

"There was a gold rush in Dahlonega, Georgia, in 1828 but mostly the mountains are full of quartzites, slates, schists, gneisses. Slate can produce profit, but you have to mine it. There's nothing where someone could walk around and pick up treasure, if that's what you mean?"

"I wasn't being very precise. I look around and it seems no one will come here. All along Chapel Cross Road, the Blue Ridge comes down on the west side. If you know the area, I think you would know where to stash things or people."

They turned to walk back.

"I wasn't much help," Sister remarked.

"If the rocks had value, you would have told me. You were a help."

They reached Yvonne's, knocked on the door.

"Finished? Come on in."

Sam was there with Ribbon, the Norfolk terrier.

"Sit down, please."

They sat in the enclosed sunroom, which had a fireplace warming the glassed room.

Ben lifted his right hand slightly. "No answers, except that it's an easy place to hide things if that's one's purpose. Oh, and the cameras have been shot out."

"That's not good." Yvonne grimaced.

"You are probably safe. But someone has been back there. Someone who doesn't want to be identified," Ben said. "Stay out of there, which I expect you will."

"I wonder if we should change the joint meet at Tattenhall Station?" Sister asked. "On the one hand, I think all will be well. People selling contraband would be stupid to interfere. We know so little."

Ben reassured her. "The only way anyone would come back would be if there was more of value left somewhere. I doubt they would find it during our foxhunt."

CHAPTER 30

November 15, 2024 Friday

Georgia parked by the attached garage connected by a walk-way to Bradford Hall. The style matched the Georgian century architecture so it didn't look out of place. She looked across the fields, the new kennels, unpainted, looking tidy, well thought-out. Beagles played in the separate yards. Some slept in special outdoor dog boxes. As with Sister's kennels, if anyone wanted to go inside, they could. And like Sister's kennels, some hounds wanted their own box or a box big enough to share with a few others. Hounds are sociable animals.

Looking across the fields she did not feel like a sociable animal. Those Leyland cypress were going in fast. It wasn't two men on the job, it was eight. At least she counted eight. Shaking her head she walked to the side door, knocked, opened it.

"Knock, knock."

A voice came from within the house. "Come on in. I'm in the sewing room."

"I'm going through the kitchen, do you need anything?"

"No," Beryl answered.

"Where did you get that fabric?" Georgia admired the beautiful tweed, once in the sewing room.

"Hugh Brown and Joe Manning sent it to me from Scotland. They took a month this summer to explore that beautiful, tough country. Can't be a weakling and live in Scotland."

"I guess." Georgia sat next to Beryl, who stopped sewing.

"Come on, let's go into the living room."

"Not until I touch this fabric." Georgia rubbed the tweed in her fingers. "Nobody does it as good as they do. Jacket?"

"Yes. My old one, which I bought at Horse Country forty years ago, can you believe it, forty years, is finally showing its age. So I'm trying to match the pattern with this fabric. I hope I haven't bitten off more than I can chew."

"That machine is professional."

"It is. An anniversary gift years ago from Winston. But I have realized over those years that I'm not as professional as the machine. Come on, let's sit by the fire. Getting colder here."

"Good for hunting although tonight is a full moon." Beryl laughed as the two old friends dropped into comfortable chairs facing the fireplace with a decorous marble fire surround.

They sat in silence for a bit enjoying the flames dancing at different heights. Old friends, bound by marriage to brothers, which is how they met. Even Georgia's tempestuous divorce hadn't rocked their bond. Then again, the divorce wasn't Georgia's doing.

"Who's here for a pat?" Georgia reached down to pat Tidbit, a demanding Yorkshire terrier. The retired beagle, Miss Priss, slept on her bed.

"I swore I would never get a little dog. Did. Don't know how I lived without her. What have you been up to?"

"Sy Sharpie?"

"Oh." Beryl's eyebrows raised hearing the name of a particularly aggressive lawyer, who Winston had considered using, but finally chose a young woman at McGuire Woods, a large firm.

"Can you imagine going through life with that name?"

"Georgia, I think there are worse names than Sy's." She then shrugged. "And if mud gets slung my way, I'll fight back, even if I'm not accused of anything. By the way, I can't believe that tree line is going in so fast."

After a pause, Beryl's eyes narrowed. "Solange doesn't want to see us or maybe us to see her. Or maybe she needs a project. She's going to hunts, heard she, Ann, and Scott drove to Washington to go to the galleries with friends up there. The story of her beloved husband's demise is getting heavy circulation."

"God help us." Georgia exhaled. "Well, Sy Sharpie will help me. He asked interesting questions. Questions that would have never occurred to me. Like did Andrew and I when married have separate bank accounts?" She paused. "Boy that launched a discussion. I didn't have my own account, as you know. I had to ask him for every penny. He always gave it to me, but I hated being the supplicant. I wasn't a supplicant; I was his wife. So, as you know, I took a job down at the FedEx Center behind the counter. Everyone who came into the building to send something or pick up boxes, mailing envelopes, saw me."

Beryl laughed. "You were so smart. God that was funny. He roared up here, pulled Winston into his office. Of course Winston told me everything. But Andrew felt humiliated. His wife working. Working like a commoner. Ha. Plus so many men came to FedEx. That didn't make him happy."

"I got my own bank account very quickly. Gave FedEx, and I liked working for them, two weeks' notice. And to Andrew's credit, he would put fifty thousand dollars in every quarter. He didn't want me feeling poor. Those were his exact words. I saved a lot of it. You know, looking back, Beryl, on one level I never thought he'd cheat on me. I did trust him there. That was a mistake."

"It wasn't your fault." Beryl was quick to defend her former sister-in-law.

"I don't think so. I mean, I never denied him anything. I did my best to keep in shape, all the girl stuff, which takes so much time. And money."

"Men have no idea."

"Drag queens do."

"Well, Georgia, what else did Sy ask?"

"Was there ever tension with people hired to work here?"

"Like the gardener? Maid? You didn't have a lot of people." Beryl cast her mind back.

"No, because I did most of it. I didn't mind. And there wasn't tension because I was the one who dealt with what help we had. Then he asked did I ever feel Andrew's business associates were doubtful, that's the word he used, *doubtful.*"

"Like crooks?"

"I wasn't sure, so I asked, people who might be drug dealers? He nodded yes. And I can't say that I thought anyone was shady. I didn't like all of his business associates but I didn't really have to socialize with most of them. If Andrew were on drugs, I would have known."

"Probably, but if he was selling them, probably not."

"Beryl, why would he sell drugs? The Bradfords have a lot of money," Georgia said.

"Yes, they do but the boys didn't make it. Winston put his efforts into nonprofits especially environmental stuff. He wants to be useful. Andrew wanted to have a good time. It got to Andrew, that Winston had more respect than he did," Beryl responded.

"Drove him crazy, really," Georgia recalled. "He didn't have a business brain, but he wanted to look like he did. He never really stuck with anything."

"True." Beryl nodded her head in agreement.

"We think of drugs first. I expect there are other ways to turn a no-tax profit. Like what if you put together a land deal and took a percent under the table in cash?" Georgia then added, "Sy came up with that. I would have never thought of it."

Georgia couldn't understand why people put all that effort into committing crimes, when hard work at an honest trade would make you money. Maybe not as much, but there wouldn't be a risk.

"Anything else surprise you?" Beryl asked.

"Yes." Georgia frowned in agreement. "Sy did say that murder, being so serious, pushed law enforcement. Maybe it won't take that long, but it won't be a trial in a couple of weeks, that's for sure."

"My poor husband." Beryl folded her hands together.

"Back to money." Georgia sat up straight. "Have you seen that line of trees out there?"

"Can't miss it."

"I started to count them before knocking on the door. Too dispiriting. And expensive. Those are already eight feet tall. Looks like it to me. The taller the tree the more money. Solange is blowing a lot of money."

Beryl sighed. "I haven't counted them but, dogwoods, certain bushes, the cost is up there. Landscaping will get you."

"It makes me think that Andrew learned from me. I bet he gave Solange her own account. If she's spending like she's spending on the trees, how long can it last? He gave me two hundred thousand dollars per year. Factoring in time, inflation, what did he give her, if he did?"

Beryl shrugged. "I bet he did give her her own account, plus he hired her two friends who seem to be doing a lot of work. Now they have to watch over her."

"It always comes down to the money, doesn't it?" Georgia reached down to Tidbit, the Yorkie, picking her up, putting her in her lap.

"Most times. Do you think Andrew was involved in something criminal?"

"Oh." Georgia scratched Tidbit's chin. "Well, it could be but you'd think he'd slip somewhere along the way."

"Maybe he did," Beryl said, conclusively.

Kathleen Sixt Dunbar, sitting in her office at the 1780 House, put down the phone, slapped her hands in happiness. Her Welsh terrier, Abdul, barked. She called Aunt Daniella.

"Hello, my whipper-in buddy."

"Oh, Kathleen, you called me in the nick of time. I was getting ready to dust with the feather duster. After a rousing conversation that urge will pass." The old woman laughed.

"Good. Have you ever seen in a graveyard a tombstone that read 'She was a good housekeeper'?"

"No. I'm closer than you are. I'm thinking Dorothy Parker's tombstone is the best if in fact that's what's on her tombstone."

"Aunt Dan, what is that?"

" 'If you can read this you're too close.' "

The two of them laughed, then Kathleen said, "I just got off the phone with Solange Bradford. She and her two friends are going to rent out my small apartment for that long weekend. The November 30 and December 1 hunt. They want to come down a day or two early, she said she's not sure, visit the university, maybe drive to Richmond to the Museum of Fine Arts. She also said to send her videos of what I have for sale here. She wants to redo her house. And here's the best part, she said she'd send me three thousand dollars for the three of them for four days whether they stay four days or not." She then added, "That apartment comes in handy."

Aunt Daniella heard Abdul bark, "Gracious." Abdul barked again as Kathleen patted him. "She hardly sounds like a bereaved widow." A silence followed this, then Aunt Daniella remarked, "Loss takes people in different ways. Some go on as though nothing has happened. Others collapse. I don't know her enough to make a guess, although it does appear unseemly. That's the only word I can think appropriate."

"Does. Maybe that's why Scott and Ann are with her. To pick her up if she does fall apart."

"I thought the world of Olivia. Never had a cause to criticize or dislike her sons. Neither one was ambitious, although Winston has worked hard for good causes. It's difficult to be the son of a rich man or a powerful one."

Kathleen considered this. "You're right. But at least neither of them died in a drug-induced stupor."

"You don't have to be rich to do that," Aunt Daniella came back.

"Guess not. Anyway, I am happy. The fall has been slow, and I swear it's because the color came late. This place fills up when the leaves turn on the Blue Ridge. I do well."

"You do, and you have magnificent stuff. Hepplewhites, Sheratons, Chippendales. The end tables alone. Oh, that bird's-eye maple big table you had years ago! Completely original and yet it made sense being the kitchen table for a farmer who did carpentry on the side in the 1820s. Then that chest of drawers. Sheraton. That had to be worth a fortune. That was before you and I whipped-in."

"It was. I received cash for that, as three people were bidding on it. Three. Walked away with eleven thousand dollars. Which would be higher today, thanks to inflation."

"I know the dog food bill has shot up for Jefferson Hunt. Gray mentioned it. They don't want to raise dues." Aunt Daniella thought of raising costs. "Everyone is under pressure. It comes and goes. I've lived through four steep downturns. Crawling out of that is not easy and the government will never use the word *depression*. Recession, bull. Well, I'm nattering on but I am thrilled for you, Kathleen. If that girl's spending money, you sell her the best. Redo her house for her. Sister said she inherited Ashton Hall. Winston stays at Bradford Hall. She also said that when Andrew remarried, Olivia updated her will, split everything in half except for her jewelry, some personal items."

"Wise." Kathleen looked at Abdul in the eyes, which he loved. "Are you ready for tomorrow's hunt?"

"Ready as I'll ever be. It's picking up. The cooler temperature helps. We need more moisture."

"I'll see you tomorrow."

"You will, babydoll, and we can celebrate." Aunt Daniella hung up, happily relieved of the impulse to clean.

CHAPTER 31

November 16, 2024 Saturday

Zorro, nose down, slowly walked in a circle around a brush pile. *"Nothing."*

Pickens, a few steps ahead of the determined hound, grumbled, *"We've been out here, sun getting higher. You'd think scent would lift."*

"Yeah." Zandy, coming up next to Zorro, agreed.

The day should have been good. The first cast had been at ten o'clock. The mercury had nudged over into the higher thirties. A low cloud cover promised that scent would hold longer than in bright sunshine. So far, nothing.

The fixture, Philo, newer, had been opened over the summer. It seemed like a good balance between rolling hills, a low bridge, streams. Good soils.

The fifty-three numbered field walked along. A bracing run would have snapped them all wide awake. As the season wore on, the weekend numbers increased. Holiday weekends, so tricky, could be a handful of people or it seemed like a regiment. One never knew.

The hounds cared not at all for the people. Nothing distracted them from their mission to pick up scent and run that line.

A small stream feeding into a larger creek created an angle, forty degrees. It was low enough for hounds and horses to cross. On the other side harvested corn stood, old kernels on the ground.

Weevil, seeing the harvested corn, leapt over the stream, landed on the other side, urged his hounds into the corn stalks.

Noses down, they trotted in, eager. The field crossed the wider part of the creek, where the stream joined in. No point jumping if there's a decent crossing, which there was. Sister had the feeling things were going to heat up. There'd be plenty of chances to jump. For people who hunt to ride, those jumps thrilled them. For Sister, who rode to hunt, she took them feeling they were obstacles between her and her hounds. Then again, she had great horses. No need to worry, she was going over.

"*Gray,*" Zorro, keen today, announced.

A group of the made hounds drew near, opened, and off they ran. The two couple of young entry, smack in the middle of the pack, were learning fast. Grays run a bit different than reds, and this gray proved no exception.

Hounds shot straight as an arrow down a harvested corn row. Out of the corn row, they continued on a straight line, dipping into a slight swale, then out and then a half circle.

"*Is he going back?*" Arnie, a young entry, asked.

Twist, battle hardened, told the youngster, "*Up to a point. He'll probably run in a figure eight and use every obstacle he can. If there was a dead cow, he'd run over it.*"

The run was on the first loop of the circle eight. Then the line straightened out heading back, over the convergence of the stream into the creek, straight on and then another loop curving back from the direction in which they came.

What a good run for the young ones. The gray might go out of the territory, but this wouldn't be a straight shot, like a coyote; staff would run a coyote, of course, but these were foxhounds and they wanted to run foxes.

They were getting their wish. Back at the top loop again everything changed.

"Another fox," Trooper called out, stopped a moment.

Dasher, nose down, investigated the two scents as did Diana, his littermate.

"This one's hotter," Dasher told his sister.

"Not our original fellow, but the humans don't know the difference." Diana, baying at the top of her lungs, tore off, heading slightly away from the loop.

Zorro, good nose, knew they had switched foxes.

And this fox mimicked the original fox, but ran his figure eight east and west instead of north and south.

What a run. They dipped into the low fields, then the earth rose slightly, harder ground; they blasted over that. Easy footing, and then a jagged line of old stone confronted them. This was the remains of the original stone fence from the late seventeen hundreds. The owners of Philo swore that when all the other stuff was completed, they would restore this fence line. Is there anything more appealing than a well-laid stone fence, loose stone? Maybe a zigzag fence, but the original fences charmed people.

As all of this was new territory the original settlers used what they could find. Clearing fields of stones, especially larger ones, was an important chore. Hard to plough with stones in the field. They will bend the blade. What a job that must have been.

Sister cleared the still straight line. The fallen stone stood at maybe two feet. Other spots were lower, but anyone could take this fence, including Second Flight. Bobby wasn't about to find a low spot. Two feet isn't a lot to ask.

Those people in his field who were scared had the good fortune of a seasoned rider coming alongside them, telling them to grab mane and follow. Everyone made it. The experience emboldened people. Sometimes you have to push someone, they do it and gain confidence.

The pace picked up. This fellow was burning the wind.

Weevil, on Showboat, felt a trickle of sweat run down his face. Cool though it was, he was riding hard.

The whippers-in, thankful for the easy roll of the land, kept up. As there were no pastures fenced this far back on the farm, no jumps other than the fallen stone fence.

The fox was flying. Sister, eyes ahead, kept a loose rein on Rickyroo. He was fine and appreciated no pressure on the bit other than that he could feel her hands. Light hands make for a happy horse.

Hounds roared toward an old farm road. Kathleen and Aunt Daniella sat far enough away.

Seeing the road, Weevil realized the fox had just run out of the fixture. He had to call his hounds off a hot line. No huntsman ever wants to do that.

He slowed, blew the three long notes, as both Tootie and Betty crossed over the road. They might need to get ahead of the pack to turn it back. No one really knew this landowner, and no one wanted a fuss over hoofprints on his land. New people, and they were new people, could be extra protective of their acres. The smaller the plot of land, the more protective. Occasionally someone with five acres enjoyed seeing the well-turned-out field. That was a blessing.

As it was, masters felt like law clerks having to deliver and explain the state's hunting laws, the club's liability waivers, and the insurance policy. Country people in the old days knew you were as good as your word. No more.

"Hold hard," Betty called.

"*No.*" Zorro was furious.

Tatoo, now up with them, commanded him, "*It's terrible but you have to do it. Have to.*"

The pack stopped, both whippers-in excelling at a hard job.

As the hounds walked back, Zorro asked Tatoo, "*Back there when we switched foxes. That's okay?*"

"*Usually, the problem is if you come upon a second line and the line you are on is not as hot. Sometimes the huntsman and whippers-in can tell if one line is hot and one not. They want you to stay on the original line but usually they'll give in. A good run keeps everyone happy and a fading line can poop out. So it's almost always not a problem. The problem that you just encountered is when everything is great but the fox runs out the territory,*" Trooper explained.

"*Does the fox know?*" The youngster was astounded.

"*I don't know but I do know they are so smart. And remember, wherever we hunt, that's where those foxes live. They know things we don't.*"

Everyone got their wind walking back.

Weevil lavishly praised his hounds for being obedient.

The original gray, a young male, secure in his den, one opening of which was under the fallen stone fence, listened for the horses and hounds to go away. He had been out courting, as had the fox who ran off the fixture. The minute the hounds, horses, and people were well out of the way, he was going back to find her. He was the right one. He needed a present. He hoped, once free, he could find something, anything.

Back at the trailers, a few people upon dismounting realized how tired their legs were. The makeshift breakfast was much needed.

The trailers shielded the wind. Didn't do much to warm the

air, but everyone had changed into a heavy tweed or even a warmer non-hunting coat. Sister, much as she liked tradition, felt better for people to be comfortable. Cold can eat at you.

Kathleen and Aunt Daniella drove up.

Gray immediately walked over to his aunt, opened the door, grabbed her shawl, which he placed over her fitted coat, a tweed. Aunt Daniella, although not a rider, knew the traditions and stuck to them. Also, she looked great in hunt kit.

The breakfast, happy, gave people time to talk, laugh, recount the wonderful day. Started out lackluster and ended up just great.

The new members, Dinah Jamison, Lorraine Shoemaker, and Pete Jensen, were full of questions about the upcoming joint meet, followed by beagling the next day, also a joint meet.

"You'll love it," Yvonne told them. "So many people, all of them fun to meet, most of them really good riders. It's so much fun. And if you decide to attend the beagling, you'll be part of a different kind of hunting, still a pack. But your legs might be tired from the day before. I always bring a walking stick. If I get a little sore, I lean on the stick. Have to catch up, but there are flight leaders, same as with foxhunting."

"What do I wear?" Lorraine wondered.

"For beagling some people wear britches and a green coat, especially if they're staff. If it's raining, most everyone wears a Barbour or a good raincoat."

Dinah, surprised, asked, "We still go?"

Yvonne answered. "Unless it's a downpour, yes. Same for the foxhunting. Sister allows people to wear raincoats. She herself doesn't, but she knows some people really take a chill if they get wet. Now, granted, the coats from England repel the rain. Marion at Horse Country has jackets and coats from England. Fewer than years ago, because of Labour's attack on hunting. Businesses closed, but she still has them. Sister is really good about it but she, herself, never."

"No kidding?" Pete's jaw slacked a bit in surprise.

"She obeys traditions. To the letter." Yvonne smiled. "She and Sam taught me. There's quite a bit of good sense involved. And then again, who doesn't look great?"

"Can we wear gloves with rubber undersides?" Lorraine liked clothing.

"If the backsides are mustard. No black or dark brown gloves. You can wear knitted gloves, the special white or tan ones. My experience is, they do get soaked but your reins don't slip. The problem can be solved with leather reins with the back of the reins covered in pebbled rubber. You don't really notice it but it sure works. I used the knitted gloves and the special reins."

"Don't your hands get cold?" Pete hated cold hands.

"Well, if it's bitter, they do. Then I pull out my heavy leather gloves with fur lining and take my chances. But the rubberized reins usually keep me okay. I actually quite like the look of the knitted gloves. Again, old tradition."

"I have a lot to learn." Dinah grabbed a ham biscuit.

"Never stops." Yvonne grinned. "Sister, who has hunted longer than any of us, always says there is no such thing as a hunt where she doesn't learn something. For me that's part of the appeal. That and the beauty. Those rolling acres today, the harvested cornfield, all those kernels on the ground, a special kind of beauty. I grew up and lived in a big city. Not until I moved here, which I thought I wouldn't much like, did I realize how gorgeous, exciting, fields, forests, the creatures are." She then blushed. "Forgive me. I nattered on."

Pete, like most men, enchanted by Yvonne's beauty, remarked, "Your enthusiasm is contagious. And the run we had, I'm glad I stayed on."

Yvonne, beaming from the praise, said to the three, "Did you notice we ran figure eights?"

"We did." Dinah's eyes grew larger.

"I thought we were turning. Well, we were, but I didn't notice the figure, so to speak." Lorraine was rethinking the hunt.

"Figure eights. We were on a gray."

"Wow." Pete was getting the picture.

"Well, let me give my fellow a break. His aunt is giving him way too many chores." She excused herself, walking over to Aunt Daniella, who was in her element.

"Aunt Dan, what would you like?" Yvonne asked the glowing woman.

"Sam will get it. Sam, bring me a bracing Old Fashioned."

"Of course."

"You know what I need," Aunt Daniella simply added.

As everyone was catching up, Ronnie asked Kasmir, "If you have any extra old blankets, may I have them? I have one for each stall, but in case someone tears one up during turnout, a few extra will help. We are going to be mobbed."

"I do have a few. It will be a big weekend, plus right after Thanksgiving, which I think is a plus."

"Now, if we get a run like we had today, perfect." Ronnie held out his hand like an actor accepting applause.

Ben Sidell and Bobby gladly sat in their foldout chairs.

"Walter, any deer hunting problems at Mill Ruins?"

"No, but down by Shootrough you know they are across the road there. No one bothers me, but my neighbor did tell me there was a bad feeling between some of the clubs. Accusations of being on the other guy's territory. Even accusations of stealing guns, wrecking traps."

"No good will come from it," Ben noted.

Bobby, corn bread in hand, said, "It does seem to get worse

every year. When prices go up, they go up for everything including renting hunt lands."

"Any ideas on those guns?" Walter asked Ben.

"No. Jude and Jackie," he named his young assistants, "have already questioned the clubs south of Charlottesville. Now they're working on those north of town. Those two both just tipping thirty and they're keen."

Walter, kind, urged the sheriff, "Time for promotions at the beginning of the new year."

"Those kids are good. We need good people in law enforcement." Bobby seconded the notion.

"It's on my agenda." Ben smiled. "No one seems to know about guns with serial numbers filed off."

"That's hard to believe," Bobby came back.

"It is, but do I think hunters are selling those expensive guns? Probably not." Ben took a breath. "Why? If I picked them up they'd be in real trouble. There is a competition over who had the best rifle. For some guys, it's their grandfather's gun; for someone else, a Purdy. Another guy wants a brand-new, expensive Beretta. Kind of like cars. A stolen, unregistered rifle would get a man in a world of trouble."

Alida and Freddie listened as Betty described what she saw during the hunt.

Everyone remained energized, thrilled with the day.

And the home gray fox was thrilled, because when people left, they picked up their garbage but did leave some food for the foxes. He even got a deviled egg, plus biscuit bits, which he took to the vixen. She accepted his gifts.

CHAPTER 32

November 17, 2024 Sunday

"I'm too young to be a widow," Betty complained as she and Sister pored over pedigrees in the kennel office.

"You poor thing." Sister shot a rubber band at her.

"Every Sunday, we go to church. We sometimes go to the Home Place for dinner. Then we go home, and he races for that TV. It's not that I don't like football, it's only that I don't like it that much."

"Yes. What did you think of Reverend Taliaferro's sermon this morning?"

"She surprises me. Where does she find her quotes?"

"Me too. She's obviously a reader."

"You're a reader. I'm not, unless it's mysteries."

"Mostly I like history, geology, but I wouldn't go so far to say I'm a serious reader. But she quoted G. K. Chesterton. That isn't an everyday quote. Most people don't even know who he was."

"A big bug in England at the end of the nineteenth century. That's the limit of my knowledge."

"Better than many," Sister praised her.

"I remember that quote word for word because it so surprised me. He said, 'When a man ceases to believe in God, he does not believe in nothing, he believes in anything.'" Betty's voice lifted up a bit. "Makes you think. I think it's true."

"I do, too." Sister shuffled papers. "That's it. Didn't take as long as I'd anticipated."

"That's because you carry most of the bloodlines in your head. I can look at a hound, I have a rough idea of what type of foxhound it is. Well, I do better with ours. You can look and often know the bloodlines."

"Betty, given how many years I've studied bloodlines and gone to other hunts for what, forty-five years, I should know something. I fear paper breeders whether it's hounds or horses. One needs to see the animal. No, I will never see Squire Osbaldeston's famous Furrier, but for my time I've seen a lot." She'd cited a famous master, breeder, huntsman from the late eighteenth century to nineteenth-century England. He died in 1866.

"I suppose. Back to Chesterton. What do you think people believe now?"

Sister blew air out of her mouth, thought, then replied. "Whatever they can hold on to that makes them feel superior to someone else. They can parrot an idea but they don't really think. It's a dangerous time."

"Isn't every time dangerous?" Betty got up, threw two more logs on the fire.

"Yes, but some times are more dangerous than others. The 1930s were more dangerous than the 1950s. England after 1815 entered into a prolonged peace as did the rest of Europe. It ended in 1914. We'll never see anything like that again. Am I worried? I am, but I don't think there's much I can do about it."

"Me neither. I'll stick to what I know, the printing business and foxhunting. Printing. Well, paper and ink prices go up. Special occasions stay the same, birth, graduation from high school and college, marriage, death. People once again want those special occasions to have elegant, printed announcements, stuff you can't do on a computer. That's what I know."

"It's more than I know. No one cares about geology unless it's an oil company." Sister half smiled. "What else do I know? Gardening. I'm not a businessperson. You and Bobby are." She inhaled. Took the papers, returning them to their folders. "We all have different brains, different gifts. Mine aren't worth money."

"I don't know."

Sister looked at her friend. "What's saved me are the men I have married. They do know business. It's not that I was kept from it by my being a woman of my generation. I'm not interested in it."

"What you do, you do better than the rest of us," Betty reassured her. "Speaking of doing something better, Ronnie, Kasmir, and Alida are working on the temporary beagle barn as we work here."

"He told me they would be doing that. Given that none of us are really beaglers, you and I go sometimes, it's especially kind of the Barbhaiyas. It will be clean; warm, thanks to all that straw and old blankets; and convenient. Neither beagle club will have to drive their pack very far from Wolverhampton."

"Are you worried we'll end up in that rough patch across from Beveridge Hundred?"

"Betty, if we do, we're fine. The guns are out. Why would anyone come back?"

"Yeah." Betty considered this. "So you think whoever is behind this knows the guns are gone?"

"Sure. My bet is whoever these people are, they know the area. They aren't worried about us. What do we want with guns?"

"We could sell them."

"Betty, to whom? If we peddled those guns we'd be sitting ducks. This is some kind of organized operation like the old country waters, people were organized including the warned." She meant the moonshiners.

"You're probably right," Betty agreed.

"All right. Done. Come on in the house with me. You can help me feed the cubs."

The walk from the kennels to the house, one hundred yards, wasn't far, but it was far enough to know it was cold outside. The two stepped into the mudroom, took off their coats. Hung them on the wall pegs, then stepped inside to the welcome warmth of the kitchen.

Golly, asleep on the counter, opened one eye then closed it.

The two women could hear Gray in the library, watching the game. The two dogs watched with him.

"Must be winning." Sister smiled. "No loud curses."

"Sometimes I think I'll need to give Bobby amyl nitrate to revive him when it's bad."

They laughed, and Sister prepared the milk. She handed Betty a jar of baby food, as well as a dish towel.

Then, sitting on the floor, they put the dish towels on their laps. Sister opened the screened door. The cubs squeaked, wobbled out.

Sister and Betty picked them up, one for Betty, two for Sister, put them on their laps. First they fed them the milk. Next Sister opened the jar of baby food. She dipped in a finger then held it to a cub. Betty did the same.

"Something new." Betty loved animals as much as Sister.

"Here, little one." Sister put a tiny bit of baby food on the cub's nose, which she licked off. "There we go."

Betty did the same.

All three babies quickly figured out this was good.

"They've grown," Betty remarked.

"I'm hopeful. If they all make it, I have to decide what to do. I can't really turn them out. Because they're so little, they bonded to me, not afraid of humans."

"How about me?" Golly meowed. *"They know who I am. I sit by their cage."*

"I guess Gray will have to build bigger lodgings."

"Maybe. Part of the old back yard is fenced in. I can fix that so they can't get out and no one can get in. Raptors can be the very devil. Well, I don't have to make up my mind today."

"Full stomach. Sleep." Betty rubbed one sleek, red head.

The three, put back into their dwelling, curled up next to one another and fell asleep.

The two made the ever-ready pot of tea and sat to once again discuss the sermon.

"I need a good sermon," Betty declared.

"Me too. Something to take my mind away from daily chores, troubles, the detritus of daily life. Something to make you think, to make you feel. And Betty, we've been asking these questions for thousands of years."

"So we have. Speaking of questions, we'll have Winston and Beryl here. Georgia, too. And have you heard from Aunt Daniella today at dinner that Solange, Ann, and Scott will be renting Kathleen's top floor?"

"Which reminds me." Sister rose, opened the door to the mudroom, returning. She handed Betty fifty dollars. "Had cash in my Carhartt pocket."

"What's this for?"

"You bet Solange would come to the big joint meets and I said I didn't think she would. So here."

A big grin covered Betty's kind face. "Wasn't I smart."

"Yes. You know what's occurred to me? We don't really know who killed Andrew. Solange believes it was Winston, obviously, but maybe she's in danger. Maybe Andrew was deep into trouble."

"Could be but wouldn't she know?"

"I have no idea. She doesn't appear stupid but then again, think of how many men have engaged in theft, criminal activity, affairs and the wife never knew."

"Possible. I'll have to think about that. You know what I was thinking about sermons? I remember the good ones."

"I do, too," Sister agreed.

"Remember the one Reverend Taliaferro gave last summer? Who was stronger Samson or Delilah?"

"That was a goody."

They were off and running.

As two old friends luxuriated in each other's company, Ben Sidell, football game on in the background, sound off, stared at his computer.

He caught the sight of a long pass deflected at the end zone by the defense. Smiling, he returned to his computer. Ben, dogged, kept chipping away at things. Finally, he found out who the man was caught in the trap. Mort Ricalton had used many aliases; addresses also changed, as did cars, some stolen. He was a low-level crook, mostly a thief by opportunity, although he did get arrested twice, once in North Carolina and once in Virginia for transporting illegal liquor.

Reading the details of a demolished life, Ben didn't jump to conclusions but he was getting a larger picture of events. Mort could have been a mule for contraband and that could mean contraband guns. Whoever he'd crossed had killed him. Yes, he stepped in a trap. Had that been all, Mort would have probably screamed until someone found him. As it was, someone made sure he was dead. His manner of death was not an accident.

Ben did know the county was a stopping place, given its ideal location for contraband coming from the east or west, north or south. The roads were good. No big city. Lower law-enforcement numbers. Charlottesville proved perfect in many ways. One could drive, say, high-quality illegal liquor from southern Virginia, switch carriers in Charlottesville, out on a country road, hop back on 81 or 95 or 29 if going north and south, 64 or 70 if going east and west. Since no crimes were committed here, no attention drawn to the product, easy. Cigarettes were another in-demand product. Sold cheaper in the South, all one had to do was haul them across the Mason-Dixon Line.

So if nothing else, Ben knew he was dealing with an organized group, probably small. The fewer the number the less opportunity to split off, become a rival. Then again Mort could be a dead rival.

His other theory was that Mort might have done low-level jobs for an organization. Or he may have learned about it and thought he could steal a load of guns, booze, something. He certainly was dead.

Ben's immediate worry was not finding Mort's killer. His immediate worry was watching Chapel Cross Road. Surely they wouldn't come back. Each week crimes in the city and county were posted online. When Charlottesville had a daily newspaper they would be printed. No reporter hopped on the online report for a story. This lack of internet reportage might embolden the cartel or criminals to keep using the area.

CHAPTER 33

November 29, 2024 Friday

Ronnie was at Wolverhampton for those people who came in early. As it was the day after Thanksgiving, most people didn't have to work, so they loaded up their horses, clothing, brought food, and drove to Chapel Cross Road. Everyone was eager to hunt.

The Bull Run people settled in, building fires in all the fireplaces for latecomers. The stable could hold eight horses. The group from Bradford came next, so there remained two empty stalls in the stable. Marianne Casey and Susan filled those. The extra horses went to Kasmir's stable, which was beautiful. That was a two-mile drive. The beagles snuggled into the makeshift but lovely little stable, converted for them. While Susan settled her horse, Jim helped with the beagles. It was good they had married each other. Each one had to be doing something.

Beryl took charge of the evening meal, with Georgia pitching in. Others set the table, kept the fires going. Winston fixed the drinks. What a party.

Everyone talked about hunting, the weather, ever the weather, who was tapped for Trump's cabinet. That set off questions, fussing, laughing, but everyone really could talk without fear.

It became a convivial evening with people united by a shared passion.

Ronnie stayed for the party, then left at eight. He figured he'd better rise early the next morning for the hunt at Tattenhall Station. If anyone needed anything he wanted to provide it.

He called Sister once home, gave her an update. She thanked him over and over for all he had done. He enjoyed it, and hoped the hunt would be a barn burner.

She hung up the phone, gave the report to her husband.

Gray, looking up from his *Barron's*, folded it in quarters. "He's been especially busy."

"He has. I think he's lonely. He has all of us, but Ronnie needs someone to love."

Gray put the paper in his lap. "We all do. He's a giving man, but it's got to be harder when you're middle-aged and gay. He had a lot of guts to come out in college, but he's paid for it."

She thought. "If RayRay were alive, he would have helped him. My son, young though he was, didn't have a prejudicial bone in his body. His father made up for that."

"Different generation plus your late husband had to convince people to give him their money to invest. That makes one naturally conservative, I think. But I don't remember Big Ray ever being racist or saying unpleasant things about gay men. If he did, I never heard it. Well, given that I'm Black, no, I wouldn't hear that."

"He didn't say much around me but I could tell when someone made him nervous. Gay men made him nervous. I figured it was because he was good-looking. Anyway, how would I know?"

"You're sweet to think about Ronnie."

"I love him. He and Xavier, another of RayRay's best friends, kept coming around after my son died. I think they were looking out for me in their own way. Fourteen years old. They'd ask me to their junior high school events. When they were in high school I didn't miss a football game. Xavier played right tackle."

"They're your boys." He smiled at her. "You know you can always talk to me about things. Things in the past. Your life has been full, pain, sorrow, excitement, joy, success. Neither you nor I were born when much was expected of us."

She looked at him. "Yes. I try not to think about that because it gives me excuses if I want to use them."

"Me too." He smiled. "Aunt Daniella would set me straight. As for Ronnie, I don't know, honey, where would he even look? Where would we look? He has little Atlas," Gray mentioned Ronnie's exuberant Chihuahua. "You'd think someone would come out hunting. But I guess not."

"We take dating for granted. Or did. Well, I'll keep him in my prayers."

"You have a long list." He put his paper on the coffee table, got up, came over, and kissed her. "You pray for all of us."

"The Good Lord can do more than I can." She kissed him back.

As they sat there thinking of other people's lives, Kathleen could hear something on her top floor, where the apartment was. The three came in two days ago, a day early, but she'd had everything ready.

Scott drove the ladies wherever they wanted to go. Kathleen quite liked him. He was handsome and helpful.

Solange examined everything in the shop. She bought a lot of stuff, good stuff. Kathleen was happy for that. She thought Scott did as the girls, as Kathleen thought of them, asked. Ann, married to Scott, didn't boss him around or vice versa. She seemed to take him for granted.

Kathleen thought it none of her business. She certainly didn't want to get involved in the uproar at Bradford Beagles. She was astonished that they came to be a part of the blowout weekend. Then again, the hunting should be terrific, the company wonderful. As long as the three hunted, didn't push Winston, Beryl, or Georgia, why not?

Still, she felt something was off. She couldn't identify it. But she truly wanted to stay out of it.

CHAPTER 34

November 30, 2024 Saturday

Hounds screamed along the creek running by the railroad tracks at Tattenhall Station. Hounds struck after five minutes from being cast. Sister, Midshipman stretched out, gave thanks to Artemis. A large meet with a good run was something worth praying for, or at least acknowledging the goddess of the hunt. After all, former hunters, like Xenophon, all appeased the goddess. Thucydides even built a small temple for her. Anyone who hunted with him left a bit of money there. At the end of the year, Thucydides collected the money and the fellows enjoyed a big party after paying their respects.

Sister didn't have a temple, but flying along at this moment, she certainly considered it. Parker, at full maturity, led the pack for the first time, a big deal for him. The fox ran straight, heading south, within a five-minute span the huge field had already strung out. Adrianna, Marianne, other guests who were invited to ride up front, hung behind Sister. Lynne and Alida, side by side, rode right behind the other masters, up front. A big knot of people followed the front-runners. Given the large pasture they almost looked like a regiment as they covered a lot of that field. Behind them rode the last of First Flight, people not on Thoroughbreds. The pace was so fast, the Thoroughbreds surged ahead, but those in the rear hung in there. Bobby Franklin, maneuvering Second Flight, stared at the woods up ahead. The trails, cleared, were not very wide. People were going to have to take that into account.

Those on draft crosses, or older horses, formed an impromptu Third Flight. Jefferson Hunt didn't have a Third Flight, but they did now. Freddie, wisely, fell back to keep this group together. Ever generous, Freddie gave up riding up front to tend to those who couldn't keep up, some unwilling to jump. A stout one loomed up ahead.

The fox blasted straight into the woods, crossed a cleared trail, now heading westerly. Midshipman didn't blink. Sister thought about using him today although he was young. This was a huge field, but she had brought him and Matchplay along carefully. She trusted his mind and importantly, he trusted her. This boy was so talented and smooth, he made any gait a pleasure. Sometimes a horse has a wonderful ground-covering trot but a shorter-stride gallop. Other horses have terrible trots. You can feel your fillings rattle. But Midshipman was a dream. He also loved leading everyone. Sister could just see Weevil's scarlet coat up ahead, but he, on Hojo, another Thoroughbred, was pulling away.

Behind her, the field had to sort itself out. The Jefferson Hunt members gave way for the visitors, as it should be. Walter and Ronnie brought up the rear. So far so good, but both knew not everyone was going to make that jump, a tiger trap. This jump has the boards up and down instead of horizontal. Not every hunt built tiger traps. Sure enough, a few horses refused. Fortunately, the riders turned, going back to the rear, which was proper. It only takes one refusal for the horses behind that horse to get tetchy.

Hearing hoofbeats behind her, Sister did not look back. It

doesn't do a bit of good. The cry filled the woods, which was mostly replanted pines, as that part of Tattenhall Station had formally been used for timber, a good crop and essentially an easy one, until the pine beetles got you. You never know about those devils.

Lower branches had all been cleared in the summer. It was a great trail but the fox could have cared less. He hooked right, zig-zagged through the woods. Hounds never lost the scent, but some of his maneuvers slowed them. Sister knew if she slowed down, she could well lose the hounds, because sooner or later this boy, she was pretty sure it was a courting male, would go out into a pasture again.

Finding a cross up ahead she turned right. She couldn't see Betty or Tootie, but she knew they were in the right place. They almost always were.

She listened intently. Weevil, slowing, had to have turned back. No need to urge Midshipman. He knew his job was to stay behind the huntsman and the hounds. He put on the afterburners, reached another trail, and turned hard right. Fortunately, her leg was tight.

So now they paralleled the direction on which they'd started, but about a quarter of a mile west.

Boom. Out into the pasture again. She couldn't see where Weevil was then she heard him once again scream at the top of his lungs. He'd crossed Chapel Cross. A simple coop in the old fence line was up ahead. They cleared it, hit the road where Aunt Daniella and Kathleen sat far back, out of the way. Then over a hand-laid stone fence into Old Paradise. Now she could see her huntsman, the pack, all on, and her two much-loved whippers-in. God, they were all screaming.

If she had turned around she would have noticed some riders fell back but it appeared no one had come off.

Flying across Crawford's rich pasture, she leaned back, to charge down a swale.

Once out of the swale, she could once again see her hounds.

As the fox was running like a demon, Earl watched from the carriage house. Sarge, with him, gave thanks they weren't being chased, because the pace was blistering. Although in good shape, both foxes had gotten spoiled living at Old Paradise. Lots of food, blankets to snuggle in, and impenetrable dens.

The fox they watched, they didn't know.

"Romance," Earl declared laconically.

"He's heading for the Main Stable."

"Your old den is still there." Sarge thought the Main Stable smashing.

"If he doesn't find it he'll have to head up the mountainside." Earl flicked his red tail with the white tip. *"I don't think romance is worth this."*

The chased fox shot straight into the Main Stable as the large doors were opened. He didn't know there were two den openings inside, one in a stall leading to a den, the other under blankets in the tack room, the den immediately underneath. So he ran through it, then circled behind it. He was smart enough to know this was a good place for someone to live. Lucky for him he found the outdoor opening, plunged down, and kept going through the tunnel.

The entire pack charged down the main aisle. Weevil was right behind them. Both of the whippers-in, outside each on a side. Betty saw the fox duck down into the den opening. She pulled up, as she knew the pack would be there in a moment. She took off her cap, outstretched arm pointing at the den. She'd wait for Weevil. He appeared in a minute, understood her gesture, so she moved farther up field.

Weevil dismounted, blew "Gone to Ground," and praised his pack. They had shown good sport and, yes, were a little strung out, a few older ones bringing up the rear, but they looked good. If he wanted it to be perfect he probably should have left Trinity and

Tinsel, not really old but also not particularly fast. He knew they were true blue, so he'd put them in the pack.

Sister did not ride through the stable. She waited outside, thinking she might have to go around the building, but she knew of the old den. Hearing "Gone to Ground," she walked to that side of the stable as Weevil was patting everyone's head.

She rode up to him. The field stayed put.

"We'll have to come back here and make sure there are no damages."

"Yes, Madam." He nodded. "I don't think there are, but there will be dirt and," he pointed to the den opening, "they dug furiously."

"Right. Well, fortunately we are chasing rabbits on foot tomorrow, so we aren't spoiling Sunday's beagling."

"Would you like me to leave Old Paradise?"

"Yes, if we pick up a line, we'll hunt it, obviously, but we should jump out and head over toward Beveridge Hundred. That gives everyone time to renew." She smiled. "Hell of a run. And we've only been out a little more than an hour." She checked her grandfather's pocket watch.

Weevil sprung up into the saddle, Hojo standing still. "Come along."

Dreamboat followed right behind him, the others walked behind him. They could use a bit to catch their breath as well.

As Sister rode by the field she noticed a grin on each face. What could have been better?

Weevil jumped over the stone jump, then back into Tattenhall Station. Best to hunt toward Beveridge Hundred than to walk on the road, even though traffic was light out here.

In the middle of Second Flight, Solange, Ann didn't chat but stuck close together. Winston, Beryl, and Georgia rode in First

Flight in the middle. Scott, an okay rider but not as strong as the others, rode with the new Third Flight.

"How many people do you think there are?" Kathleen asked as she watched the group go over the jumps.

Aunt Daniella guessed. "A company? A hundred?"

Bobby unlatched the gate and Freddie guided Third Flight through it when her turn came. She waited, then latched the gate. Fortunately, the staff horses were all good with gates.

"What?" Diesel asked.

Trinity came over. *"Bear."*

Zorro also took a big sniff. *"We'll find a fox."*

Hounds knew bear was legitimate game, or Weevil would pull them off, or the whippers-in would. But this day, mid-forties, low clouds, couldn't have been better for scent. Surely they would pick up another fox, and they did.

The fox blew through Beveridge Hundred then into the land just west of that. He turned. Almost retraced his steps and slunk under the fence at the old estate. Hounds were closing. He ducked into Yvonne's wonderful feeder box, so designed that nobody could get a fox who was in there. Yvonne was popular with foxes.

Ducking in, he stayed still. The kibble smelled enticing, but he'd wait for the hounds to leave.

Yvonne, in the middle of First Flight, watched as the large, well-defended box was surrounded.

Weevil rode up, spoke to the hounds. He couldn't really blow "Gone to Ground," as the fox wasn't in a den. So he called them away. Reluctantly, they came. Heading back toward Tattenhall Station, he cleared the coop in the fence line between Yvonne's and Kasmir's.

First Flight, one by one, got over. Georgia's horse balked and that fast Solange, who had moved up throughout the hunt being on a fit Thoroughbred, ran right in front of her and took the coop. Georgia's horse reared, and off she came.

Walter rode up as he saw the whole thing. So did everyone else.

Georgia, furious, wind knocked out of her, was attended by Ronnie, now off Pokerface, his super horse.

"You're sure you're all right? No broken bones? Walter will kill me if I move you too early." Ronnie had his arm around her waist.

"I'm fine. Have to get my wind back." She sucked in a large amount of air, shook her head. "Really, I'm okay."

Walter looking down said, "Okay, Ronnie."

Ronnie lifted her up. She stood there for a moment.

"Let's go to Second Flight. We'll let the other people over. Can you take a leg up?" Walter asked.

"I can. He's a good boy. I'm lucky she didn't ram him. Twelve hundred pounds slamming into my boy."

"And you." Ronnie cupped hands under her boot as she took the reins.

"I don't much care about me, but I will get that bitch."

Up she went as riders passed them. Everyone got over and everyone couldn't wait until after the hunt to discuss what they had seen.

Walter remained at the rear while Ronnie rode with Georgia to Second Flight. Bobby opened the gate, waited for them.

"I'll stick with her. She had a hell of a jolt," Ronnie informed Bobby.

Bobby hooked the latch. "Saw part of it."

Sister, up ahead, didn't know what happened. Her job was to stay behind her huntsman, unless there is a terrible calamity. This could have been that, but fortunately it wasn't.

Weevil urged his hounds on. They were heading back to the trailers, but a fox could have crossed the pasture. Noses down, the keen animals tried. A fading whiff here, a fading whiff there. Nothing to push.

Back at the trailers, Walter gave Sister the story of what happened. This was emphasized by Ronnie, who came up. Other people also came over to tell her. She thanked them all.

"What a damn mess," Sister said once she, Walter, and Ronnie were alone.

Bobby came over. "You heard?"

"Did."

Winston also heard, and Beryl hung on to him because he was going into the train station to get Solange. Gray, trailer by Winston's, helped Beryl restrain him.

"She could have killed Georgia!"

"Yes, she could have, but she didn't. This is a master's job. Let them handle it." Beryl tried to calm him down.

"She's right." Gray seconded her thoughts. "You're in enough trouble, thanks to her. My wife will take care of it."

Sister and Walter, both masters, decided to handle it together. The other masters observed when the two walked into the potluck breakfast.

Walter and Sister, lockstep, reached Solange, who had just picked up her plate. At about that time, Aunt Daniella and Kathleen came in. They had witnessed the event from the car. It was distant, as they were on the road, but they clearly saw Solange's dangerous actions.

"Solange," Sister started.

The beauty looked up at her with a beatific smile. "Fabulous hunt."

"We are excusing you from this breakfast and future hunting with Jefferson Hunt," Sister calmly ordered.

"Her horse balked." Solange's jaw stuck out, she knew what she had done.

"You ran right in front of her. If her horse had gone forward, it would have been a horrific collision. We ask that you leave." Walter backed up protocol.

Without warning, Solange threw her plate on the floor, breaking it. She grabbed Ann by the arm, pulling her along. Scott, mouth full, looked at the two women, swallowed reluctantly, then followed.

As Solange left the building, Georgia couldn't help it, she clapped. To her surprise others clapped with her.

Sister and Walter did as they should have, no prevarication. A dangerous rider, especially one choosing to be dangerous, has got to go. In the old days, a woman could be excused for too much makeup. This was a real outrage.

After that drama, everyone got to talking, eating, wondering what the hell was going on. People talked to Winston, sympathizing. Beryl, too. Beryl did expand on what they had been dealing with, the sign by the driveway, the demand for the hounds, the telescope, the Leland Cypress. If they had desired, they would have a rapt audience. Shaken as he was at what could have happened to his friend, Winston held it together.

Marianne and Russ, along with Susan and Jim, breathed a sigh of relief. Not that they had wanted something like this to happen, but they felt at least tomorrow would be uneventful.

Marianne, Susan sat across from Sister. As it turned out, the masters sat close to each other at the table.

"Good job." Hugh Brown, Master of Rockbridge, knew it could have been worse.

"Hugh, protocol is protocol," Sister replied.

The other masters nodded. While there could be arguments about safety in the field especially concerning helmets, a ride at another rider could stir no argument. What most of the masters knew was that some people can't handle confrontation. If they become a master, and there isn't a joint master to deal with conflicts, the hunt falls apart.

The room, jammed, felt warm as the two great fireplaces blazed.

Everyone agreed the hunt had been spectacular.

The breakfast broke up after two hours, a long breakfast, but it was so good, the people so happy. Everyone needed a good night's sleep for tomorrow's hunt, which fortunately wouldn't start until two in the afternoon.

Once home, having fed her fox cubs, who now squeaked when they saw her, extra goodies for Raleigh and Rooster, special crunchy fishies for Golly, plus raspberries and lettuce for J. Edgar Hoover, Sister finally showered and in her plush robe dropped on the library sofa.

Gray turned on the college game.

"Honey, I'll watch with you."

"In a minute. What do you make of that crisis today?"

She quietly thought then said, "I don't understand. Georgia was her rival? Georgia never said anything to that effect. She has said they got along, distant but not hostile. The only reason I know of the constant harassment up there is because Marianne usually tells me or Beryl calls. Seems to me Solange is carrying on the grieving, endangered widow too far. Beryl's not going to shoot her, although at this moment I expect Georgia would."

"Right." He stroked his military moustache. "It seems to me the lady doth protest too much."

CHAPTER 35

December 1, 2024 Sunday

With pale sun peeping from behind clouds, the joint meet with Bradford Beagles and Nantucket-Treweryn Beagles started slow. A little wind made the dried brown leaves on the oaks rustle.

Russ and Winston encouraged their hounds. The packs blended nicely together, one reason being that both of the huntsmen hunted more alike than differently. Those noses were down, tails up. As the hunt moved along, faster now as a waft of scent gave hope, the people walked faster. Then trotted.

Happy, an NTB hound, first picked up the scent of a rabbit. Within seconds all the beagles were on. The two huntsmen, in shape, stayed as close as they could. The whippers-in, on the sides, scrambled for the territory, rolling, tested one.

Sister, in the middle of the foot followers, admired Marianne and Beryl leading the people. Georgia was whipping in. On the edge of the woods, behind the Main Stable, the pastures remained unmowed along the edge for those edge feeders. Rabbits are edge feeders. They don't look forward to being out in the open for hawks, owls, coyotes, and other predators that liked rabbits.

Being on the bottom of that food chain meant one had to be careful. The rabbits' first defense is to sit still. Predators notice a flicker of movement, so while this strategy may seem strange to a human, it worked quite often.

Hounds followed the edge, running now, all speaking. The ground became hillier. They were well past the Main Stable and the grand house. Sister, knowing the land intimately, thought they were headed for Chapel Cross West.

If the rabbit turned right, they would wind up at the crossroads and the church. If he turned left, the trees would become thicker, the road would peter into a foot trail zigzagging up to the top of the Blue Ridge, at this point eighteen hundred feet.

Old trails fanned off of that road even when the macadam turned to packed dirt. For years an elaborate still, well concealed, nestled in the ravine with crystal-clear mountain water running by it. The result proved to be some of the best county waters in the state. For years Sophie Marquette's progeny, now numerous, made liquor. As laws changed the descendants paid off the authorities. Even during Prohibition the still produced liquor, more than ever. All was well until Arthur and Alfred DuCharme, immediate descendants who did not speak for decades to each other, decided each should get a percent of the profits. Given that they had exhausted most of their inheritance, they sought easy money. The distiller, a now very distant descendant, had no choice but to pay off each brother. The water was too good. The revenue man knew better than to come their way. It would have taken so much time for Dinwiddie Buzzwell to move his equipment, and could he find water this pure? So he paid up. Although a distant relative of the DuCharmes', Dinwiddie Buzzwell was squeezed hard. No family feeling there.

The uneasy truce lasted for fifteen years. Dinwiddie's son took over. The locals knew about the still, gave them good business. Sister often bought a jug or two for friends visiting from the North. The stuff was under the table at the Gulf Station, owned by Arthur and his wife. So as not to play favorites, Sister also purchased mason jars full from Alfred by calling on him at the Main Stable.

To avoid problems, if not gunshot, Sister did not go back there. Wise in country ways, she called on Buzzwell's wife, a pleasant lady who could hold her liquor as well as sell it. Sister called on her, gave her a wrapped box of pretty cotton fabrics so she could make her dresses, and also handed her an envelope containing a thirteen thousand dollar check for the damages hounds did to two stills during a wild hunt. This way Sister could keep the fiction going that she herself did not know where the still was located but she knew her hounds had wrecked the place. Within a week after that, everything was replaced, barrels of corn delivered as well as secret substances, supplying the distinctive admired taste.

RayRay, still alive at twelve, was fascinated when he and his mother drove back to the farm.

"Do they really shoot people?" he asked, hoping it was like the movies.

"Now, how would I know? But I do know if I were a Federal agent, I wouldn't set foot on any still in the state of Virginia."

"Mom, why do people drink?"

"We'll get to that later, but for some people it makes them feel good until they drink too much. It's how the phrase goes, 'It's an icebreaker.'"

Hearing the cry of the beagles, remembering the discussion with her son, Sister felt a surge of energy. Life is full of surprises, dreadful, fabulous. You just go on. RayRay taught her that.

Trotting now, the hounds had slowed a bit, so people could catch up without running flat out, she thought for a moment how she loved those conversations with her boy. Sometimes RayRay, Ronnie, and Xavier would sit outside, Co-Colas in hand, and all three young men would pepper her with questions. They felt they could talk to her about sex, politics, the people they all knew, relatives getting cancer, all the events, questions a young person has. She didn't have all the answers, but she respected their questions.

Snapping herself out of her reverie, she broke into a lope. Sneakers would have been easier to run in but one would slip and fall, thanks to various changing footing. Her work boots, heavy, kept her upright.

They were tiring. The pace weeded out the followers, as many people were at yesterday's foxhunt.

"Tally-ho," Susan, pushing along her group falling behind Marianne, called.

A big rabbit slipped right by everyone. It wasn't the hunted rabbit for the beagles, at the top of their lungs, ran a now scorching line.

As the entire group came out on the public road, Sister noticed Aunt Daniella and Kathleen. How good of them to follow, just in case. To her shock, behind them, in a now muddied, apparently brand-new Porsche SUV, came Solange, Ann, and Scott.

How many Porsches did Solange have?

Sister couldn't count the expensive cars in which she had seen Andrew, Solange, together and then individually. Big-ass Range Rovers, a Maserati for Andrew, a perfect 911 for Solange. The family Mercedes. Every truck was brand new.

Adrianna and Lynne, back with Sister, noticed as well.

Hounds paused. Good thing. People needed a break. They'd covered a lot of ground with their own two legs. Using four was better.

Lynne blurted out, "Is she crazy?"

"I begin to wonder," Sister answered. "Technically, she could have hunted behind the beagles. I am not their master. I'm starting to be surprised that she didn't try."

"I half expect her to have his jar of ashes with her." Adrianna had had enough of Solange's sufferings.

The other two couldn't help it. They laughed.

Betty caught up with them. "Did I miss anything? Had to show some people the way back. They're worn out."

Lynne pointed Betty toward the retreating Porsche SUV.

"Jesus Christ." Betty couldn't help herself, when seeing Solange, Ann, and Scott.

"I don't think even he could help her now." Adrianna shook her head.

"Found the line again." Sister took a deep breath. "Ready?"

"Ready but fading," Betty confessed. "If I were to do this every week, I'd need to start running, build up my legs and wind."

Still, she managed to walk faster as they headed up the macadam road, which turned into a tertiary state road, then stone, then dirt.

Bradford's Barnaby along with NTB's Happy led the pack. Hounds ran together. They were filtering into the woods, not deep but off the road. The going was getting rough for the whippers-in on the side.

Winston surged ahead, as did Russ. The field tried to catch up. The grade and the woods slowed people. Legs began to burn. Marianne looked for a better path. Sister, who knew the ground, ran up to her as fast as she could given the conditions, plus she too was tiring.

"Master."

Marianne looked around. "Is there a better way?"

"Yes." Sister walked next to Marianne. "Follow me. We'll wind up on a hard-packed dirt road into the woods."

Beryl joined them. The three women fought their way through

brush and creepers until hearing a car up ahead. It was Kathleen and Aunt Daniella acting as road whips for the beagles.

Kathleen Sixt Dunbar wondered what to do.

"Kathleen, it's a bit tight, but pass this turn, stop then, park. If hounds surge up the mountain, we can follow for a bit. And if the masters call them back we can drift down, plus we can pick up stragglers. Your car will get dirty," Aunt Daniella instructed her.

"I don't care." Kathleen followed instructions. "What's in there?"

"Well, either the remains of the old still or a rebuilt new one. One doesn't go back there. Know what I mean?"

"I'm getting the picture." Kathleen stopped her SUV, cut the motor.

The two women listened, hearing the full cry of the two packs. The hounds sounded as though they were heading for the still area.

Kathleen strained. "Aunt Dan, do people know of this place?"

"Older people do. I think younger generations of Buzzwells know, the distiller family. As to poachers, that I don't know but you just don't come back here and poke around."

"Who owns the land?"

"Technically, Crawford, but he would be a fool to intrude. He could timber it, but he doesn't need the money and if any of those men or their progeny use this place, they would take their revenge."

"Kill him?" Kathleen's eyebrows rose upward.

"No. Burn down the main house of Old Paradise, undo all Crawford has done on that majestic place." Aunt Daniella spoke low as if they could hear her were they around.

"Dear God."

"You don't screw around with these people. And if you shut up, buy their product, all is well. So if county waters are again being made, or whatever they are selling, Crawford would do well to buy thousands of dollars' worth. Insurance."

"Is there an alternative?" Kathleen was morbidly fascinated.

"Yes. You can try to kill them." Aunt Daniella said this as though it was the most normal thing in the world.

In their world, it was. Violence was a way of life.

As Sister, Marianne, and Beryl, up ahead, battled through, they heard a deep, throaty motor. This one turned left.

"Girls," Sister always called younger women girls, "we can get near that road, but we've got to stay out of sight. In case. That vehicle, sounds like a truck, could be doing business back here if business has revived. Best we stay hidden."

Unfortunately, Russ and Winston didn't know what lay up ahead. The hounds roared forward.

As hounds burst into the road, the car driven by Scott, Ann, and Solange in the back, passed them, holding them up. It also fouled the scent. Under the circumstances, this was a good thing.

Shots fired out.

Scared the hell out of the hounds. The first hound back, straight for Russ, was Gatsby, followed by the rest of the NTB hounds. Bradford hounds fled to Winston, also stunned by the sound of the shots.

They heard a car strike something then stop, the motor still running. They also heard two more shots.

Then another vehicle started up, a truck by the sound of the motor.

"Hold hard." Both men soothed their hounds but gave a firm command. Those hounds weren't going anywhere. A few were shaking. Hounds hate gunfire.

"Winston, let's get them out of here. Whatever is up there can't be good."

The two men turned, blowing their horns. Hounds eagerly followed. Georgia turned back to get the people to stop, go back.

Listening to the truck, Sister, perhaps foolhardy, perhaps not, felt whoever was in there defending their turf or product was getting out. Someone who had a lot to lose. Something else was in there. She figured she'd know if it was again illegal liquor. She'd be offered the opportunity to buy some, using the old coded language.

Kathleen and Aunt Dan saw a beat-up Ford 350 pull out. They couldn't see the driver or passenger and luckily for them, they were not seen as they were far enough away from the turn. That truck was hauling ass.

Sister reached the road. She ran past the two bodies of Solange and Ann still in the SUV as was Scott. The two women were obviously dead.

Marianne said to Beryl, "We can't leave her up there. Come on."

"What if we get shot?"

"Oh, we'll hit the ground first," Marianne called over her shoulder.

The two women, running hard, had heard the truck. They also heard Kathleen pull into the road. She, too, was taking a chance, encouraged by Aunt Dan, who opined that whoever was behind this was in the Ford 350 and getting the hell out.

Sister reached the Porsche SUV. Scott, slammed back in the seat, had his chest crushed by the impact. He, too, had been shot.

He couldn't turn off the motor. Sister reached in and cut it. She thought the vibrations added to his pain.

She opened the door. "Don't move. There's a doctor in the field."

No sooner were the words out of her mouth than Walter reached them. He said nothing, looking at the handsome young man with deep concern. "I'm going to unfasten your seat belt. This will hurt."

Turning his head, Scott, tears in his eyes, replied quietly, "I'm dying. I know it."

Sister reached for Walter's hand. He squeezed hers, looking at her, and nodded that Scott was dying. Blood covered his jacket.

"I have a confession to make. Then will you pray for my soul?"

"We will." Sister was hoping that Reverend Taliaferro and Father Mancusco would be close enough to run up. Time was running out.

"Solange and Ann killed Andrew. I helped them. Andrew was beginning to suspect they were in love. My marriage was a cover for Ann. We were old friends. She"—he gasped—"was afraid to be gay. Solange wanted the money for them. Seduced Andrew. I jammed his body on the spider wheel tedder. I have sinned. Pray for me."

"We will." Sister realized how conventional she was, as love between the women had never occurred to her.

Scott looked up at Sister, tears running down his face, then looked toward Walter. "Solange stabbed him with her letter opener. I did nothing to save him. I deserve hell."

"God will forgive you." Sister believed that.

She didn't know what she could or could not forgive, but she believed the Lord would forgive.

Marianne and Beryl reached them, and moments later, Scott took his last breath.

They saw the two women sprawled in the car. Whoever shot them was a good shot.

"We need to stay put. Can't move anybody." Sister was shaken by the confession, thinking Andrew must have figured out the relationship.

"I'll call Ben." Walter speed-dialed the sheriff. "Next let me call Yvonne. She can get everyone back, with Kasmir's help. I'll tell them all to go into Old Paradise. Tell Crawford and Marty." Walter instructed Yvonne, reaching her on her cell.

The four people stood there.

Marianne then pulled out her phone. She didn't like carrying a phone while hunting, but this time she was glad she had. "Susan, get everyone back to Old Paradise."

Sister walked up to Kathleen and Aunt Daniella. "I expect Ben will be here as soon as he can. You all should go back and stay by the turn into here. He'll need to know what you saw and what you heard and where you were."

Kathleen, pale, nodded and pulled out, looking over her shoulder to back out.

Jude and Jackie reached them first, as they worked this weekend. Ben, home missing the beagles as he was trying to catch up on paperwork, reached the scene in forty minutes.

Sister, Marianne, Beryl, and Walter told Ben, Jude, and Jackie what they knew when Ben arrived. The two deputies wisely, carefully inspected the place, should there be anyone else hiding there. Jackie found two former intact cabinets used to store equipment for making liquor. Grips for old guns were in the cabinet. This location was designed to cover illegal activity, and it had done so.

Ben then questioned Aunt Daniella and Kathleen, who had remained parked on the road. Sister, Beryl, Marianne, and Walter walked out, as going would be easier on the road.

Once finished with the wheel whips, Ben told them he'd be in touch.

Kathleen crept up in the car to Sister, Marianne, Beryl, and Walter, now walking down the road. "Come on. We can all squeeze in here somehow."

Walter, the tallest, sat in the back. Beryl sat on his lap, and Sister sat on Marianne's. Once at Old Paradise, they unkinked themselves, each one more shaken than they'd realized.

Crawford prudently started the breakfast. The large dining room, fabulously restored, impressed everyone. Ben spoke to him first.

"Crawford, there is illegal activity back there, but it's not moonshine as one non-Southerner calls it. This may be connected to the contraband found across from Beveridge Hundred. This isn't going to be easy. Those involved are smart, well-armed, and making money. I expect they've bought off people. My first responsibility is to sort out the three victims."

A stunned Crawford replied, "I understand. I offer whatever services you need."

"Thank you. I'll address the assembled. Better they hear the details from me than allow their imaginations to run away with them."

"Of course."

"Folks, there have been three unexpected deaths. Some of you know the deceased, Solange Bradford, Ann Howlett, and Scott Howlett. We have to notify next of kin. At this time I have no more information."

That was enough, everyone talked at once.

Crawford quietly asked Ben, "Should I have security?"

"You are probably safe but, yes, best you do."

"Right."

Sister, now with Gray, Sam, and Yvonne, didn't go into elaborate detail but did say that although she couldn't prove it, the three people had surprised people engaged in criminal activity. You don't shoot people for nothing.

They agreed, and also figured it was best to mingle, talk to people about other things.

Sister walked over to Marianne with her Nantucket-Treweryn people. "Can we help you with your hounds? You have a long way to go home."

"Thank you. We've got it. Best to leave soon before the light leaves us."

"Marianne, thank you for coming up when you did."

Marianne nodded. No point in going into detail in front of others.

Sister then offered Jefferson Hunt services to Bradford Beagles. Beryl, still pale, said like Marianne, they were going to leave now to get on the road.

"Thanks for coming up."

"Sister, Marianne was the brave one. I followed."

"I'm grateful. You could have been shot."

Beryl laughed. "Marianne said if we heard a shot, we could hit the ground."

Sister smiled. "She would. If nothing else, Winston is in the clear."

Beryl nodded, choked up. "I've been so worried. He's borne it with fortitude, a few lapses of temper, but my husband is a remarkable man."

Sister kissed her on the cheek. "He had you."

Later, driving back with Gray and Betty and Bobby in the car as they left her Bronco at the farm, the four, still shocked, talked about what had happened.

"Would you have guessed it?" Betty asked the others.

Everyone said no.

"Solange probably felt he was getting too close." Bobby found the entire episode dreadful, and the guys who had shot them were just as bad. "Money. Always money. Maybe Andrew had just figured it out."

"America worships the golden calf," Sister replied. "Are we Calvinists? If God loves you, you're rich or maybe if you are rich then God loves you."

"Funny, we don't immediately think of women as killers," Gray suggested.

"True," the others agreed.

"Men in love with women kill over them. I guess it happens sometimes in reverse." Bobby was trying to figure it out. "Not reverse. You know what I mean."

"What I know is three young people are dead over the almighty dollar." Sister sighed. "Wasted lives. Look at the soft golden light as the sun sets. Early now. It's soft and beautiful. They will never see it."

"Maybe they didn't see it when they were alive." Gray was thoughtful. "Some people feel nothing for the natural world. It's all their bank account, jewelry, trips to brag about, big cars. I'm sure that makes someone happy, but for how long? Until your car breaks down, or your friend buys a better one?"

"I wonder." Betty did, too.

"We aren't three young people. We're four uh, middling, I mean middle-aged ones." Bobby stopped.

"Oh, Bobby, up here in the front seat, we're getting old. So what?" Sister smiled into the rearview mirror.

"You never seem old," he replied.

"That's a very kind thing to say, but where we are, what we notice and appreciate, we're fortunate. All we have to do is walk out the door or look out the window on a snowy day. Makes me happy," Sister said.

"Well, we're certainly richer than those three kids who are dead," Betty pronounced with finality.

C H A P T E R 3 6

December 2, 2024 Monday

S itting at the breakfast table, second cup of coffee, Gray picked up a wrapped present off the kitchen chair. "You have wanted this."

She took it, carefully opening it, as Sister saved wrapping paper. "What? You didn't."

"I did."

She hopped out of her chair, taking the small skateboard with her. Opening J. Edgar's cage, she gave him a treat, then picked him up, placing him on the center of the skateboard.

Golly jumped off the counter to observe.

J. Edgar wiggled his legs, then touched the ground. He rolled a bit.

"This is the best." Sister watched with glee.

Golly ran beside the fellow, touching his shell. J. Edgar didn't seem to mind. He was getting the hang of moving with speed. Golly ran along, giving him little pats.

"I thought you didn't like my turtle." Sister stood to kiss her husband.

Laughing, Gray kissed her back. "I've grown accustomed to his face."

"Here come the dogs."

Rooster and Raleigh now watched.

Golly brushed by them. *"I'm teaching him how to roll. Leave him alone."*

The two dogs walked to the table and plopped down. Best stay out of the way. Golly could be imaginative in revenge.

Golly then turned to walk back to J. Edgar's cage. The turtle didn't have the turn down yet.

Sister got up, turned him around, and the fellow scooted after the long-haired calico.

Gray and Sister couldn't help but laugh. The three fox cubs, asleep because they ate their own good breakfast, opened their eyes at the commotion. This was too good.

Sister, again next to Gray, took his hand. "You know, it's the little things, the unplanned things. Just makes me happy."

"Me too." He admitted to himself he might not love the turtle but he accepted him.

They both broke into the song from *My Fair Lady* about growing accustomed to her face. Then they burst out laughing.

It need not be said by either of them, but to kill or die for money seemed the most absurd thing in the world.

Sister watched a bit more. "I'd better put him back in. He'll tire himself out."

Gray watched as Sister gently lifted J. Edgar off his new toy. She placed him in his cage, then put the skateboard in, too. Golly sat right by the door.

Then Sister rejoined her husband. "You think of such wonderful things. It's funny, but Gray, I feel younger with you than I did when I was younger. We don't need a lot to be happy."

"All we need is each other." He kissed her hand.

ACKNOWLEDGMENTS

Marianne Casey, MB, Russell Wagner, MB and huntsman of the Nantucket-Treweryn Beagles, provided me with nonstop support plus tins of special teas. William Getchell allowed me to tag along with him in the hunt field. He's one of those whippers-in who puts you in the right place. Susan Watkins and her husband, Jim Rose, juggled all my questions.

Thank you also to Peter J. Cook, MB of NTB, for giving me time with his hunt staff and for making me laugh.

Because of NTB, Waldingfield Beagles, Farmington Beagles, and the ever forward Ashland Bassets, I have learned to love hunting on foot. This is a debt I can never repay so I am trying to pay it forward.

To the foxhunter and foot hunter reader, we are in many ways the last defense against environmental despoilment. Every one of us must work to protect wildlife, plants, soil, water as best we can. We are also part of a dwindling number to understand the canine pack mentality. Hound packs are one of the reasons humans survived.

My agents, Emma Patterson and Emily Forland, continue to shelter me and all their authors. How lucky can you get?

Special thanks to Elinor Carrington Lyon, for taking an interest in foxhunting and beagling. She's been a good sport.

Biggest thanks and kisses to Holly, my very busy mutt, who gives up her play whenever I go to my desk. Even if the other dogs bark she sticks with me while I write. She feels some claim to authorship. No doubt she's right.

ABOUT THE AUTHOR

RITA MAE BROWN is the bestselling author of the Sneaky Pie Brown mysteries; the Sister Jane series; the Runnymede novels, including *Six of One* and *Cakewalk; A Nose for Justice* and *Murder Unleashed; Rubyfruit Jungle;* and *In Her Day;* as well as many other books. An Emmy-nominated screenwriter and a poet, Brown lives in Afton, Virginia, and is a Master of Foxhounds and the huntsman.

ABOUT THE TYPE

This book was set in Baskerville, a typeface designed by John Baskerville (1706–75), an amateur printer and typefounder, and cut for him by John Handy in 1750. The type became popular again when the Lanston Monotype Corporation of London revived the classic roman face in 1923. The Mergenthaler Linotype Company in England and the United States cut a version of Baskerville in 1931, making it one of the most widely used typefaces today.